THERE IS CONFUSION

by

JESSIE REDMON FAUSET

There is confusion worse than death,
Trouble on trouble; pain on pain—
                                        Tennyson

MARTINO FINE BOOKS
Eastford, CT
2020

Martino Fine Books
P.O. Box 913,
Eastford, CT 06242 USA

ISBN   978-1-68422-502-6

Copyright 2020
Martino Fine Books

Cover Design Tiziana Matarazzo

Printed in the United States of America On 100% Acid-Free Paper

THERE IS CONFUSION

THERE IS
CONFUSION

by

JESSIE REDMON FAUSET

There is confusion worse than death,
Trouble on trouble; pain on pain—
Tennyson

BONI and LIVERIGHT
New York
1924

THERE IS CONFUSION

CHAPTER I

JOANNA'S first consciousness of the close understanding which existed between herself and her father dated back to a time when she was very young. Her mother, her brothers and her sister had gone to church, and Joanna, suffering from some slight childish complaint, had been left home. She had climbed upon her father's knee demanding a story.

"What sort of story?" Joel Marshall asked, willing and anxious to please her, for she was his favorite child.

"Story 'bout somebody great, Daddy. Great like I'm going to be when I get to be a big girl."

He stared at her amazed and adoring. She was like a little, living echo out of his own forgotten past. Joel Marshall, born a slave and the son of a slave in Richmond, Virginia, had felt as a little boy that same impulse to greatness.

"As a little tyke," his mother used to tell her friends, "he was always pesterin' me: 'Mammy, I'll be a great man some day, won't I? Mammy, you're gonna help me to be great?'

"But that was a long time ago, just a year or so after the war," said Mammy, rocking complacently in her comfortable chair. "How wuz I to know he'd be a great caterer, feedin' bank presidents and everything? Once you know they had him fix a banquet fur President Grant. Sent all the way to Richmond fur 'im. That's howcome he settled yere in New York; yassuh, my son is sure a great man."

But alas for poor Joel! His idea of greatness and his

9

Mammy's were totally at variance. The kind of greatness he had envisaged had been that which gets one before the public eye, which makes one a leader of causes, a "man among men." He loved such phrases! At night the little boy in the tiny half-story room in that tiny house in Virginia picked out the stories of Napoleon, Lincoln and Garrison, all white men, it is true; but Lincoln had been poor and Napoleon unknown and yet they had risen to the highest possible state. At least he could rise to comparative fame. And when he was older and came to know of Frederick Douglass and Toussaint L'Ouverture, he knew if he could but burst his bonds he, too, could write his name in glory.

This was no selfish wish. If he wanted to be great he also wanted to do honestly and faithfully the things that bring greatness. He was to that end dependable and thorough in all that he did, but even as a boy he used to feel a sick despair,—he had so much against him. His color, his poverty, meant nothing to his ardent heart; those were nature's limitations, placed deliberately about one, he could see dimly, to try one's strength on. But that he should have a father broken and sickened by slavery who lingered on and on! That after that father's death the little house should burn down!

He was fifteen when that happened and he and his mother both went to work in the service of Harvey Carter, a wealthy Virginian, whose wife entertained on a large scale. It was here that Joel learned from an expert chef how to cook. His wages were small even for those days, but still he contrived to save, for he had set his heart on attending a theological seminary. Some day he would be a minister, a man with a great name and a healing tongue. These were the dreams he dreamed as he basted Mrs. Carter's chickens or methodically mixed salad dressing.

His mother knew his ideas and loved them with such a fine, albeit somewhat uncomprehending passion and belief, that in grateful return he made her the one other consideration of his life, weaving unconsciously about himself a web of such loyalty and regard for her that he could not have broken through it if he would. Her very sympathy defeated his purpose. So that when she, too, fell ill on a day with what seemed for years an incurable affection, Joel shut his teeth and put his frustrated plans behind him.

He drew his small savings from the bank and rented a tiny two and a half room shack in the front room of which he opened a restaurant,—really a little lunchstand. He was patronized at first only,—and that sparingly—by his own people. But gradually the fame of his wonderful sandwiches, his inimitable pastries, his pancakes, brought him first more black customers, then white ones, then outside orders. In five years' time Joel's catering became known state wide. He conquered poverty and came to know the meaning of comfort. The Grant incident created a reputation for him in New York and he was shrewd enough to take advantage of it and move there.

Ten years too late old Mrs. Marshall was pronounced cured by the doctors. She never understood what her defection had cost her son. His material success, his position in the church, in the community at large and in the colored business world,—all these things meant "power." To her, her son was already great. Joel did not undertake to explain to her that his lack of education would be a bar forever between him and the kind of greatness for which his heart had yearned.

It was after he moved to New York and after the death of his mother that Joel married. His wife had been a school teacher, and her precision of language and exactitude in small matters made Joel think again of the education and subsequent greatness which were to have been his. His wife was kind and sweet, but fundamentally unambitious, and for a time the pleasure of having a home and in contrasting these days of ease with the hardships of youth made Joel somewhat resigned to his fate.

"Besides, it's too late now," he used to tell himself. "What could I be?" So he contented himself with putting by his money, and attending church, where he was a steward and really the unacknowledged head.

His first child brought back the old keen longing. It was a boy and Joel, bending over the small, warm, brown bundle, felt a gleam of hope. He would name it Joel and would instil, or more likely, stimulate the ambition which he felt must be already in that tiny brain. But his wife wouldn't hear of the name Joel.

"It's hard enough for him to be colored," she said jealously guarding her young, "and to call him a stiff old-fashioned name like that would finish his bad luck. I am going to name him Alexander."

Alec, as he was usually called, did not resemble his father in the least. He was the average baby and the average boy, interested in marbles, in playing hookey, in parachutes, but with no determination to be a dark Napoleon or a Frederick Douglass. Two other children, Philip and Sylvia, resembled him, and Joel Marshall, now a man of forty, gave up his old ideas completely and decided to be a good business man, husband and father; not a bad decision if he had but known it.

Then Joanna came; Joanna with a fluff of thick, black hair, and solemn, earnest eyes and an infinite capacity for spending long moments in thought. "She's like you, Joel," Mrs. Marshall said. And because the novelty of choosing names for babies had somewhat worn off, she made no objection to the name Joanna, which Joel hesitatingly proposed for her. "She certainly should have been named for you," the mother told him a month later; "see how she follows you with her eyes. She'd rather watch you than eat."

And indeed from the very beginning Joanna showed her

preference for her father. The two seemed to have a secret understanding. After the first child, Mrs. Marshall had fretted somewhat over the time and strength expended in caring for the other little Marshalls, but she never had any occasion to worry about Joanna. Joel had his office in his residence, and after Joanna was dressed and fed, all she wanted was to lie in her carriage and later to ride about on the kiddie-car of that day in her father's office, where she watched him with her solemn eyes.

Joel never forgot the first time she asked him for a story. He was in the habit of regaling his youngsters with tales of his early life, of himself, of boys who had grown up with him, of ball-games and boyish pranks. The three older children had a fine catholicity of taste. "Tell us a story," was all they asked, its subject made no difference to them.

But on that certain Sunday before Joanna was five years old she perched herself on her father's knee and commanded astoundingly:

"Tell me a story, Daddy, 'bout somebody great."

Joel didn't know what she meant at first, so far removed was he from the thought of his old dream. And yet the question did seem something like an echo, faint but recognizable of a longing that had once loomed large in his life.

"Great," he repeated. "How do you mean great, Baby? Tall, great big man, like Daddy, hey?" He stood six feet and was broad with it.

Joanna shook a dissenting head. "No, not great that way. I want to hear about a man who did things nobody else could do,—maybe he put out a fire," she ended doubtfully, "but I mean something greater than that."

Joel had her taught to read after that. She was a little frail for school, and did not start until later than the other children, though she was far the most studious. So she had three or four years of solid reading, and always her choice of subject was of some one who had overcome obstacles and so stood out beyond his fellows.

At first she thought nothing of color, and it was not until she had gone to school and learned something of discrimination that she began to ponder.

"Didn't colored people ever do anything, Daddy?" But Joel was prepared for that. He told her himself of Douglass and Vesey and Turner. There were great women, too, Harriet Tubman, Phillis Wheatley, Sojourner Truth, women who had been slaves, he explained to her, but had won their way to fame and freedom through their own efforts.

Joanna had a fine sense of relativity. Young as she was, she could understand that the bravery and courage exercised by these slave women was a much finer and different thing from that exercised for instance by Florence Nightingale. "They were like Joan of Arc," she thought to herself, "Joan, wonderful Joan with the name almost like mine." Only an innate, almost too meticulous sense of honesty had kept her from changing her own name to the shorter form.

She used to lie in her bed at night, straight and still with her eyes fixed on the stretch of sky visible even from a house in Fifty-ninth Street and dream dreams. "I'll be great, too," she told herself. "I'm not sure how. I can't be like those wonderful women, Harriet and Sojourner, but at least I won't be ordinary."

She spoke to her father like a little piping echo from the past, "Daddy, you'll help me to be a great woman, somebody you'll be proud of?"

Her words made him so happy; they renewed his life. She was so completely like himself, and he could help her. "Thank God," he used to murmur over his books that daily showed an increase in his earnings.

He took Joanna everywhere with him. One Easter Sunday a great colored singer, a beautiful woman, sang an Easter

anthem in his church, lifting up a golden voice among the tall
white lilies. Afterwards she went home with Mr. and Mrs.
Marshall and stayed to dinner. Joanna never moved her eyes
from her during the ride home.

After dinner she stood in front of the singer in the comfortable living-room. "I can sing like you," she said gravely,
"and I can remember the tune of most of that hymn you sang
this morning. Listen."

And with no further introduction she sang most of the
anthem. She was only ten then, yet her voice was already
free of the shrillness of childhood and beginning to assume
that liquid golden quality which so distinguished it later.

Madame Caldwell gasped. She had won her own laurels
through bitter experience in various studios, meeting insult,
indifference and unkindness with an unyielding front, which
brought her finally consideration, a grudging interest, sometimes a genuine appreciation.

She was well on her way to recognition now. Colored people
acclaimed her all over the country and she had some local
reputation in her home town where black and white alike
were very proud of her.

"But no daughter of mine," she used to say bitterly, "if
she has the voice of an angel shall go through what I have
suffered."

Yet when she heard Joanna sing that Easter Sunday, she
seized Joel Marshall's arm. "Get her a teacher, Mr. Marshall.
She has a voice in ten thousand. Poor child, how you will
have to work!"

But Joanna wasn't listening, her eyes sought her father's.
Both of them knew at once that the road to glory was stretching out before her.

CHAPTER II

JOANNA was like her father not only so far as ambition was concerned but also in her willingness to work. She had a fine serious mind, a little slow-moving at first, but working with a splendid precision that helped her through many a hard place. Her quality of being able to stick to a problem until she was satisfied served in the long run as well as her sister Sylvia's greater quickness and versatility. Eventually, too, Joanna's laboriousness and native exactness produced in her the result of an oft-sharpened knife. The method which she applied to one study, she remembered to apply to another, and if this failed then she was able to make combinations.

Usually she had to have things explained to her from the very beginning, either by a teacher or through directions in a book. But to offset this slowness she had a good sense of logic, a strong power of concentration, and a remarkably retentive and visualizing memory.

Sylvia and she, destined to be such perfect friends in their maturity, were not very sympathetic in their childhood. The older girl was thoughtless, quick to jump at conclusions, natively witty and strongly disinclined toward seriousness. "Joanna makes me sick," was her constant cry, "always thinking of her lessons and how important she's going to be when she's grown-up. So tiresome, too, wanting to talk about what she's going to do all the time, with no interest in your affairs."

Which was not quite true, for Joanna was mightily interested in people who had a "purpose" in life. Otherwise not at all.

16

This was where she differed most from her father. With Joel success and distinction had been his dream, his dearest wish. But always he had realized that there were other things which might interfere. With Joanna success and distinction were an obsession. It never occurred to her that life was anything but what a man chose to make it, provided, of course, he did choose to make it something. Her brothers' and Sylvia's haphazard methods were always incomprehensible to her, and this gave her the least touch of the "holier than thou" manner.

Her mother insisted on each child's learning to do housework. Even the boys were not exempt from this, indeed they rather liked it. Sylvia made no complaint though she occasionally bribed Alec or Philip to do her stint for her. Joanna never complained, either, yet she made up her mind early that as a woman she would never do this kind of work. Not that she despised it, she simply considered it labor lost for a person who like herself might be spending her time in more beautiful and more graceful activities. Yet in spite of her dislike, she always lingered longest over her work, and the room or the silver which she had cleaned always looked the best. It is true she never learned to iron especially well, but this was about the only thing in which she yielded place to Sylvia.

Sylvia was like a fire-fly in comparison with Joanna's steady beaconlike flood of light. Sylvia dashed about, worked as quickly as she thought and produced immediate and usually rather striking results. Sylvia with a ribbon, or a piece of lace and a ready needle and thread could give the effect of possessing two dresses, whereas she had only the one. Sylvia dressed the dolls, hiring Joanna's remarkable and usually disregarded assembly of these so that she might make them new clothes. She drove an honest bargain. If Joanna would let her play store with her dolls for a week, one of them could keep the new dress which Sylvia would have made for her; Joanna's dolls were usually in Sylvia's care.

2

Yet when Joanna did sew or knit, her stitches and pieces bore inspection much better than Sylvia's. By the same token, however, they missed Sylvia's dash.

In one thing only did Joanna show real abandon, that was in dancing. Sylvia was as light as thistle-down on her feet, but Joanna was like the spirit of dancing. She had grace, the very poetry of motion, and she could dance any step however intricate if she saw it once.

"If you want to get Joanna to play," Maggie Ellersley, Sylvia's chum and school-mate would say impatiently, "you must start some singing or dancing game. She wouldn't play 'I Spy' or 'Pussy wants a corner' with you for worlds."

Any sort of folk-song or dance, though she did not know them by that name, delighted the child. Usually she held herself aloof, but in summer down on Fifty-ninth Street Joanna was one with the children in the street, singing, dancing, jumping rope in unexpected and fancy ways.

Sylvia's and Maggie's and even her brothers' rougher scoffing affected her not at all, not only because she had the calm self-assurance which is the first step toward success, but also because of old Joel's strong belief in her.

Joel believed that all things were possible. "Nothing in reason," he used to tell Joanna, "is impossible. Forty years ago I was almost a pauper in Richmond. Look at me to-day. I spend more on you in a month, Joanna, than my mother and I ever saw in a five-year stretch. One hundred years ago and nearly all of us were slaves. See what we are now. Ten years ago people would have laughed at the thought of colored people on the stage. Look at the bill-boards on Broadway."

It was in the first part of the century when Williams and Walker, Cole and Johnson, Ada Overton and others were at their zenith. Old Joel believed them the precursors of greater things. Since Joanna's gifts were those of singing and dancing, he hoped to make her famous the country over. Of course he would have preferred a more serious form of endowment. But such as it was, it was Joanna's, and must be developed. Joel Marshall believed in using the gifts nearest at hand.

"And don't think anything about being colored," he used to say.

"It might be different if you lived in some other part of the country, but here in this section it may not interfere much more than being poor, or having some slight deformity. I have often noticed," said Joel, who had used his powers of observation to no small advantage, "that having some natural drawback often pushes you forward, that is if you've got anything in you to start with. It might even happen," he added, launched now on his favorite theme, "that your color would add to your success. Depend on it if you've got something which these white folks haven't got, or can do something better than they can, they'll call on you fast enough and your color will only make you more noticeable."

Joanna used to listen interestedly. Not that in those early years she always understood fully everything her father said, but his talk created for her a kind of atmosphere which created in turn a feeling of assurance and self-confidence which was really superb.

Another theory of Joel's which he had worked out for himself, and which in no small degree contributed to Joanna's education was his early understanding of the natural rights of men inherent in the mere fact of living. He told Joanna that no class of men remained static throughout the ages,—he had not used these words, it is true, but he had come pretty near it. Somewhere in those early days of his in odd scraps of reading he had learned that Greece had once been enslaved; that Russia had but recently freed her serfs; that England possessed a submerged class.

"All people, all countries, have their ups and downs, Joanna," he would tell her gravely, "and just now it's our turn to be down, but it will soon roll round for our time to be up, or rather we must see to it that we do get up. So everyone of us has something to do for the race. Never forget that, little girl."

Joanna was a memorable type in these days. A grave child, brown without that peculiar luminosity of appearance which she was to have later on, and which Sylvia already possessed. She had a mop of thick black hair which was actually heavy, so much so that the back of her head bulged. Joanna knew next to nothing at this time of those first aids to colored people in this country in the matter of conforming to average appearance. If she had known them, it is doubtful if she would have used them, for she had the variety of honesty which made her hesitate and even dislike to do or adopt anything artificial, no matter how much it might improve her general appearance. No hair straighteners, nor even curling kids for her.

"Joanna's ways are so straight, they almost sway back," Sylvia used to say aptly. And indeed Joanna wanted one to see her at her very worst. She did not like to take people by surprise. But as her worst included a pair of very nice brown eyes, with thick, if somewhat short, and curling lashes, an unobtrusive nose, small square hands and exquisite feet, it was not hard to look at. She was always intensely susceptible to beautiful people and to beautiful things. It was the beauty inherent in Joel's ideals, and in all ideals which really underlie success, that most attracted her. And this passion for beauty while informing and indeed molding her character, yet by a strange twist influenced adversely and warped her sympathies.

CHAPTER III

IT was Joanna's love for beauty that made her consciously see Peter Bye. It is true that almost as soon as she saw him she lost sight of him again, for the boy did not come up to her requirements which, even at the early age at which these two met, were quite crystallized. Joanna liked first of all fixity of purpose. The phrase "When I grow up, I'm going to be" was constantly on her lips. She got into the habit of measuring people, "sizing them up" Joel would have said, in accordance with the amount of steadfastness, perseverance and ambition which they displayed. She had little time for shiftless or "do-less" persons. Sylvia used to say, half angrily, "Joanna, when the bad man gets you, he isn't going to torture you. He's just going to shut you up with lazy, good-for-nothing folks. That will be torture enough for you."

Peter Bye, in spite of the dark arresting beauty which first drew Joanna's glance to him across the other white and pink faces in the crowded schoolroom, was undoubtedly shiftless. "Not lazy," Joanna said to herself, looking at him from under level brows before she dismissed him forever from her busy mind. "It's just that he doesn't care; he just doesn't want to be anybody."

She was too young to understand the power of that great force, heredity. She had no notion of the part which it played in her own life. Peter was the legitimate result of a heredity that had become a tradition, of a tradition that had become warped, that had gone astray and had carried Peter and Peter Bye's father along in its general wreckage.

It is impossible to understand the boy's character without some knowledge of the lives of those who had gone before him.

As far back as the last decades of the eighteenth century there had been white Byes and black Byes in Philadelphia. The black Byes were known to be the chattels of Aaron and Dinah Bye, Quakers, who without reluctance had set free their slaves, among them black Joshua Bye, the great-grandfather of Peter. This was done in 1780 according to the laws of Pennsylvania, which thus allowed the Quakers to salve their consciences without offending their thrifty instincts.

Aaron Bye, most people said, was unusually good to his slaves. He had something of the patriarchal instinct and liked to think of himself as ruler over the destiny of many people, his wife's, his children's and more completely that of his slaves. Certainly he was very kind to Joshua's mother, Judy. She was a tall, straight, steely, black woman with fine inscrutable eyes, a thin-lipped mouth and a large but shapely nose. She bore about her a quality of brooding, of mystery, embodying the attraction which she exercised for many men, white and black. But apparently she knew little of this. Her only weakness, if such it might be called, was an inexplicable attachment to the white Bye family. She married, a few years before receiving her freedom, a man named Ceazer, a proud, surly, handsome individual, who refused to adopt the surname of his master; he had belonged to white people named Morton. Since even after freedom Judy would not hear to leaving the Bye family, Aaron Bye greatly pleased by this loyalty offered the position of coachman to Ceazer, which the latter, with his customary surliness, accepted. Later he not only threw up his job, but ran away, vanishing finally into legend.

His was a strange truculent character; he hated slavery,

hated all white people, hated particularly the Mortons, hated ineffably Aaron Bye. He wanted nothing at his hands. Once he knocked down another Negro who referred to him as "Mist' Bye's man." He was no man's man, he assured the stricken narrator, least of all the man of that damn Quaker. His enmity went to ridiculous lengths. Aaron Bye taught Joshua how to write and gave him a little black testament for a prize. In it he wrote "The gift of Aaron Bye." Joshua, delighted, wrote his own name under the inscription and ran and showed it to his mother. She, it turned out, had not been watching his making of pothooks without purpose. Underneath her boy's name she fashioned in halting crazy characters her single attempt at writing, her own name, Judy Bye. Nothing would serve Joshua then but that he must have Ceazer's name in the book, too. Remembering that his father could not write, Joshua wrote out himself with a fine flourish "Ceazer Bye" and showed the name to its owner, entreating him to make his mark beside it. Ceazer took up the pen in his strong, wiry fingers.

"Which one ob dese did you say were mine?"

Joshua pointed it out, waiting for the cross. Ceazer made a mark, it was true, but it was a thick broad line drawn through his name with a fury which almost tore the thin page. *He* was no Bye!

It was not long after this that he disappeared, a strange, brooding, intractable figure.

Joshua, although born in slavery, had never known the institution in its more hideous aspects. He had been a very little boy when his freedom came to him. And Ceazer, old Judy told him, had fought in the Revolution! So that Joshua knew more of warfare to set people free than of slavery for which war was later to be waged. From him his son Isaiah heard almost nothing of the old régime, though there were many vestiges of it on all sides. All he knew was that Joshua had kept on working for Dinah and Aaron Bye after his emancipation, and that they had given him on the occasion of his marriage to Belle Potter a huge Family Bible, bound in leather and with an Apocrypha. On the title-page was written in a fine old script: *To Joshua and Belle Bye from Aaron and Dinah Bye. "By their fruits ye shall know them."*

For a long time to Isaiah, who used to pore absorbedly as a boy over this book with its pictures and long old-fashioned S, this inscription savored of vineyards and orchards. The white Byes, as a matter of fact, were the possessors of very fine peach-orchards in the neighborhood of what is now known as Bryn Mawr, and Isaiah, even as a little fellow, had been taken out there to pick peaches.

His father Joshua had spent his life in making those orchards what they were; a born agriculturist, he had an uncanny knowledge of planting, of grafting, of fertilizing. Many a farmer tried to inveigle him from Aaron Bye. But although Joshua's wages were small, he had inherited his mother's blind, invincible attachment for the Byes. His place was with Aaron.

It was young white Meriwether Bye, youngest son of Aaron's and Dinah's ten children, who told Isaiah what the inscription meant. Joshua had not married until he was nearly fifty and his single son, black Isaiah, and white Meriwether were boys together. Meriwether used to come to the Bye house at Fourth and Coates Streets, which is now Fairmount Avenue, as often as Isaiah used to appear at the Bye house at Fourth and Spruce.

Isaiah showed the inscription to Meriwether, "By their fruits ye shall know them."

"Yes," said young Merry tracing the letters with a fat finger, "that's our family motto." Isaiah wanted to know what a motto was.

"Something," Meriwether told him vaguely, "that your whole family goes by." The black boy thought that likely.

"Everybody knows Bye peaches, ain't that so?   'Cause of that everybody knows the Byes."

Meriwether, though impressed by this logic, didn't think that that was what was meant.   A subsequent conversation with his father confirmed his opinion.

"It means this, Ziah," he said one hot July afternoon walking home with the colored boy from the brickyard where Isaiah worked, "it means it shows the kind of stuff you are.   It means—now—you see a bare tree in the winter time don't you, and you don't know what it is?   But you do perhaps know an apple blossom when you see it, or a peach blossom.   In the spring you see that tree covered, let's say, with apple blossoms. Well, you know it's an apple tree."

"But what's that got to do with us?"   Isaiah wanted to know.   He was interested, he could not tell why, but his slow-working mind clung to its first idea.   "Your father wrote it in the book he gave my father.   My father hasn't any fruit trees."

Isaiah never forgot the answer Meriwether made him in the unconscious cruelty of youth.   "When it comes to people," said the young Quaker, "it means pretty much the same thing. Now when I grow up, I'm going to be a great doctor," his chest swelled, "but nobody will be surprised.   They'll all say, 'Of course, he's the son of Aaron Bye, the rich peach-merchant. Good stock there,'" he involuntarily mimicked his pompous father; "and I'll be good fruit.   That's the way it always is: good trees, good fruit; rich, important people, rich important sons."

"What'll I be?" asked Isaiah Bye, grotesquely tragic in his tattered clothes, the sweat rolling off his shiny face, so intent was his interest.

"Well," Meriwether countered judicially, "what could you be?"   He pondered a moment, his own position so secure that he was willing to do his best by this serious case.   "Your father and your father's father were slaves.   'Course your father's free now but he's just a servant. He's not what you'd call his own man. So I s'pose that's what you'll be, a good servant. Tell you what, Isaiah, you can be my coachman. I'll be good to you. And when you're grown up," said Meriwether with more imagination than he usually displayed, "I'll point you out to some famous doctor from France and say, 'His father was a good servant to my father, and he's been a good servant to my father's son.' How'll you like that?" Meriwether tapped him fondly if somewhat condescendingly on the arm.

"You'll never," said Isaiah Bye, drawing back from the familiar touch, "you'll never be able to say that about me." And he turned and ran down the hot street, leaving Meriwether Bye gaping on the sidewalk.

After that his father could never persuade him to enter again the Bye house, or the Bye orchards. Fortunately his mother upheld him here. " 'Tain't as though he had to work for them old Byes," she said straightening up her already straight shoulders. "He makes just as much and more in the brick-yard and in helpin' Amos White haul."

"I know that," Joshua would reply impatiently, "but old Mist' Aaron says—now—he likes to have his own people workin' roun' him. And I don't like to disappoint him."

Belle Bye told Isaiah. "I'm not one of his own people, Ma," he answered stubbornly, "and after that I'm not ever goin' back." Belle was rejoiced to hear this. She would have been an insurgent in any walk of life. Joshua was the genuine peasant type—the type, black or white, which believes in a superior class and yields blindly to its mandates. But Belle had seen too many changes even in her thirty-five years—she was far younger than Joshua—not to know that many things are possible if one just has courage.

Isaiah, on being questioned, told his mother with considerable reluctance about his conversation with Meriwether. Belle, while regretting the breach, understood. She had been glad to have her boy the associate of young white Bye. Without expressing it to herself in so many words she had realized that association with Meriwether was an education for Isaiah. Already he was talking more correctly than other colored boys in his group, his manners were good, and though his work was of the roughest kind, his vision was broad, he knew there were other things.

"I don't believe," his mother told him wisely, "that you kin go as fur as you dream. Too many things agin you fur that, boy. But you kin die much further along the road than when you was born. Never forget that."

So Isaiah was saved from the initial mistake of aiming too high and of coming utterly to smash. Yet he accomplished wonders. Who shall say how he increased his slender store of knowledge? How he learned to read wise books borrowed and bought as best he might? How he learned geography and history that made his heart-beats go wild since it told him of the French Revolution and how a whole nation once practically enslaved arose to a fuller, richer life?

The inspiration for all this lay in those careless words of young Meriwether. Although Isaiah met the young fellow many times after that incident, and apparently with friendliness, he never in his heart forgave him. Like Ceazer he developed a dislike for white people and their ways which developed, however, into a sturdy independence and an unyielding pride. No amount of contumely ever made him ashamed of his slave ancestry. On the contrary, to measure himself against old Ceazer and Judy gave him ground for honest pride. "See what they were and how far I've gone," he used to say, pleasantly boastful.

He resented as few sons of freedmen did the assurance with which the white Byes took their wealth and position and power. "Hoisted themselves on the backs of the black Byes." He resented especially the ingratitude of Aaron Bye to Joshua.

For himself he asked nothing; being content to fight his own way "through an onfriendly world."

The white Byes had gone far, but the black Byes having now that greatest of all gifts, freedom, would go far, too. They would be leaders of other black men.

The upshot of all this was that Isaiah Bye opened a school for colored youth down on Vine Street. No name and no figure in colored life in Philadelphia was ever better beloved and more revered than his.

CHAPTER IV

ISAIAH did not marry until he was thirty-one, which was an advanced age for his times. Even then he had married earlier than his father. Old Joshua, who died long before Isaiah's marriage, had been inordinately proud of his one son.

"Jes' wouldn't work fer white folks," Joshua used to say, "that weren't good enough fer him."

Isaiah and Miriam Sayres Bye had one son. "Meriwether," Isaiah wrote in Aaron and Dinah Bye's old gift, and under it in a script as fine and characteristic as that of the original inscription: "By *his* fruits shall ye know—*me.*" It was a strange but not unnatural bit of pride, the same pride which had made him name this squirming bundle of potentialities, "Meriwether,—Meriwether Bye," a boy with the same name which old white Aaron Bye's son had borne and with as good chances. The Civil War was on the horizon then and Isaiah Bye, with that calm expectation of the unexpected which was his mother's chiefest legacy, was sure that in that grand mêlée all his people would know freedom. So black Meriwether Bye, born like himself in freedom, would know nothing but that estate when he began to have understanding.

Isaiah had accumulated a little, though how that was possible, no one aware of his tiny stipend could guess. It is true he not only taught school, but he had outside pupils, ex-slaves, freedmen, men like himself born in freedom, but unable through economic pressure to enjoy it except in name,—all these crowded his home at night on Vine Street, and sweated mightily over primers and pothooks and the abacus. Twenty-five cents an hour he charged them, giving each a meticulous care such as would bring a modern tutor many dollars. He wrote letters, pamphlets, too, for that marvelous organization already well established, the A. M. E. Church. His wife had a sister whose husband kept a second-hand shop and from this source he earned an occasional dollar. When Meriwether was eight, Isaiah owned two houses in Pearl Street, the house in Vine Street, a half interest in his brother-in-law's store and a plot in Mount Olivet Cemetery.

From the very beginning Meriwether knew he was to be a great man—a doctor, his father had said emphatically. And Meriwether repeated it by rote. He was a clever enough child though without his father's solid trait of concentration. But he liked the idea of greatness—that and the profession of medicine came to be synonymous with him as it was already with his father. Otherwise it is likely that both of them would have seen earlier the boy's inaptitude for the calling thus thrust upon him.

Meriwether went to his father's school, to Mr. Jonas Howard's catering establishment, which he loved, to Sunday-School and to his Uncle Peter's second-hand store. In any one of these places he was at home. He might have made a good teacher, caterer, minister or storekeeper. Yet he meandered on, doing absolutely mediocre work, never failing, never shining, and always rather purposely waiting the day which should bring him to the Medical School.

He was waiting for something else, too, though this Isaiah never guessed. He was waiting for some sign of help or recognition from the white Byes. His father had told him of the slaveholder's great debt to old Joshua; he had taken him riding past the Bryn Mawr peach orchards. "By rights part of them ought to belong to us. But I don't mind, no sir-ee! Let 'em have 'em. See where we are to-day without their help. Think of it!"

Meriwether did think of it and did mind it. He learned that he had been named after the son of his grandfather's patron and somehow it seemed impossible to him that that mere fact should not result in something tangibly advantageous. He lacked the imagination to understand the pride which actuated Isaiah to name his boy as he had. The year before Meriwether was to enter medical school, Isaiah, fortunately for himself, died.

A few months later Miriam died, too. Meriwether was left sole heir to the three houses and two or three hundred dollars. He was tired of school and not at all displeased with the idea of being his own master. He would like a little vacation, he fancied, and a chance to see the world. Somebody told him of a good way to do this—why not get a job as train porter? The idea pleased him; there was travel, easy money, besides his little property in Philadelphia. And afterwards perhaps there would be the patron for whom he had been named, Dr. Meriwether Bye of Bryn Mawr.

Isaiah's mother, Belle Bye, used to say, "Things you do expect and things you don't expect are sure to come to pass." It took Isaiah many years to see the reasonableness of this apparently unreasoned statement. Certainly one of the things he never expected to come to pass was that his boy Meriwether should, first, give up altogether his project of studying medicine and, second, that bit by bit, through sickness, gambling, and a hitherto unsuspected penchant for sheer laziness, he should run through his Philadelphia property, thus wiping away all that edifice of respectability and good citizenship which Isaiah Bye had so carefully built up.

Colored Philadelphia society is organized as definitely as, and even a little more carefully than, Philadelphia white society. One wasn't "in" in those old days unless one were, first, "an old citizen," and, second, unless one were eminently respectable,—almost it might be said God-fearing. Meriwether having been born to this estate suffered all the inconveniences coming to a member of a group at that time small and closely welded. His business was everybody's business. His Uncle Peter had upbraided him for not studying medicine. Jonas Howard, the caterer, knew about his first real estate transfer. The young Howards and his cousins knew about his gambling and rebuked him admiringly. On one of his "runs" Meriwether spent a week in New York. This was in 1889. Not a single colored person knew him or cared about him. He rented a room in Fifty-third Street and made that his headquarters. Later he rented two rooms and married a young seamstress who died in 1891 when her boy was born.

Meriwether did do two things after that. First he wrote to Dr. Meriwether Bye telling him who he was and implying he would not disdain a little aid. It is doubtful if the doctor, who at that time was traveling in Europe with his tiny grandson, ever received the letter. Second, he took to drink. More than anything else he fell into a deep, ineluctable mood of melancholia. Here he was, Meriwether Bye, destined to be a great man, a famous physician. Why, he had been a man of property once, with money in the bank! And now he was just a poor nobody, picking up odd jobs, paying his room rent fearfully from week to week, sometimes pawning Isaiah Bye's chased gold watch.

How he worked it out he himself could not have told. But he saw himself a martyr, "driven by fate" from the high eminence of his father's dreams to his own poor realities. Think how he had struggled, sacrificed—he believed it—the fun and freedom of youth to come to this! "How," said Meriwether Bye harking back to Sunday-School days, "how are the mighty fallen!" And how easily might they have remained mighty.

He named his boy Peter after his Uncle Peter, in whose

second-hand shop in Philadelphia he had spent delightful hours.

Now see the perversity of human nature. Just as his father Isaiah Bye had talked to his son Meriwether about the reward of effort and faithful toil, just so Meriwether talked to Peter about the futility of labor and ambition. And in particular he talked to him about the ingratitude of the white Byes—of all white people.

"It makes no difference, Peter, what you do or how hard you work. The rewards of life are only for such or such. You may pour your heart's blood out,"—he had a fine gift of rhetoric—"and still achieve nothing. Think of your great-grandfather. Fate favors those whom she chooses. Blessed is he who expects nothing, for he shall not be disappointed."

Or, "Peter, if life has any favors for you, she'll give them to you without your asking for them. The world owes you a living, let it come to you, don't bother going after it."

How completely his son might be absorbing all this, Meriwether never knew, for Peter, vocal enough with his playmates and others, maintained an owlish silence when his father thus harangued him.

But his aunt knew. She was a tall, stout, yellow woman, with that ineffable look of sadness in her eyes characteristic of a certain type of colored people. She was the sister of Peter's mother, and when Peter's father died, suddenly, inconsequently, she accepted uncomplainingly his son along with her other burdens.

Peter was then twelve; extraordinarily handsome, vivid and alert. Miss Susan Graves riding home from the cemetery reflected that he might be not such a burden after all. Clearly he would soon want to be taking care of himself.

"Peter," she said thoughtfully, "what do you want to do when you grow up?"

"Oh, I don't know," her nephew replied, temporarily remov-

ing his gaze from the window-pane where it had been glued
for twenty minutes. "I'm not bothered about that, Aunt
Susan. You see the world owes me a living."

She noticed in him then the first fruits of his father's shiftlessness. But far more deeply rooted than that was his deep
dislike for white people. He did not believe that any of them
were kind or just or even human. And although he could not
himself have told what he wanted from the white Byes, if
indeed he wanted anything, he grew up with the feeling that
he and his had been unusually badly treated. His grandfather's connection with white people resulted in pride, his
father's in shiftlessness; in Peter it took the form of a constant
and increasing bitterness.

CHAPTER V

IT may seem a cold-blooded thing to say, but the dying of Meriwether Bye was about the best thing he could have done for his son, Peter. Certainly that was what Miss Susan Graves thought as she viewed rather grimly the small and motley collection of belongings which Peter transferred to her home in his little express wagon from his father's former landlady, Mrs. Reading. The collection consisted of a well-worn extra suit of clothes, another pair of shoes, some underwear in sad need of patching, some books chiefly on physiology and anatomy, the Bye Family Bible, a little old black testament, and a box of letters. There was also a big railroad map which Peter lugged along under his arm and from which he stubbornly refused to be parted. Meriwether, in his brighter moods, used to refer to his "runs" as "business-trips" and would point out to Peter just where he would go on such and such a date. The boy learned a lot of geography in this way, and was talking to his playmates about Duluth and Jacksonville, Sacramento and Denver, before most of them knew that they personally were living in the country's metropolis.

The books on medicine and anatomy had been well thumbed by Peter, too. Meriwether had received them from old Isaiah, his father, and had carried them around on his runs to impress his co-workers in the Pullman service.

Later he got into the habit of reading from them to Peter who always listened in the grave silence which he usually reserved for his father's effusions. For some reason the little boy's brain retained the various and amazing things which his

father read to him from the dry old books. Long before he
knew his multiplication tables he knew the names of the principal bones of the body and the course of the food. In fact
these books were his first readers, for Meriwether, more interested in this dry stuff, now that it was too late to profit him
anything, taught his boy how to pronounce the difficult names,
so that the latter could read to him. Perhaps the poor fellow,
dissolute and weak failure though he was, thought that some
of the old "greatness" might still accrue to him by this fiction
of studying at medicine.

The Bible was the one thing that Peter knew least about.
He looked into it once or twice and hitting on Isaiah Bye's
tragically proud inscription: "By *his* fruits ye shall know—
me," spelled it out laboriously,—he always had trouble in reading script,—and asked his father with some natural perplexity
what it meant. But Meriwether snatched the book away from
him with such a black look and took such pains to put it out
of his reach, that Peter for a long time thought the Bible, or
at any rate that inscription, must be something decidedly off
color. He waited until his father had gone on his next
"business-trip" before investigating again, but finding the
book nowhere as exciting as his beloved Anatomy, he gave up
the puzzle and attributed his father's defection to the inscrutable whims and vagaries of the genus called parents. He
valued that old Bible the least of all his possessions. That
was the bitterest day of his life when he found out what it
ought to mean to him.

Miss Susan, though not an "old Philadelphian" herself, knew
something of colored Philadelphia's pride in the possession of
family and tradition. She would have been glad of course if
Meriwether Bye had left Peter some money. But of the two
she would very much rather have had the Bible with its absolute assurance of the former standing and respectability of the
black Byes. She had a family tradition of her own, for she

was a member of the Graves family of Gravestown, New Jersey, a clan well known to colored people not only in that vicinity, but also throughout Pennsylvania.

The story is that two white sisters in the middle of the eighteenth century fell in love with two of their father's black slaves. The Negroes may have been African Princes for all any one knows to the contrary. Since nothing they could do or say would win their father's consent to such a union, the girls ran away with their lovers, and married them, with or without benefit of clergy it is impossible to relate. Nature and God alike, instead of being disconcerted at this utter contravention of the laws of man, presented each couple with numerous children. When these reached mating age, finding themselves out of favor with both black and white of their community, the cousins solved the problem by marrying each other. The children of each generation did the same, whether driven to it by like necessity or not, history does not say. But by the time the next brood appeared a precedent had been established, and Graves married Graves not only as a matter of course, but as a matter of pride. They were able to do this, being automatically rendered free by the fact that a white woman had married a black man.

Miss Susan Graves had not married for the simple and sufficient reason that in her day there were not enough male Graves to go around. She would as soon have thought of marrying outside her family as a Spanish grandee would have thought of marrying an English cockney. In those days the position of old maid had its decided disadvantages—few people if any gave her the benefit of the doubt that she might have remained single from choice. Yet Miss Susan Graves, in spite of three other offers, soared on family pride above all this and made her career that of housekeeper for the family of a wealthy merchant on Girard Avenue, in Philadelphia. (You must marry a Graves, but obviously you obtained work where you could find it.)

There was a younger sister, Alice Graves, not as direct in purpose as Susan, yet in some respects curiously strong. She had always considered the Graves' tradition silly: it was so unexciting marrying someone whom you had known and seen all your life. What was marriage for if not for a change?

When the oldest son of Merchant Sharples of Girard Avenue married and went to New York, Susan Graves went along as housekeeper. And thither Alice Graves followed shortly to do sewing for that intricate but orderly household. Meriwether Bye, who had known both ladies in Philadelphia—for Miss Susan Bye was a frequent visitor both at his father's and his Uncle Peter's house—came to see them in his rare fits of loneliness, and between runs courted Alice Graves in Central Park. Of course it would have been better if Alice could have married a Graves, but Susan resigned herself easily to the matter—for Bye belonged to old stock and must, she thought, make good eventually. But she developed a strong dislike for him before his death, and took Peter not only for his mother's sake but also to dispel if possible his father's doubtless harmful influence.

Peter was a surprise to his aunt. She found him kind but thoughtless, industrious on occasions but unspeakably shiftless, not too proud, not very grateful and with no sense of responsibility. His father of course spoke there. Yet the boy was indubitably charming, never complained, and usually did as he was told. Miss Susan found herself between two minds— she had an impulse to work her fingers to the bone and thus spare Alice's beautiful son the tussle with poverty which he must know, and again a desire to speak and act forcibly and drive him into an acknowledgment of what her loyalty to her sister was leading her to do for a homeless, friendless lad. Actually she struck a medium, made him keep clean, insisted on his regular attendance at school, took him to Sunday-School and Church entertainments and induced him to work on Saturdays and holidays by refusing pocket-money to "a boy as big as you."

She could not understand why he chose a job in a butcher's shop. Doubtless Peter hardly knew himself. "I like to watch the man saw the bones," he would have said vaguely. "I can do it, too. I can cut up a chicken or a rabbit just as neatly!"

CHAPTER VI

IT was Joanna who first acquainted Peter with himself. But neither of the children knew this at the time. And although Peter came to realize it later it was many years before he told her so. For, though he went through many changes and though these two came to speak of many things, he kept a certain inarticulateness all his lifetime.

Joanna and all the older Marshalls went to a school in West Fifty-second Street, one after another like little steps, with Joanna at first quite some distance behind. They were known throughout the school. "Those Marshall children, you know those colored children that always dress so well and as though they had someone to take care of them. Pretty nice looking children, too, if only they weren't colored. Their father is a caterer, has that place over there on Fifty-ninth Street. Makes a lot of money for a colored man."

Peter, unlike Joanna, had gone to school, one might almost say, all over New York, and nowhere for any great length of time. Meriwether had stayed longest at Mrs. Reading's but as, in later years, he more and more went off on his runs without paying his bills, Mrs. Reading frequently refused to let Peter leave the house until his father's return.

"For all I know he may be joinin' his father on the outside and the two of them go off together. Then where'd I be? For them few rags that Mr. Bye keeps in his room wouldn't be no good to nobody."

This enforced truancy was the least of Peter's troubles. He did not like school,—too many white people and consequently, as he saw it, too much chance for petty injustice. The result

40

of this was that Peter at twelve, possessed it is true of a large assortment of really useful facts, lacked the fine precision, if the doubtful usefulness, of Joanna's knowledge at ten. When Miss Susan settled in the Marshalls' neighborhood and brought Peter to the school in Fifty-second Street he was found to be lacking and yet curiously in advance. "We'll try him," said the principal doubtfully, "in the fifth grade. I'll take him to Miss Shanley's room."

Miss Shanley was Joanna's teacher. She greeted Peter without enthusiasm, not because he was colored but because he was clearly a problem. Joanna spied him immediately. He was too handsome with his brown-red skin, his black silky hair that curled alluringly, his dark, almost almond-shaped eyes, to escape her notice. But she forgot about him, too, almost immediately, for the first time Miss Shanley called on him he failed rather ignominiously. Joanna did not like stupid people and thereafter to her he simply was not.

On the contrary, Joanna had caught and retained Peter's attention. She was the only other colored person in the room and therefore to him the only one worth considering. And though at that time Joanna was still rather plain, she already had an air. Everything about her was of an exquisite perfection. Her hair was brushed till it shone, her skin glowed not only with health but obviously with cleanliness, her shoes were brown and shiny, with perfectly level heels. She wore that first week a very fine soft sage-green middy suit with a wide buff tie. The nails which finished off the rather square-tipped fingers of her small square hands, were even and rounded and shining. Peter had seen little girls with this perfection and assurance on Chestnut Street in Philadelphia and on Fifth Avenue in New York, but they had been white. He had not yet envisaged this sort of thing for his own. Perhaps he inherited his great-grandfather Joshua's spiritless acceptance of things as they are, and his belief that differences between people were not made, but had to be.

Joanna clearly stood for something in the class. Peter noted a little enviously the quality of the tone in which Miss Shanley addressed her. To other children she said, "Gertrude, can you tell me about the Articles of Confederation?" Usually she implied a doubt, which Gertrude usually justified. But she was sure of Joanna. The tenseness of her attitude might be seen to relax; her mentality prepared momentarily for a rest. "Joanna will now tell us,—" she would announce. For Joanna, having a purpose and having been drilled by Joel to the effect that final perfection is built on small intermediate perfections, got her lessons completely and in detail every day.

It was at this time and for many years thereafter characteristic of Peter that he, too, wanted to shine, but did not realize that one shone only as a result of much mental polishing personally applied. Joanna's assurance, her air of purposefulness, her indifference intrigued him and piqued him. He sidled across to the blackboard nearest her—if they were both sent to the board—cleaned hers off if she gave him a chance, managed to speak a word to her now and then. He even contrived to wait for her one day at the Girls' entrance. Joanna threw him a glance of recognition, swept by, returned.

His heart jumped within him.

"If you see my sister Sylvia,—you know her?—tell her not to wait for me. I have to go early to my music-lesson. She'll be right out."

Sylvia didn't appear for half an hour and Peter should have been at the butcher's, but he waited. Sylvia and Maggie Ellersley came out laughing and glowing. Peter gave the message.

"Thanks," said Sylvia prettily. Maggie stared after him. She was still the least bit bold in those days.

"Ain't he the best looker you ever saw, Sylvia? Such eyes! Who is he, anyway? Not ever Joanna's beau?"

"Imagine old Joanna with a beau." Sylvia laughed. "He's just a new boy in her class. He *is* good looking."

Some important examinations were to take place shortly and Miss Shanley planned extensive reviews. She was a thorough if somewhat unimaginative teacher and she meant to have no loose threads. So she devoted two days to geography, two more to grammar, another to history, one to the rather puzzling consideration of that mysterious study, physiology. Perhaps by now the class was a bit fed up with cramming, perhaps the children weren't really interested in physiological processes. Joanna wasn't, but she always got lessons like these doggedly, thinking "Soon we'll be past all this," or "I'm going to forget this old stuff as soon as I grow up." Poor Miss Shanley was in despair. She could not call on Joanna for everything. Pupil after pupil had failed. Her eye roved over the room and fell on Peter's black head.

She sighed. He had not even been a member of the class when she had taught this particular physiological phenomenon. "Can't anyone besides Joanna Marshall give me the 'Course of the Food?'"

Peter raised his hand. "He looks intelligent," she thought. "Well, Bye you may try it."

"I don't think I can give it to you the way the others say it,"—the children had been reciting by rote, "but I know what happens to the food."

She knew he would fail if he didn't know it her way, but she let him begin.

This was old ground for Peter. "Look, I can draw it. See, you take the food in your mouth," he drew a rough sketch of lips, mouth cavity and gullet, "then you must chew it, masticate, I think you said." He went on varying from his own simplified interpretation of Meriwether Bye's early instructions, past difficult names like pancreatic juice and thoracic duct, and while he talked he drew, recalling pictures from those old anatomies; expounding, flourishing. Miss Shanley stared at him in amazement. This jewel, this undiscovered diamond!

"How'd you come to know it, Peter?"

"I read it, I studied it." He did not say when. "But it's so easy to learn things about the body. It's yourself."

She quizzed him then while the other children, Joanna among them, stared open-eyed. But he knew all the simple ground which she had already covered, and much, much beyond.

"If all the children," said Miss Shanley, forgetting Peter's past, "would just get their lessons like Peter Bye and Joanna Marshall."

She had coupled their names together! And after school Joanna was waiting for him. He walked up the street with her, pleasantly conscious of her interest, her frank admiration.

"How wonderful," she breathed, "that you should know your physiology like that. What are you going to be when you grow up, a doctor?"

"A surgeon," said Peter forgetting his old formula and expressing a resolve which her question had engendered in him just that second. He saw himself on the instant, a tall distinguished-looking man, wielding scissors and knife with deft nervous fingers. Joanna would be hovering somewhere—he was not sure how—in the offing. And she would be looking at him with this same admiration.

"My, won't you have to study?" Joanna could have told an aspirant almost to the day and measure the amount of time and effort it would take him to become a surgeon, a dentist, a lawyer, an engineer. All these things Joel discussed about his table with the intense seriousness which colored men feel when they speak of their children's futures.

Alexander and Philip were to have their choice of any calling within reason. They were seventeen and fifteen now and the house swarmed with college catalogues. Schools, terms, degrees of prejudice, fields of practice,—Joanna knew them all.

"Yes," said Peter, "I suppose I will have to study. How did you come to know so much—did your father tell you?"

"Why, I get it out of books, of course." Joanna was highly indignant: "I never go to bed without getting my lessons. In fact, all I do is to get lessons of some kind—school lessons or music. You know I'm to be a great singer."

"No, I didn't know that. Perhaps you'll sing in your choir?"

Then Joanna astonished him. "In my choir—I sing there already! No! Everywhere, anywhere, Carnegie Hall and in Boston and London. You see, I'm to be famous."

"But," Peter objected, "colored people don't get any chance at that kind of thing."

"Colored people," Joanna quoted from her extensive reading, "can do everything that anybody else can do. They've already done it. Some one colored person somewhere in the world does as good a job as anyone else,—perhaps a better one. They've been kings and queens and poets and teachers and doctors and everything. I'm going to be the one colored person who sings best in these days, and I never, never, never mean to let color interfere with anything I *really* want to do."

"I dance, too," she interrupted herself, "and I'll probably do that besides. Not ordinary dancing, you know, but queer beautiful things that are different from what we see around here; perhaps I'll make them up myself. You'll see! They'll have on the bill-board, 'Joanna Marshall, the famous artist,'—" She was almost dancing along the sidewalk now, her eyes and cheeks glowing.

Peter looked at her wistfully. His practical experience and

the memory of his father inclined him to dubiousness. But her superb assurance carried away all his doubts.

"I don't suppose you'll ever think of just ordinary people like me?"

"But you'll be famous, too—you'll be a wonderful doctor. Do be. I can't stand stupid, common people."

"You'll always be able to stand me," said Peter with a fervor which made his statement a vow.

CHAPTER VII

SYLVIA and Joanna, walking through Sixty-third Street on an errand for their mother, came upon groups of children playing games. Italians, Jews, colored Americans, white Americans were there disporting themselves with more or less abandon, according to their peculiar temperament.

"Look," said Joanna suddenly, catching at Sylvia's hand. "See those children dancing! Wait, I've got to see that!"

Out in the middle of the street a band of colored children were dancing and acting a game. With no thought of spectators they joined hands, took a few steps, separated, spun around, smote hands sharply, and then flung them above their heads. One girl stood in the middle, singing too, but with an attentive air. Presently she darted forward, seized a member of the ring:

"Say, little Missy, won't you marry me?"

Their voices were treble and sweet, though shrill, and rang with a peculiar, piercing quality above the street noises and the sounds of the other children's games. The little players were absorbed, enraptured with the spirit of the dance and the abandon of the music. Joanna, too, was in a transport. She watched them going through the motions several times. Presently she caught all the words:

"Sissy in the barn, join in the weddin,'
Sissy in the barn, join in the weddin' "

The child in the center here chose a partner. The others sang:

47

"Sweetest l'il couple I ever did see.
Barn! Barn!

They stamped here.

"Arms all 'round me!
Barn!

The two children in the center embraced each other while the rest sang:

"Say, little Missy, won't you marry me?"

Then the two in the center pointed fingers at each other, shrilling:

"Stay back, girl, don't you come near me
All them sassy words you say!

Then all:

Oh, Barn! Barn!
"Arms all 'round me!
Say, little Missy, won't you marry me?
Marry me?"

The last line came as a faint echo.

Joanna rushed forward: "I can play it! Girls let me play it, too!"

The children stared at her a moment, then, with the instinct of childhood for a kindred spirit, two of them unclasped hands and took Joanna in. She outdid them all in the fervor and grace of her acting. Two white settlement workers stopped and looked at her.

"Come on, Joanna," Sylvia called impatiently.

Joanna came running, a string of the children after her. She bade them good-by. "I must go now, but I'm coming back sometime soon, to learn some more." She blew them a kiss, "good-by, oh, good-by!"

She came up to Sylvia flushed and excited. "We'll play it home, Sylvia! Wasn't it lovely and dear? Oh, I could dance like that forever!" She went almost all the entire remaining distance on tip-toe.

Life in Joel Marshall's house was not always a serious discussion of the Marshall children's future. Like many of the better class of colored people, the Marshalls did not meet with the grosser forms of color prejudice, because they kept away from the places where it might be shown. This was bad from the standpoint of development of civic pride and interest. But it had its good results along another line. The children took most of their pleasures in their house or in those of their friends and devoted their wits and young originality to indoor pastimes.

The Marshall house was a great center for this kind of thing, and already Friday and Saturday nights were being regularly set apart for the children's amusement and for the reception and entertainment of the various young people who dropped in.

Joanna taught her dance. Sylvia and Philip and Alexander were willing pupils; Joanna was magnetic when in this kind of mood. By the time Harry Portor and Maggie Ellersley arrived, they were all singing and stamping and twirling. Peter came in late, held up by the butcher. "Had to go on an errand for the grand white folks," he explained briefly.

"You'll wear out my carpet to-night for sure," said Mrs. Marshall, but she loved the dancing as much as any of them, and got up and took a turn. Joanna taught the tune to Peter, who had a good ear, and he ran over to the old-fashioned square piano and rattled it off to a wild thumping accompaniment. When Brian Spencer came in, who even in those days was pretty sure to be where Slyvia was—the fun was at its height. Peter, strumming a haunting, atavistic measure; Joanna, dancing like a faun, instructed Maggie Ellersley.

"Now, Maggie, dance up to one of them. All right, take Philip. You point your finger at him,—no both of you. Yes, you're right, Peter. I forgot that. See, Phil, Peter's learned

4

it already. Here I'll do it by myself; all of you stand back."

She went through an elaborate pantomime, stretching out her hands as though clasping a partner on each side. She described an imaginary circle for the ring and ran into the midst of it. An imaginary partner was before her and she drew him in, pointed a slim, brown finger at him, rested both hands on her young hips, pirouetted, sang to him gayly:

"Stand back, boy, don't you come near me!"

"My," laughed Brian Spencer, clapping loudly. "Can't you see it all just as plainly? Really, Jan, you ought to go on the stage as an impersonator, I don't believe you could be beat." He was a tall dark boy with fine proud features that looked chiseled. He and Alexander were home from college for the Easter vacation.

Maggie Ellersley, as it happened, had been at a matinée the week before. "It was vaudeville, Joanna, and there was an actress there who took off different people and then she did some Irish folk dances, but she couldn't hold a candle to you. Too bad we're colored."

"It's not going to make any difference to me," said Joanna determinedly. "Mother and father are willing. If I want to go on the stage I'll get there."

"Joanna has the faith that moves mountains," laughed Peter. "If anybody can make it she can."

Peter was a regular visitor at the Marshall home now. Ever since that day four years before when he had told Joanna of his new-born determination to be a surgeon, he had spent all his spare time near her. Miss Susan Graves did not like this at first, not that she resented Peter's absence from her so much, but he was a Bye and she did not choose to have him associate too much with people whom she did not know. It was no part of her plan for Peter to retrograde into the wreck which Meriwether had become. She made it her business to meet Mrs. Marshall at a church affair

"I think," said Miss Graves, eyeing Joanna's mother with her clear, square gaze, "that my boy has spoken to me of you."

Mrs. Marshall looked puzzled. She thought this was a *Miss* Graves.

"Peter Bye," his aunt continued, "he's my nephew. He often speaks of Joanna Marshall."

"Oh, Peter! Yes, we like to have him at the house. The girls find him great fun. So you're his aunt. You must come to see us, too. Get him to bring you."

Miss Graves came and was impressed enough to let Peter continue, though he would have continued without her permission. But Miss Susan, like Belle Bye nearly a century ago, recognized atmosphere when she saw it. She was poor; Peter was penniless. These were the sort of people her nephew ought to know. She liked Joel's success, his pride, his air of being somebody. She estimated rightly the correctness of the old-fashioned walnut furniture, the heavy curtains, the kidney table in the parlor, the massive silver service and good linen. It is true Sylvia changed much of this—except the silver—for cretonnes and wicker chairs and gay rugs. But as Miss Susan went to the house only a few times she did not know of this.

What she especially liked was the spirit of life, of ambition and hopefulness that pulsed in that household. As Miss Graves grew older, she began to see that her younger sister had had some pretty good views after all, that it did not do to stick to settled views,—"this for me, and that quite other thing for you." The great things of life were for the taking, it was true, but the result of deliberate planning. One did not simply stumble into success. She had lived too long with "the best white people" not to find that out.

Joel knew this, too, she realized. His whole life was devoted to the mapping out of his children's future. His own and Joanna's high enthusiasms had borne fruit. Of late the boys, Philip and Alexander, had talked good solid man-talk.

"Colored people will be going big pretty soon. We'll have to get in it, too, Pa."

Miss Susan decided this was a good place for Peter. Even if she had the money to do so, she could not send him to a school where he would meet with more inspiration in both precept and actual concrete example. Already in the lesser things this association was bearing fruit. Peter was too handsome, too graceful, too charming ever to be considered a boor. But he had lacked finish, that fine courtliness of manner which Miss Susan noted could convert a man of most ordinary appearance into a prince. She had marked it among Jacob Sharples' grandsons. Peter had not possessed a knowledge of that delicacy, of that attention to trifles which, once gained by a man, gives him passport everywhere. Miss Susan had noticed, to her regret, the boy's tendency to let her carry bundles, to look after even the heavier household duties. It had never occurred to him if the weather were cold or stormy, to offer to go errands for her. And his aunt, practical though she was, shrank from calling his attention to these things. She did not want him to think of her as exacting a return for her kindness.

Now the Marshall boys were fine gentlemen. Joel had made them so by teaching, as well as by his attitude toward their mother and sisters. Joanna and Sylvia, particularly Sylvia, helped the boys out with an occasional stitch, an occasional sewing on of a button. When Alexander was getting ready for college, and was working at nights to help with his expenses, Sylvia used to arrange sandwiches and milk for him when he came in late. And Joanna had recopied his chemistry and history notes. These were only kind trivialities, but the boys treated their sisters like queens. Philip was a little like Sylvia, only neither as handsome nor as lithe and quick. Alexander—Alec, Sandy, the girls called him variously—was slower, like Joanna. Both boys were tall and well set-up.

The girls used to thrill a little—sisters to them though they were—over the very real and thoughtful gallantry of these two young men.

Miss Susan had remarked this quality as soon as she met them. And she was beginning now to see its reflection in Peter. And as he had beauty and great personal charm to go with it, it distinguished him even more than the Marshall boys. She half way suspected a conscious assumption of this on his part.

"But if he keeps it up, it will become part of him," she thought to herself, "and then—girls be careful." She would have been a little fearful for Joanna had she not noticed immediately in the young girl that indomitable desire for distinction. "Joanna will never fall in love with anybody," she said once to a common friend of herself and the Marshalls. "She'll never be able to take her mind off long enough from her high falutin dreams."

Of course Peter had no conception why his aunt liked him to visit the Marshalls. He was only too glad that she didn't disapprove. He was seventeen now and beginning to know himself in some ways pretty well. He liked Sandy and Philip and Sylvia Marshall—liked them very well, and Joanna! It could hardly be said that he loved her at this time. But he knew that what he liked best of all in the world was to be near her, to watch her, and to listen to her plans. She had little shadowy gleams in her dark thick hair, glints of light that ended abruptly in wavy blackness. He would like to touch it. He remembered that he had once pulled her hair. He had done it often! But now, though she was only fifteen, he did not dare. Yet he often touched Sylvia's.

The night that Joanna taught them all the barn dance, Peter maneuvered until he got Harry Portor at the piano, and said:

"How does that part go, Joanna? Here I am in the center. Then I take you in. Then——"

"Put your arms around her," said Sylvia. "That's it. Now,——

Barn! Barn!"

He went home and fairly babbled to his aunt about it. "Joanna is the most wonderful!"

CHAPTER VIII

IF Peter was unconscious of the utter desirability of association with the young Marshalls, Maggie Ellersley was
not. Ever since her childhood when she had overheard
a conversation between a cousin and her mother, she had made
up her mind to attach herself to some such family and see
what came of it.

The cousin and her mother worked together for some
wealthy white people. Maggie's mother was a laundress, a
spare hard-working woman to whom life had meant nothing
but poverty and confusion. On Thursdays and Fridays of
each week she washed and ironed and gossiped with "my
cousin Mis' Sparrow" who was cook at the house on Madison
Avenue. Maggie used to come there for dinner and go home
with her mother.

"Mis' Sparrow," small and spidery, had a perpetual complaint against the world. In particular she experienced envy
toward those who were better off than herself. Her jaundiced
disposition may be excused, however, when one reflects that hers
was a lot which had been hard ever since she could remember. She was poor, she was weak, she was ignorant. Add to
that the fact that she was black in a country where color is a
crime and you have her "complex." Some people would say
she had really done well in one sense with her life. She had
attained by her own unaided efforts to a comfortable, even
if menial, position, where she had heat, light and enough
to eat. They would ask: Considering her beginnings what

more could she want? Alas, in that dull soul unknown aspirations stirred, amazing questions took form. "Why, why, why?" asked Mis' Sparrow in her own peculiar dialect, "are all the sweetness and light of life showered on some and utterly denied to me?"

At present Mis' Sparrow had fastened a resentful eye on Mrs. Proctor, the bride of the son of the "white folks" for whom she worked. Edmonia the maid had told her about the newcomer, and over the supper table she retailed it to Mrs. Ellersley.

"She wan't nobuddy. Jes' a little teeny slip of ole white gal. No money, no fambly, no nuthin'."

"Where'd he meet her then?" asked Mrs. Ellersley, uninterested but polite.

"Young Mr. Proctor's sister met her in boardin'-school, poorest thing there," replied Mis' Sparrow, wiping a puckered mouth with her apron. " 'Monia says Miss Dorothy sorry for her and got her a job in her father's office. Mr. Harry was jes' home f'um college; he saw her, took a fancy to her and jes' married her. Jes' wouldn't listen to nobuddy a-tall."

"Don't it beat all," pondered Mrs. Ellersley, "how some people have all the luck? Now if that kind of thing could just happen to my Maggie."

Mis' Sparrow was unmoved by the irrelevant allusion to Maggie. Where would she get such a chance?

" 'Monia says she don't even love him. Liked some young travelin' salesman she'd known all her life. 'Monia declares she cries about him when she's by herself."

"What she marry him for then?" asked Maggie Ellersley, aged twelve, and an interested listener.

"H'm child, wouldn't you do anything to get away f'um hard work, an' ugly cloes an' bills? Some w'ite folks has it most as bad as us poor colored people. On'y thing is they has more opporchunities."

Maggie, visualizing the life which she and her mother endured, thought she probably would. She thought it again after they had reached the tenement in Thirty-fifth Street where the two of them lived. It was the famous "Tenderloin" of those days and Maggie's spirit revolted with a revulsion of feeling which never ceased to amaze her mother against the sordidness of that place. There were three rooms. The front one looked on the street and so was well lighted, but the other two got light only from the air-shaft. Mrs. Ellersley, a widow who considered herself fortunate to be one, rented the front room out, usually to train-men (perhaps some of Meriwether's acquaintances were among them), occasionally to a married couple.

She and Maggie slept and lived in the two wretchedly ventilated rooms, in a perpetual gloom penetrated ever so slightly by a flickering blue flame. A confusion of clothes, obscene old furniture, boxes, stale newspapers was littered about them. For some reason the rooms were everlastingly damp, perhaps because, although rain could get down the air-shaft, the sunlight never could. The rooms gave Maggie a constantly eerie feeling, which in later more fortunate years she was always able to recall by the sight of a gas-flame burning low and blue.

They never, in those days, enjoyed a really bright flame. Saving was Mrs. Ellersley's insistent because necessary fetish. Maggie's tea was always weak, and never sweet enough. The bread—baker's with holes in it, yesterday's, two loaves for five cents—was always stale; the meat usually salt and sometimes tainted.

Out of it all Maggie bloomed—a strange word but somehow true. She was like a yellow calla lily in the deep cream of her skin, the slim straightness of her body. She had a mass of fine, wiry hair which hung like a cloud, a mist over two gray eyes. Her lips, in spite of her constant malnutrition, persisted unbelievably red. When she met excitement those gray eyes darkened and shone, her cheeks flushed a little, her small hands fluttered. And she was nearly always excited. Something within her frail bosom pulsed in a constant revolt against the spirit of things that kept her in these conditions.

"I will not always live like this, Ma—I'll get out of it some way."

And her mother, though always scoffing, believed her with a dreary hopefulness. "If there's a way to be found out, Maggie'll find it."

Maggie found early that one avenue of escape lay through men. They were stronger than women, they made money. They did not give the impression of shrinking from spending the last penny lest when that cent was gone there should be no more. All the train-men liked her. She could not get much order in that abominable home, but she could and did keep herself clean and neat. She washed her few garments over night; she wound a stray ribbon, from a box of cigars or a box of candy, through her hair. Some of the men, young students, "on the road" during their summer vacations, used to flirt with her.

"Hurry and grow up, Mag. When I get through school I'll come back and marry you. How'd you like to live in a little house—not like this!—in Washington?" Or Wilmington or Savannah as the case might be. "I'd give you pretty dresses."

Poor Maggie. Her calla-lily charm visibly lessened in those days when she opened her pretty mouth. She disclosed herself then for what she was, a true daughter of the Tenderloin.

"Aw quit your kiddin'!"

But she came slowly to realize that here was a way out. If she could only grow up—if she were—say—seventeen.

She was persistently frail, else her mother might have put her to work. As it was she was sent to school very regularly —to save fuel and gas. Evenings she went to the houses where her mother worked and got her dinner.

On the night after she had listened to Mis' Sparrow's comments about young Mrs. Proctor, she sat thoughtful a long time. She had sense enough to know that very often these train-men stayed poor. They made pretty good money—they did, too, in those days—but not enough to save their wives from labor. Maggie did not want to wash and iron, to go through the dreary existence which had been her mother's when her father was living; he had run on the road.

Suppose, just suppose, there were some colored men who were fortunate, successful, who had enough to eat, who could give their wives help. Her mother knew of ministers like that. There were colored doctors and lawyers somewhere. Their very titles connoted prosperity.

"Ma," she spoke out of her brown study, "are there any very rich colored men?"

"Not any very rich ones, I don't think," Mrs. Ellersley replied thoughtfully, "but lots very well off, comfortable, with servants to wait on 'em." She sighed.

"I'm going to meet one," said Maggie solemnly, and henceforth she thought, she dreamed of nothing else.

When she was fourteen young John Howe, who was occupying the front room, came down with a spell of typhoid fever. He begged Mrs. Ellersley not to send him to the hospital, and it was impossible to get him to his home in Oklahoma. He had enough money to see him through, and he put his fortunes and his case into her withered hands. All the trainmen knew of Mrs. Ellersley's absolute honesty. She did what she could for him, sat up long nights, gave him his medicine faithfully, "counted out his money."

But it was Maggie who gave real service. She stayed out of school to attend him. The doctor gave her a list of directions which she followed with meticulous care. In that shabby house down in that terrible district John Howe met with an attention, a devotion from the humble woman and her delicate daughter, such as no money could have bought him in the seats of the mighty.

John Howe was a Lincoln divinity student, intermittently working his way through college. He sat up gaunt and weak in the scratched bed of cheap cherry wood and picked with long skeleton fingers at the thin blue and white checked coverlet.

"Maggie, you and your mother've been mighty good to me. Look here, I've got to pay you back somehow. After this illness I'll have to stay out of school a year. What do you want?"

Maggie stared at him, her gray eyes going black in the yellow oval of her face.

"There's only one thing I want, Mr. Howe, and you couldn't give me that."

"I could try. What is it?"

"Oh Mr. Howe, if you could just get us out of this awful place, this house, this street! If I could just get to know some decent folks——"

"Well, I don't see how I could arrange about the folks. Where do you want to live, if you go from here? There're not many places for colored folks in New York."

"There are houses for colored people up in Fifty-third Street, and decent folks living in them."

"But my goodness, Maggie, it costs a fortune to rent one of those houses."

"I know, oh, I know. But if we could just get started. Mother could fill the house with roomers. Why there've been twelve men here for this room since you've been sick. The rest of the rooms aren't much, but mother always keeps this room tidy, and we're honest. They all know that. Never missed a penny here, any of them. And they tell their friends about us. Lots of times they tell Ma if she only had more room she'd have all the roomers she wanted."

"But you've no furniture."

"We could buy on the instalment plan." She had her scheme all worked out. Clearly she had nursed her project. "Mr. Howe, if you could just help us to begin."

He would, he told her, convinced by her earnestness. "What exactly do you want me to do, Maggie?"

She wanted him to make his headquarters with them for the year, and to pay as much as he could in advance. It was still early summer. He must write and tell other men, who would want rooms, and get a few of them to pay in advance, too. "Train-men won't mind that," she told him shrewdly, "they'll like to know they have some place to go to when they've cleaned themselves out at cards, or whatever it is they do. That will pay a month's rent, and leave something, and with what we pay on this—this *hole,* we'll have something to put on the furniture."

"I guess you're right," said Howe, "I'll speak to your mother about it."

But that was useless. Mrs. Ellersley was sure of her livelihood, her mere existence here, but she was doubtful about a great venture. "Of course, for Maggie's sake I'd like to get away."

"Oh, Ma, do—do, Ma," Maggie had pleaded in an ecstasy of longing. "This is our one chance. You see if we don't take this we'll never get away."

Fortunately she had Howe to back her. "She's right, Mrs. Ellersley, and this is no place for a young girl to grow up.

You can count on me. I'll go look for a house, and see about some furniture. I know plenty of fellows would be glad to come."

Miraculously the scheme worked. It gave Maggie her first insight into the workings of life. If you wanted things, you thought and thought about them, and when an opportunity offered, there you were with your mind made up to jump at it.

Of course they were poor, but at least they were decent. John Howe, staying for that year in New York, realizing more and more how truly he was indebted to Maggie and her mother, took a proprietary interest. He laid the cheap rugs, he set up the cots, three in a room, he did mysterious jobs in the bath-room which to Maggie was always so marvelous. He bought tools and fixed window-cords which the landlord neglected. Maggie darned his socks for him, and he bought some wall-paper, cheap but clean and virginal, a soft yellow, and papered her square box of a room. A good job he made of it, too. Another roomer at his instigation made a dressing table out of a packing box which Mrs. Ellersley, re-invigorated, covered with scrim.

Gradually, word of her rooming-house spread among the better class of transients. All her lodgers gave her their mending to do, she washed for some of them, gave breakfast to a few chosen spirits, and they paid willingly and well.

Maggie was in transports. This was something like a home. Of course, she had to attend school in the district. Her mother took her as soon as matters were settled. She looked fresh and neat in a dark blue serge dress trimmed with black braid, the gift of melancholy Mis' Sparrow who in turn had had it from young Mrs. Proctor. The dress was worn, but it was whole, and Maggie had tacked a tiny turn-over of white lace in the high collar.

She was assigned to the eighth grade. There were two of them in the school. Her star was in the ascendant, for she was assigned to the one of which Sylvia Marshall was a member. She would have fared differently if it had been Joanna, for unless she were markedly clever, Joanna, who was intellectually a snob, would probably never have seen her. But Sylvia spied her at once. She came over to Maggie at recess.

"You're a new girl, aren't you? Want me to show you your way around?"

Maggie looked at the pretty girl, charming in a soft dark red cashmere dress made with a wide pleated skirt. She had on little patent leather, buttoned shoes with cloth tops, and a big red bow perched butterfly fashion on her dark head. Joanna wore her hair rather primly back from her face, but Sylvia's was parted and rolled in waves over her ears, then it was caught up and confined by the bow. She had a thin gold bracelet on one arm. And about her hung the aura of well-being and easy self-assurance which marked all the Marshall children.

"I wish you would," said Maggie.

Sylvia in those days was an ardent worker in Old Zion Sunday School and had promised to help in a campaign for more students. She told Maggie about it within the next two or three days.

"My mother is going to entertain the new folks whom I get to join. Will you join?"

Maggie would and so went to Sylvia's home as her mother's guest.

She never forgot that home with its quiet dignity and atmosphere of prosperity. The Marshall children were a revelation to her. She had not known of colored people like these.

"At last I'm getting to know decent people," she told her mother.

She had a passion for respectability and decency quite apart from what they connoted of comparative ease and comfort, though she coveted these latter, too, and meant some day to have them.

"Two months ago," she thought, "I was still in that horrible house on Thirty-fifth Street, and I got away. If that could happen, anything could happen." She lay in her bed at nights in the little yellow room and saw visions.

CHAPTER IX

SHE played her cards with an odd mixture of deliberation and spontaneity.

"Maggie adores you, Sylvia," said Joanna.

"I think she does," Sylvia replied modestly. "I don't know why, I'm sure. She certainly is nice to me."

Maggie's obvious admiration and Sylvia's naïve acceptance made the way easy. It is hard not to be nice to someone who shows plainly that you are her ideal, your company her supreme satisfaction. Maggie wore her hair like Sylvia's, she copied when she could her manner of dressing, she spent half her time at the Marshall house.

She saw the value of absolute honesty. No need to pose when telling the exact truth brought what one wanted without the strain of living up to a false position. The Marshalls soon knew of Maggie's poverty, of the quick wit and determination which had brought them from that "dump-heap"—Maggie's word—to the respectable and comfortable if still cheap boarding-house. Sylvia used to talk to her mother about it. Mrs. Marshall suggested that she hand over to Maggie one or two of her perfectly good but discarded dresses.

But Sylvia objected with a very real delicacy. "She goes to the same school I go to and to Sunday-School. I wouldn't want the other children to see her in my things, she'd feel so badly."

Her mother saw the justice of that. "I suppose I have one or two things. There's that old brown Henrietta of mine and the silk poplin. How'll she get them made over though, Sylvia? Now don't expect me to help."

"Oh, mamma, you darling! You really are a brick! That poplin is old rose, isn't it? She ought to look lovely in it. I can fix them. You know how I love to fix things over and Maggie knows how to sew on the machine. If she stayed here three or four days, the rest of this week, we could finish them."

Mrs. Marshall agreed, Maggie's mother was consulted, Maggie came in an ecstasy. Her first sojourn away from home! And what a sojourn! Naturally neat though she was, she learned of toilet mysteries, of rites of which she had never dreamed. Nightly hair-brushings and the discovery that of course each one had her own brush and comb! Frequent washings of both, talcum powders! Joanna the ascetic used scentless ones, but Sylvia's were highly fragrant. These Maggie preferred. A bath every night.

"If you don't mind," said Sylvia, "I'll take mine first and then you can stay in as long as you like. I hope that pig Joanna hasn't used up all the hot water!"

Delicacies for breakfast, lunch, and dinner! Dinner at six instead of the middle of the day! Mrs. Marshall complained of a headache Saturday morning and Joanna took her breakfast up to her on a silver tray. Mr. Marshall kept box on box of cigars in his den. Sandy and Philip wore superlatively blackened shoes.

Maggie looked, listened, stored in her memory. The dresses were a success. The rose poplin, being the prettier, was finished first; Sylvia had longed so to get her hands on it. Maggie put it on Saturday morning and stood in front of the cheval mirror in Mrs. Marshall's room admiring her own and Sylvia's handiwork, and herself with it.

"It's too pretty to wear in the house. Oh, don't let's have

to wait till to-morrow. Mamma, couldn't the boys take us
to the matinée? Maggie, have you seen Peter Pan?"

Maggie, it transpired, had seen nothing, had never been
inside a theater.

"What fun!" Sylvia's native delicacy hit on the right expression. "Fancy going to your first matinée. Can you spare
us, Mother dear?"

The party could be arranged. Philip and Alexander expressed their willingness. Joanna did not care to go, to Maggie's astonishment, which increased when she saw how wonderful the theater was. But there were other things. The
girl never forgot the thrill that came over her as Philip took
her arm and led her over dangerous crossings, arranged her
seat and program for her, took off her coat. He held it during the performance and wrinkled it shamelessly. Sylvia
scolded him.

"You ought to be ashamed of yourself, Phil."

"It doesn't matter," Maggie interposed happily. She was
beginning to have her good time like other people. Oh, God
bless John Howe!

The acquaintanceship progressed. All through the high
school the two were nearly inseparable. It is true, Maggie
sought Sylvia more than Sylvia sought her, but on the other
hand Maggie's presence was taken as a matter of course
by the Marshalls and their friends. Maggie went to parties
with Sylvia, the two escorted by Brian Spencer and Philip.
Often she slept at her house after the parties and at Christmas time and week-ends. Once, when Mrs. Marshall took
Joanna to visit relatives in Philadelphia, Maggie stayed with
Sylvia a whole month.

In her junior year in the high school she had a long talk
with Mr. Marshall. Of course they were still poor, the house
just kept them in comfort. Maggie had become addicted to
the wearing of good clothes. Her mother was getting older.

They needed help from time to time. If Mr. Marshall would assist her in getting some work. She was young and strong and willing.

"No, no, Mr. Marshall!" she objected as Joel—they were sitting in his office—spoke of a loan and reached for his check-book. "Not that! When could I ever pay you back? No, I mean work, real work. I could take orders, count the silver, look after the napery, pay off the men if you'd care to trust me."

Perhaps a man of another race might have stopped to consider such a proposition coming from the lips of a young and dainty girl. He might have been suspicious and realized that his younger son was working in the business with him just then and the boy and girl would be bound to be thrown together. But colored men of old Joel's type are obsessed with the idea of a progressing younger generation. "They must advance," thinks the older man, "I must do all in my power to help them. This is my contribution to mine own."

Joel taught her his simple system of bookkeeping and in-stalled her. She proved herself efficient, willing, and—her mother's teachings spoke here—absolutely honest. Her energy and interest were surprising. "You might think it was her own business," said Joel. He had no desire to see either her or any of his children become caterers, but he did like to see a job well done. Philip was the only one who had evinced any interest in the business, and that was only during his last year before entering college. He had to make some extra money somehow—both he and Sandy had a healthy dislike of burdening their father with their college expenses—and since he had to work he preferred to spend his time and energy in his father's interests.

His chief work consisted in directing his father's various squads of waiters. He met them at the house where Joel was catering, started them off, checked over necessities, looked after the thousand details which lent to Joel's service the perfection that so justly brought him fame. Maggie often accompanied Philip on these trips. Sometimes she went to one house and he to another, and he would call for her and take her home. She pondered deeply over the possibility of these meetings.

He was usually jolly, unsentimental, almost brotherly. Maggie took care to follow his lead. But to her great surprise she was beginning to be conscious of a deep affection for him. At first she had only yearned for respectability and comfort, and Philip represented such a convenient short cut to her heart's desire. But now things were different.

Sometimes when they came home quite late he would take her arm and the two would walk slowly and silently down the strangely quiet streets. A curious little sense of intimacy used to brood over them at times like these. Philip would laugh a little nervously.

"Awfully jolly being out late like this by ourselves, isn't it, Maggie?"

She would nod him a smiling yes. "Some day," she thought, "he must say more."

Her studies, her work and these trips with Philip took up most of her time just now. She and Sylvia of course still saw a great deal of each other and once in a while went out together. She went to the theater still more rarely, or to a church festival with Henderson Neal, one of her mother's boarders. A mysterious tall brown figure of a man, twenty years older than Maggie and a thousand years older in experience, he caught and not infrequently held her attention. He had lived with them two years, paid his bills regularly, asked no questions and vouchsafed no explanations.

Maggie wondered what he did. Whatever his occupation, it certainly paid him well. More than once she had seen him display without ostentation a huge roll of bills, which apparently was static in bulk. His speech was often ungrammatical, but so deliberate that one thought he must be speaking correctly. He had a rather grand air, and listened to both Mrs. Ellersley and her daughter with a somewhat ponderous attention. Maggie thought he was rather interesting for such an old man—he must be nearly forty! She was a little afraid of him, though, and decided it would be rather unpleasant for any one who chanced to make him angry.

Once he met Sylvia and Maggie on the street and offered to take them to the matinée. His interest was clearly in Maggie but he politely included her friend. Sylvia later told Philip about it.

"I hope you didn't go," he replied quickly.

"No, I didn't, Maggie didn't, either. But there's no reason why I shouldn't have. She goes with him sometimes."

"But that's different. Maggie's known different people from any you've ever known. She can take care of herself."

"What's the matter?" Joanna asked, putting her head in the door. "What's old Phil so excited about?"

"You might just as well hear this, too, Jan. I won't have you and Sylvia going about with a man like Henderson Neal. Maggie can go with men that my sisters can't afford to associate with."

CHAPTER X

SUNDAY was always an important day in the Marshall household. Its importance, it is true, took on a different character as the years sped. In the early days Mr. Marshall looked forward to it as the outward and visible sign of an inward worth. He was a steward in his church, Old Zion, and on Sundays in a long frock coat with a correct collar, a black Ascot tie surmounted by a gold horseshoe, he passed the collection box from pew to pew. He liked to bend his rather stately iron-gray head in recognition of various greetings. He felt he looked the part, as indeed he did, of an upright, ambitious, aspiring citizen.

Many a small boy unconsciously stored away a memory of the erect wholesome figure as a possible exemplar for future consideration.

His wife found Sunday a rather distracting day. It was eminently satisfying, doubtless, to be able to show off such a number of stylish costumes. Joel had always been able to have her dress well. There was one wine-colored cashmere with a polonaise and bustle which she had considered particularly fetching.

"I never put the dress on in the old days," she said to her girls, showing them the truly awe-inspiring picture, "without thinking to myself: 'I certainly am glad I married Joel.' I always did love fine clothes. Sylvia, I think you must have inherited my taste."

Sylvia groaned. "Oh, no, mamma, I don't deserve that!"

Clothes, however, had not quite compensated Mrs. Marshall

71

for the arduousness otherwise entailed in the observance of the Sabbath. There was always company. Joel, a caterer, knew "how it ought to be done." Then there were the four children to dress and get off, and the constant oversight of them when they came home to see that they did not break the thousand inhibitions which made the day sacred.

"I used to hate it so," Sandy laughed. "Remember, Phil, how we used to try to find those awful sailor collars—I think they're called Buster Browns now—and see if we couldn't hide them or mark them up before the next Sunday? Mother must have had a million of them, for we were never able to exhaust her supply."

"Weren't you sights!" Sylvia teased. "You were fat, Alec, and your face rose large and round over your collar like a full moon. You had two eyes set away back from your fat cheeks and you had to bend your head way over to look down——"

"And you wore a grayish-brownish-greenery-yallery round straw hat," interposed Joanna.

"Don't you talk," Philip jeered at them, "I remember two poke bonnets, reddish, with fuzzy stuff sticking up over them."

"Astrakhan. Yes, I remember," Sylvia told him. "Weren't they awful? And the deadliness of Sunday afternoon! You boys sitting around knocking your feet against the rungs of the chairs. Such glooms!"

"Yes, and you," said Sandy, assuming a solemn countenance. "Looking dejectedly out of the window, your face propped in your hands!"

"Joanna was the only one who got anything out of those Sundays," Philip mused. "I can see her now flat on her tummy reading the life of some exemplary female."

"Notable women of color," laughed Joanna. "I adored Sunday."

Certainly no flavor of those past days spoiled the Marshalls' enjoyment in these later years. Rather remarkably the whole family still went to church, Mr. and Mrs. Marshall from years of long habit, Sylvia because she rather liked to please her mother and because it amused her to have Brian Spencer, whom church-going bored to the point of agony, obey her wish that he should go. Sandy, now in the real estate business, thought it gave him standing in the community.

Philip's reasons were various. Chiefly he went to church as he went to many meetings, because he was interested in seeing groups of colored people together. He had a strong desire to sense the social consciousness, for he was trying to learn just what stirred mass feeling and into what channels it could be directed. A minister of the poorest type was an unfailing source of study to him. How would this man sway the people? And what would he ask of them once he had them ready to listen to his will? Philip always dreamed of a leader who should recognize that psychological moment and who would guide a whole race forward to the realization of its steadily increasing strength.

He dreamed many dreams sitting crosswise in the far corner of his pew, his back partly against the wall, partly against the seat, his lean, brown, slightly haggard face bent forward. He had already the somewhat remote glance of the thinker, though his firm chin pronounced him no less the man of action. Maggie Ellersley, sitting across the church from him, watching him a little covertly under her drooping hat brim, used to think he looked like a man who would take what he wanted.

"If only he knew *what* he wanted," she half sighed.

Joanna was the soloist of the choir these days, sole *raison d'être* of *her* church-going. Her mezzo voice full and pulsing and gold brought throngs to the church every Sunday.

"There is a green hill far away," she sang, and the puzzled, groping congregation turned its sea of black and brown, yellow and white faces toward her and knew a sudden peace. Even Philip stopped his restless inner queries.

At times like these Peter Bye felt his very heart leap toward her.

Joanna with her cool eyes and steady head cared almost nothing about this. She never saw herself in this scene. Always in her mind's eye she was far, far away from the church, in a great hall, in a crowded theater. There would be tier on tier of faces rising, rising above her. And to-morrow there would be the critics. . . .

The Sundays passed thus week-end to week-end. One of them stood out in Joanna's memory. Philip, a Harvard junior, was home on his summer vacation, but he and Sylvia and Sandy had gone to visit their mother's folks in Philadelphia.

Joanna, Brian Spencer, Peter, and Maggie Ellersley stepped out of church and walked down the torrid street. It was early June, but the weather was that of August.

"Our children are growing up," said Mrs. Marshall to Mrs. Ellersley, lingering a moment in the shady vestibule. "See how tall Joanna and Maggie have grown. They were the littlest things!"

Mrs. Ellersley followed the group with a wistful eye. Of late she had begun to have some idea of Maggie's unspoken desires. She wished it were Philip instead of Brian walking down the street with her daughter. She was very tired, tired enough to die, but she could not, she felt, leave Maggie alone, unplaced in the world.

The four young people turned the corner and prepared to separate.

"Brian is coming to the house for dinner," said Joanna. "You coming, Maggie and Peter?"

Maggie had an engagement for the afternoon. Peter refused, too, sulkily, to Joanna's vast satisfaction.

"Jealous," she thought with some pride. It was an exhibition with which she seldom met. Most of the young men of her acquaintance were a little afraid of Joanna with her intent and serious air. "High-brow" they called her and she knew it, liked it, too, though it had its inconveniences.

"Peter's mad," she laughed as the two moved off, "because I told him I was going to the benefit concert with you, Brian, and so he couldn't come to-night."

"Sorry if I spoked his wheel," said Brian, "but you just have to take pity on me, Jan, I'm so lonely without Sylvia."

"Of course. Isn't it funny that he doesn't realize that? He thinks you are making up to me. As though I would come between you and Sylvia. Great chance I'd have."

"About as much as *I'd* have, trying to come between you and Peter. Not that I know anything about you, Janna. Heaven only knows what you mean to do with the boy. But I wouldn't want to face Peter, if I were aiming to be his rival. Wonder what he'll do when he goes to the University in Philadelphia. What's he going off there for, anyway? Can't he do just as well here?"

"The penalty of being colored," said Joanna soberly. "He can get much better hospital work in Philadelphia. Of course he could take his pre-medic work here, but he thinks it best to begin where he plans to finish."

"How long will he be away?"

"Forever and ever, six or seven years, I think. Of course, we both have relatives in Philadelphia. His great-uncle Peter, for whom he was named, is still there, you know. Peter's counting on living with him. It will save expense."

"Six or seven years!" said Brian disregarding anything else. "Golly what a wait! It would kill any girl but you, Janna."

"Sylvia didn't die while you were in Harvard," Joanna returned meanly.

"Not much she didn't! But she kept me in the back of her head, I'll swear. While you with your singing and dancing and your wildcat schemes of getting on the stage! Better stick to your own Janna, and build up colored art."

"Why, I am," cried Joanna, astonished. "You don't think I want to forsake—*us*. Not at all. But I want to show *us* to the world. I am colored, of course, but American first. Why shouldn't I speak to all America?"

"H'm, I suppose you're right. You ought to win out if anyone can. You work hard enough, Janna. You're eighteen now, aren't you? Well, you've got a good ways to go. How old is Peter?"

"Twenty. He lost a lot of time when he was little. That's why he's so late entering college.

"Well look here, what are you going to do with him?"

"I may not have a chance to do anything with him, Mr. Busybody."

"Phew, isn't it hot! Thank goodness here's the house. Run along and get your brother-in-law a long, cold drink."

He stayed after dinner—they had it on Sundays at three—and talked away the rest of the afternoon to Joel in the long dark dining room.

"It's cool here," said Joel, handing him a cigar. "Light up and tell me how's Harlem?"

"Great, sir. It's the place for colored people. Let us get you a house up there. Pick you up something fine in One Hundred and Thirty-first Street." Brian, too, had gone into real estate as Alexander's partner.

Joel rolled his cigar from one side of his mouth to the other. "Don't know but what I might. This neighborhood's gone down. Let me see your house."

"Yes, sir, I will. Has—er—Sylvia said anything to you about me? I'm getting along pretty well now, sir."

"What should she say? Here Joanna, come take this love-sick boy off my hands!"

Joanna came, serene and cool, a little prim in her pale yellow dress and soft floppy hat of tan chiffon. She handed Brian his Panama.

"I'm ready, Brian."

Joel stopped them for a moment, clapped the boy on the shoulder. "It's all right as far as her mother and I are concerned, Brian."

The two went off and heard a gracious, mellow-voiced woman fill a hall with sound that made them forget the heat.

"My collar's wringing wet, and I never thought of it. Wonderful how music can make people forget."

"Even color," said Joanna thoughtfully. "Did you see that white woman next to me edge away when I sat down? But when she heard me humming after it was over, she leaned over and asked me if I knew the words."

"I wondered what you were talking about. Awfully jolly of you to have taken pity on me to-night, Janna dear. You marry Peter and all four of us will go to these concerts and sit in the gallery and come home praising God from whom all blessings flow."

"It certainly sounds nice. Only we mustn't forget Philip. Don't ring the bell, here's the key."

He took it. "All right about Philip. Maggie is fond of music, too."

Joanna, in the act of entering the door, stepped back and faced him sharply. "What's Maggie got to do with it?"

"Well, she and Phil. They've always paired off together, haven't they? Just like you and Peter, just like Sylvia and me."

"She wouldn't dare," said Joanna fiercely. "Why, Philip—

he's going to be somebody great, wonderful, a Garibaldi, a Toussaint! And Maggie, Maggie's just nobody, Brian. Why, do you know what she's taking up? Hair work, straightening hair, salves and shampoos and curling-irons."

"Joanna, you're an utter snob. I always knew you looked down on people unless they were following some mad will o' the wisp. Maggie's as good as any of us. Why look here, she graduated from high school with Sylvia. You can't look down on her."

"Sylvia's my sister, thank you. She's Joel Marshall's daughter. She has background, she knows good music and pictures and worth while people."

"You talk like a silly book. What's that got to do with it? And, anyway, you can't stop it now."

"What's the reason I can't?"

"Well, good Lord, it must be as good as settled. Why Maggie thinks—only to-day— Oh—here, I've said enough. Thanks awfully for a nice evening, Jan——"

"What'd she say, Brian?"

"Well, you know we were coming home from church and you and Bye were ahead and I said, 'Look at the lucky pair.'"

"Yes, never mind me. Well, well?"

"And she said, 'You miss Sylvia, don't you, Brian?' 'You bet,' I told her.

"And she looked at me—you know how Maggie can look— she said, 'Just like I miss Philip, I guess.'"

Joanna grew visibly taller. "You let her say that, Brian Spencer?"

"Well, how could I stop her? Of course she misses Phil. And quit acting 'offended pride,' Joanna. Heavens, doesn't Sylvia sometimes do sewing?"

"Oh, but that's different, she creates, she's an artist——"

"Artist your grandmother! Sleep it off, Janna. **Good night.**" He went off, striding down the quiet street.

Joanna closed the door and crept quietly up to her room. Seated in a wicker arm-chair in a stream of gold summer moon-light, she spent a long time in deep thought.

Maggie and Philip! Maggie! Of late she and Philip had had many a long talk. He'd lean against the mantelpiece—his restless fingers caressing a little black statuette:

"Jan, I'll talk to you, because you've always cared about this kind of thing. Raise a monument—more-enduring-than-bronze sort of business, you know. When I graduate—by the way, I think I'll be elected Phi Beta Kappa next year—I've got a scheme, I've got a plan that will work all right. Father will be proud of me, you'll see. And you, too, old girl, you've always been a bright beacon light. You stick to this stage business, you'll win out. There'll be a twin star constellation. 'The well known Marshalls, Joanna and Philip.' We'll make the whole world realize what colored people can do. Nothing short of 'battle, murder or sudden death' is to interfere."

He, too, had been bitten by the desire to make the most of his life. And now here was Maggie Ellersley.

"What ambition has she?" Joanna asked herself fiercely, forgetting to measure the depth of the abyss of poverty and wretchedness from which Maggie had sprung. "She shan't spoil my brother's chances."

Rushing over to her little desk, she pulled out a piece of tan stationery and began a note.

"Dear Maggie——"

CHAPTER XI

PETER had accompanied Maggie as far as the subway station. "You won't mind if I don't go all the way home with you, Maggie? Fact is, I don't feel so well to-day, so if you'll excuse me——" His voice trailed indeterminately.

Maggie smiled at him nicely. She was oddly happy at this moment. Linking her name with Philip's, as she had, gave her an odd sense of freedom, of sureness. "And Brian didn't seem at all surprised," she kept thinking to herself over and over.

She answered out loud, "That's all right, Peter. Go home and rest. I'm going to be in the house only a minute, anyway." She looked at him meaningly. "I guess both of us have a lot to think of. Good-by." She flashed down the steps, looked back; a second later a slender golden hand waved to him from the gloom of the subway.

"Now I don't know what she meant," thought Peter, pushing his hat back from his hot forehead, and immediately turning to another idea. "I'd like to punch that fresh Brian's head. Oh, Janna, how could you go off with him?"

Down in the subway train Maggie sat smiling a little inanely. Of late, her feeling for Philip had taken a definite form; she wanted, as always, desperately to marry, and to marry well in order to secure for herself the decent respectability for which those first arid fourteen years of her life had created an almost morbid obsession. But she knew now that the one man through whom she wanted to secure that respectability was Philip Marshall. She loved him.

"If the way I wanted him at first, dear God, was a sin, you must forgive me. Oh, Philip, Philip, have a good time in Philadelphia to-day. I bet you're at a meeting of some kind this minute." The picture of his favorite attitude came before her, and she smiled more broadly.

A white man sitting opposite mistook the smile and leaned forward, leering a little. She turned her head quickly, noting as she did so that something about his build made her think of Henderson Neal, her mother's roomer.

She was to go motoring with him this afternoon. He had asked her very often of late. Usually she spent Sundays with Philip and Sylvia and Brian, sometimes with Joanna and Peter. But since the first two were away, she might just as well spend the time with Mr. Henderson. He would have a nice car, she knew; twice before he had taken herself and her mother out. It had really been very nice. She rather fancied he must work in a garage, he came riding up to the house so often. She wished a little nervously that she hadn't promised to go, it would be nice to sit quietly in her room or in the long, sparsely furnished parlor and think.

Still it was hot, and if there were any air to be got they'd catch it in an automobile.

She ran up the subway steps and hurried toward Fifty-third Street. Somehow she didn't care to keep Mr. Neal waiting.

There was still a quarter of an hour before he might be expected. She bathed her face, shook out her short, thick hair, twisted it back from her forehead. Next she crowned her oval, deep-cream face with a wide black hat, whose somberness was repeated in a broad velvet ribbon around the waist of her white dress.

But she looked anything but somber as she ran to the door at the whirr of the motor.

"Going, Ma," she called back. Mr. Neal climbed out of the car and helped her in.

He didn't look so old—elderly—to-day, she thought to herself, noting the straightness of his flat back and the smooth bronze of his closely shaven cheek. Evidently his beard was very strong and this had lent hitherto a somewhat heavy cast to his face. But to-day he was shaven to the blood. Maggie was used to studying men. It was a legacy from the old days, when failure to analyze a prospective roomer's appearance might jeopardize a week's rent. She noticed Neal's hands at the wheel, powerful and sinewy with broad square finger-tips. He was still baffling, but not so bad, she thought.

"Of course, not like Philip, but nice enough to go around with, and this is a dandy car." She looked at him again sideways. He caught her glance.

"Thinkin' I ain't so bad maybe, Miss Maggie?"

She blushed, confused, not so much at his catching her eye as at the completeness with which he had read her thought.

"You certainly look nice in that suit, Mr. Neal. It's different from what most men wear, isn't it?"

"Likely as not. I picked it up in London last time I crossed the big pond."

"You've been to Europe?" asked Maggie all ears.

"Yes to England, France, Spain, Germany *and* Italy. They was a time," he said in his deliberately incorrect way, "when I thought I'd stay in them parts forever, but I come back. Used to valet for a rich white fellow. Took me everywhere with him. Wanted to carry me to Africa lion-hunting. But I quit him cold. If you want to hunt lions, go to it. Me, I'm a-goin' t'stay right here."

He spoke with a heavy emphasis on the last word which lent a curious whimsicality to his speech.

"This is the first time you've ever talked about yourself, Mr. Neal. Tell me some more, it's mighty interesting."

He had been everything from a farmer to a chauffeur, he told her, confirming her idea that his present occupation was concerned with the manipulation of cars.

"And I've been a lot of places and I've seen a lot of people. But you don't want to hear about me, Miss Maggie. They ain't nothing in me to interest a little lady like you. Now, on the other hand, seems to me, you might make real interestin' talkin'."

He had a nice smile, Maggie thought.

"There isn't much to tell," she smiled back at him. "There's just my mother and me. I'm twenty-one and I've been out of school three years. I work in the office of Mr. Marshall, the caterer; you know him?"

"Know of him, Miss Maggie, know of him. Son's a real-estate agent, ain't he?"

"Yes. Well, I'm a sort of overseer-bookkeeper. In my spare time I'm taking up a course in hair-dressing. You know there's a Madame Harkness who's invented a method of softening hair, and of taking the harshness out of your folks' locks." She laughed at him. "You know I think there's a big future in it. It ought to mean a lot to us. Everybody wants to be beautiful, and every woman looks better if her hair is soft and manageable."

"Reckon you don't need to use no such preparation, Miss Maggie."

"No, I don't, fortunately, but I'll be glad to help those that do. I love to see people look nice; like to look nice myself."

"You sure do, you're like a little yellow flower, growin' in that house." He gave her a keen level glance whose boldness was softened by his serious manner.

"Let's stop talking about me," said Maggie with sudden confusion. "Don't you want to hear about my mother?"

"Well, not as much as about some others."

"Anyway, she's been a wonderful mother. My father died when I was about eight, and left us nothing. Mother has been hard put to it at times. That's why I want to learn the hair-trade. I want to set up a business for myself some day. If I succeed, both mother and I can live on easy street."

"You'd ought to be living there now. A delicate little girl like you's got no business having to worry her pretty head about taking care of herself." He bent on her a long considering look. "There's many a man would be willing to take that job off your hands. I bet I know of one." An odd bashfulness seemed to descend upon him.

"Perhaps he's going to propose," thought Maggie innocently enraptured, "wouldn't that be great?" She pictured Sylvia's surprise when she should tell her. His clumsy circumlocution, his heavy deference, delighted her. Philip of course was wonderful, but he was inclined, like all the Marshalls, to be a little superior. Well, why shouldn't they be?

She sighed.

Her silence seemed to put an end to his sentimental maunderings, for he began to talk about the car, explaining its mechanism. Once, too, he turned and swore fluently at a motorist who passed him too closely. At the sudden passion which convulsed his face Maggie drew back, a little frightened. He noticed it, and immediately ironed out the lines of anger.

"You must forgive me, Miss Maggie. It made me so angry to think that that fool might have caused an accident which would have injured you."

She thought with the ignorant pride of a young girl that it would be very easy for her to manage him. Shortly after that they turned around and came home. Maggie was glad when they reached the house, for she had many things to think about. Shutting off the motor, he followed her into the hall and they stood there a minute, his powerful dark figure looming over her.

She thanked him prettily. "It was very nice of you, Mr. Neal. You've been most kind to mother and me." As she sped lightly up the stairs she forgot him completely.

Her windows were open and a full moon flooded her room with light. "Oh, Philip if I only knew how you felt," she murmured, getting up and leaning out the window, gazing into the still, hot air. The people next door were in their back yard; one of their boys was playing an accordion. A little thin tinkle of voices floated up to her. How content other people seemed!

Her mind was feverish—she had concentrated so on her other desires, a decent home, a reasonable education, the means of making a little extra money. It seemed to her she couldn't find the strength to focus the flame of her ambition on Philip's kind but immobile attitude. He was so uncomprehending. She turned back to the room again and stretched her arms to the shadowy wall.

"If you'd only say one word, Philip. I'd wait forever." It was the uncertainty that sickened her spirit. "Yet," she thought, growing suddenly cold, "suppose I should be made certain—the wrong way. Perhaps you've met a girl in Philadelphia."

She determined the suspense was best. "You've been my hope so long, if you should fail me what would I do? Besides, I love you, Philip."

She lay half the night, very still and very wakeful in her white iron bed. The morning brought back her old sanguineness, she was to have a very full day; until early forenoon there was work in Mr. Marshall's office, and in the late afternoon Madame Harkness' Method of Hair Culture claimed her.

She came home, hot and deliciously tired.

"There's a letter for you," her mother told her. "Wash your face and eat your supper first. I want to get through's quick as I can. Mis' Sparrow and me, we're going to a meeting."

Maggie spied the letter in the gloom of the hall. It was from Sylvia probably; her heart hoped it was from Philip. But she put the thought away from her as too audacious. "Now just for that," she told herself whimsically, "I won't let you touch that letter till after supper." Smiling, she washed her face and changed into something cool and old that she could lounge in later up in her room, while she read Sylvia's letter.

Supper over, the dishes washed and her mother started in the direction of Mis' Sparrow's residence, Maggie went for her letter. Even in the half gloom she descried with a sudden pang that the superscription was unfamiliar. "Not from Philip, not even from Sylvia. Well, why should they write me?" she chided herself bravely.

In the waning but clear light in her room she could see plainly that the letter must be from a stranger. Yet there was something vaguely familiar about the writing after all.

She slit the envelope.

"Dear Maggie: [the letter ran]

"You'll be surprised to get this letter, yet something tells me I should write it. It's about you and Philip. ['What's this?' said Maggie, startled.] I have learned, Maggie, that you are taking Philip's kindnesses to you too seriously, that perhaps you are thinking of marrying him.

"I think you ought to know that such an arrangement would not be at all pleasing to our family, nor would it be good for Philip. I've often heard my mother say that only people of like position should marry each other, and I hardly think that would be true in the case of you and Philip. Then you must consider the future. My father is very ambitious for us and lately Philip has shown that he means to embark on a real career. You can see that a girl of your lowly aims would only be a hindrance to him. Philip Marshall cannot marry a hair-dresser !"

The childish cruel words ran on:

"Then, too, I am sure he does not care for you in the way you care for him. Don't you go around sometimes with a Mr. Henderson, or somebody like that? Sylvia met him somehow and Phil didn't like it and raised a big fuss. Sylvia told him that you knew him and went out with him and Philip said 'That's different. Maggie Ellersley can do things that my sisters mustn't do.' That doesn't sound as though he had any serious feeling for you, does it?

"I guess this will be sort of hard for you to read, but I believe" [Joanna wrote virtuously] "that some day you will thank me for these words.

"Wouldn't it be just as well if you didn't see him for some time after his return?

"Yours,

"JOANNA MARSHALL."

"P.S. Papa is thinking of buying a house in One Hundred and Thirty-first Street, in Harlem, you know. So we may move after Sylvia and the others come back from Philadelphia. Papa would still keep his office in Fifty-ninth Street. That puts us pretty far away, so if you shouldn't come up so often, no one would think anything of it."

Maggie folded the letter carefully and put it on her mantelpiece. Then, fully dressed as she still was, she lay down on her bed.

"You poor idiot," she thought to herself, "you simpleton, you fool, why should the Marshalls want you? They're rich, respected! Mr. Joel Marshall—you see the name at the head of every committee of colored citizens, and you are nobody, the daughter of a worthless father, and a poor ex-laundress!"

Her mind dwelt briefly on her mother. "Poor Mamma, she expected so much of me! Yet if Philip really cared about me, he wouldn't care a rap if they did object." She remembered then his slighting words.

"I hate him," she said fiercely, "and Joanna and her ever-lasting ambitions and the pride of all of them. Why, you're just a beggar to them." She resumed her merciless self-attack.

Presently she began to cry great, scalding tears that burned her cheeks and hurt her throat. At eleven o'clock she heard her mother's step and forced herself to an aching quiet. About midnight she realized that her head ached, that her throat was so dry and parched that it almost rasped.

"To think I should care like this," she told herself. "Oh, Maggie, Maggie, they're proud, can't you copy their pride?"

There were some lemons on the table in the dining room, she remembered. At least she could ease her tortured throat. Hot though it was she put on her felt bedroom slippers, so that her step on the creaking stairs might not disturb her mother.

The quiet lower rooms struck her with their awful solemnity, added to her woe. She sat there at the dining room table, one hand clutching the forgotten lemon, the other flung on the red-checked table cloth, above her dark bowed head.

Two conflicts were raging within her. A two-fold stream of disappointment overwhelmed. Not only had Philip not made love to her but he had despised her, not considered her the peer of his sisters. And how was she to mend her precarious fortunes? She was not strong, her mother was aging; suppose, before she got on her feet, she should fall back into the old hateful abyss. As it was she would never enter Mr. Marshall's office again.

Her shame and despair heavy upon her, she buried her face deeper on her arm. Some one seemed to say, "Miss Maggie!"

She imagined it, she knew, but even if it were real she did not want to lift that heavy, heavy head.

A powerful but kind hand strove to lift it for her. She looked up then, a blinking figure of misery in the flickering gas flame.

"But Miss Maggie, t'aint ever you. Was you asleep or—was you crying?" Henderson Neal had come in, and spying the light in the dining room had come to investigate.

She blinked at him stupidly.

"Little Miss Maggie, what's happened to you? You ain't in trouble?"

"In awful trouble." Her lips shaped the words stiffly.

His mind, accustomed to the ways of men, jumped to one dread conclusion. "You mean some good for nothin' feller's took advantage of you?"

She didn't understand him at first. "What? Oh, that! No, of course not!" A spasm of horrible amusement crossed her tightly drawn features. "He—he wouldn't touch me."

She broke into passionate yet stifled weeping. Her mother must not hear her.

Neal's face twitched. He picked her up in his steely arms, sat down in an old cavernous morris chair and held her back against him like a baby.

"Tell me about it, Miss Maggie; some of them tony fellers bothering you to marry them?"

The supposition was balm to her spirit, but she had schooled herself to honesty. "No, not that—one of them, oh, he never knew—I hoped, oh, Mr. Neal, you see I wanted him to like me——"

"And he doesn't, and he's been leading you on? The damned skunk. I'd like to kill him."

"Don't say that. He was just being kind. He'd probably be all right if he ever thought about me. You see, it's his sisters, his sister," she corrected herself, "she doesn't consider me good enough."

"Well, what's she got to do with it? Can't the feller speak for himself?"

"That's just it, I used to go to see them, they don't come to see me. If the sisters don't want me, there's no way I can reach him, particularly since he isn't interested. I had just hoped that if he kept on seeing me, some day he would grow to like me."

Neal was nonplussed. This was a puzzle.

"What are you going to do now?"

"Oh, I don't know. And I'm losing my job now. I got it through them."

"I see." He sat silent, studying her a moment. "Look here, Maggie, whyn't you marry me? I'm old and I'm rough and you see I ain't no book-learnin'. But I can take care of you—you and your mother, too, and I can dress you pretty, like you'd ought to be, and with money and fine clothes you can do a little lordin' on your own."

She hated to offend him. He was so kind. "Mother would never hear of it," she quavered for lack of a better answer.

"You don't have to let her know about it," he said, encouraged by her failure to refuse him flatly. "I'll get a license in the morning and we'll slip out after she goes to work. You won't be sorry. I'll be kind to you Maggie—girl. I've always wanted you to give me a chance." He added a cunning afterthought.

"Show these stuck-up friends of yourn, and show 'em quick that you don't have to go beggin' for favors. There's others, yes, not a man that comes into this house that wouldn't be proud to marry you."

She began to toy with the idea. Marriage with Neal was not what she wanted, but it represented to her security, a home for herself and her mother, freedom from all the little nagging worries that beset the woman who fights her own way through the world. Perhaps she had aimed too high. This was the sort of person with whom she had grown up; he would not, because he could not, look down on her lowliness. On the contrary, he would place her on a pedestal.

"I'll think about it," she promised him finally.

But he knew if she did not take him now, she would never take him. She knew it, too.

He set her gently in the chair, and knelt in front of her, barring her escape with his powerful body.

"Listen, Maggie, marry me now, to-morrow. We'll go to Atlantic City for a few weeks, and come back and go to housekeeping. I don't have to live here. I just stayed on, first because it was clean and your mother was honest and then because I liked you. I ain't no lawyer, nor doctor, nor in none of the fine positions your friends hold, but I handle a good bit of money and I'll get you everything you want."

He did have money, she knew that. She supposed she ought to find out exactly how he made it. But of course he was honest. And anyway she was too tired, too weak to bother. She could feel his strong will impinging on her own, beating hers down.

"I'll do it, Mr. Neal."

"My name's Henderson, Maggie. You will, you mean it?"

"Yes, to-morrow. But I ought to let my mother know."

"Oh, no, she might object—mothers hate to see their daughters leave them. But after she sees how well fixed and happy you are, she won't mind."

"I guess you're right. I—I don't see how I can ever pack. I'm so tired." Her figure slacked weakly against the chair.

"You don't need to. Just wear something dark and quiet. We'll get everything you want in Atlantic City, or maybe Philadelphia."

"No, no—not in Philadelphia, we won't stop there now," she told him feverishly.

"All right. Now run up to bed. Kiss me, Maggie."

She gave him her cold, stiff lips.

"Good girl! To-morrow at ten. You ain't foolin' me?"

"Oh, no, Mr. Neal!"

"Henderson's my name. Good night, little girl."

Shaking, she got up to her room to lie vacant-eyed across the bed, watching the darkness deepen, shade into gray, vanish. The sun came bringing a new day, to her a new life.

She wrote her mother a note, then dressed herself carefully in a little tan poplin suit, a small brown hat and a white veil. "Brides wear veils," she thought to herself numbly. "Oh, I didn't think I'd be a bride like this!"

Well, it was too late now. At quarter of nine she went down stairs. Her mother had left long since. Presently she heard a taxi drive up and Neal, heavy but immaculate, got out. He was coming for her. She walked stiffly to meet him; they entered the cab together and were whirled away.

"This was marriage," she thought, murmuring some words later to a Justice of the Peace. They entered the waiting taxi again and drove to the Pennsylvania station. A surprising number of the red-caps seemed to know Mr. Neal—her husband. Well, of course, of course why shouldn't they? They walked down the steps past car after car. Neal ushered her finally into a drawing-room. She had never dreamed of traveling like this. As the train pulled out Neal hailed a passing waiter. "Bring us something to eat as soon as possible."

He sat down beside her, immaculate in a gray suit, gray tie, carefully brushed low shoes. His tan overcoat rested in the corner of the seat. He put his arms around her.

"Poor, sleepy, frightened Maggie," he said tenderly.

She burst into sharp, strangling sobs, burying her head against his shoulder.

So she left New York, weeping, to return to it one day dry-eyed but with a bitterness that was worse than tears.

CHAPTER XII

"REALLY, Joanna, you ought to treat me better. You know I'm staying in New York just on account of you!"

"How do you want me to treat you, Peter?"

"Oh, hang it all. Why can't you be nicer to me? When Brian comes to see Sylvia she runs to meet him, puts her arms about his neck."

"But Sylvia and Brian are engaged. You and I are just friends."

"Just friends! Joanna, have a heart. What do you think I spend all my spare time with you for? You know how I feel."

Joanna raised a slim, protesting hand. "None of that, Peter! You come to see me because both of us are interested in the same things. Each of us is going to be an artist in different ways. What other girl is there in New York who would let you talk to her about the joys of surgery?"

"What other girl would want me to?"

Joanna, looking at the long brown figure lying full length on the grass, thought it highly improbable that any other girl would. She had seen other girls in the company of Peter, and watched quite without jealousy their ways with him. She rather prided herself on her own aloofness from such tactics. Of course, some day she might let Peter talk to her about things other than work and art, and she might answer him, but at present the big things of life must be arranged. Love was

an after consideration, she felt, and as far as she knew she
meant it.

It was a Saturday afternoon in July and the two were in
Van Cortlandt Park. Peter was to go to school in Philadelphia in the fall, and it was important for him to earn as
much money as possible for his expenses. He might have gone
with a group of other boys to one of the watering places and
worked in a hotel. But that took him too far away from
Joanna. Ragtime was coming into vogue then, and Peter
proved himself an adept at it. The butcher shop was of
course a thing long since of the past.

"Here's where I put my gift of strumming to some use," he
laughed to Joanna. "You ought to see how glad they were
to take me on at that cabaret."

"I hope you won't learn anything you shouldn't in that
atmosphere," she had answered primly.

"Oh, of course I won't," he returned, thinking how amazed
she would be if she ever looked down from her pinnacle long
enough to understand what life really was. He would have
liked her to see that cabaret with its jostling crowds and
blaring lights, and the host of noisy good-hearted dancing
girls. He tried to give her some description of it. But Joanna
turned away.

"Men and women are like that, just the same," he protested. "Everybody isn't living on the mountain-tops like
you, Janna. I can't live there of my own accord myself.
That's why I haunt you so because you do keep me on the
heights, dear." She liked that.

"But just the same," he resumed, rolling over on the short
grass like a lithe handsome animal, "all the big things of life
smack of the earth. Your poet has to eat, or he can't write
poetry. Well, so does the commonest laboring-man. The queen
has children, in agony, Janna, just like the poorest charwoman.
And love is the—the driving force for both of them." He

mused a little. "Love is the most natural and ordinary thing in the world."

But Joanna didn't believe that. "Love is a wonderful, rare thing, very beautiful, very sweet, but you can do without it."

"Not much you can't. Better not try it, Joanna. You have to found your life on love, then you can do all these other things."

"Don't talk like a silly, Peter. You know perfectly well that for a woman love usually means a household of children, the getting of a thousand meals, picking up laundry, no time to herself for meditation, or reading or——"

"Dancing! That's through poor management. Marry a man who understands you, Janna, and he'll see that you have time for anything you want. Where is such a man? Behold him!" He struck his chest dramatically.

"Peter Bye! How you talk!"

"All right, I'll choose something else. Tell me why is it that though I've elected to stay in New York in all this hot weather just to be at your side, I see less of you than at any time since I've been coming to your house."

"Does seem queer, doesn't it? It must be because I have so much work to do. I am taking extra singing lessons from Brailoff now. And my dancing takes up a lot of my time; my classes come at such inconvenient hours, 7:30 to 10:00 three times a week."

"That *is* bad. Funny time to give dancing lessons. Where'd you say you took them?"

"At Bertully's."

"Bertully's! That's in Twenty-ninth Street, isn't it? How'd you ever make it? I didn't suppose a colored girl got a chance to stick her nose in there."

"She wouldn't ordinarily. Bertully refused Helena Arnold last year. 'I'm sorry, Mees, but the white Americans like not to study with the brown Americans. Vair seely, but so.

I am a poor man, I must follow the weeshes of my clients!' "
Joanna shrugged her shoulders, spread her hands.

"You're a born impersonator, Jan. I can see that little
Frenchman now. How'd you ever get in, then?"

"Helena and I went back this year and asked if he would
take a separate class of colored girls, if we got it up for him.
He was very decent, said he'd be glad to. So we got up a
class of eight, he only asked for six. Of course, we had to
take his hours."

"Who are in it besides you and Helena?"

"Oh, all our crowd." She named the daughters of several
prominent colored men, a physician, a lawyer, a journalist, a
real-estate man among them. "There's Gertrude Moseley,
Vera and Alice Manning, Elizabeth Beckett, Sylvia, Helena,
and I."

"That's seven."

"Oh, yes, Sylvia meant to ask Maggie Ellersley."

"H'm, she had other things in her head without bothering
about fancy dancing, hadn't she? Funny how she went off
and married without telling any of us about it, wasn't it?"

"Yes," said Joanna uneasily.

"You'd have thought she'd have let old Phil in on it. I
wonder if they had a falling out of any kind! Philip seemed
rather hard hit when he heard the news."

"Not a bit of it. Why should he be?" Joanna spoke stoutly.
But her tone belied her convictions. She hadn't forgotten
Philip's expression the day Sylvia had come rushing in with
the astounding news:

"What do you think? I just met Mrs. Ellersley. Maggie's
married—married—think of it! She ran away with that man
at her house, that Mr. Neal. And they're going to live in
Philadelphia."

Philip's haggard face had turned a trifle more wan, Joanna

had thought. "Has she written to you, Sylvia?" he asked her quickly.

"Not a word. I can't imagine why she said nothing to me about it. She must have planned it for ages. If that isn't the funniest!"

Later Joanna heard Philip asking his mother if she were sure she had given him all the mail that had come for him while he was in Philadelphia. Still later he had announced his intention of teaching summer school in South Carolina.

"Fellow whose place I'm going to fill is sick. They've been at me a long time to come. I think I ought to go, father. It will give me a chance to see the South."

Joanna's throat constricted a little at the thought of Philip's look, his general listlessness. She wished she hadn't written that letter. Though that couldn't have brought about the marriage. People don't arrange to be married over night. As Sylvia said, it must have been on Maggie's mind long since. And then, anyway, Philip couldn't really have cared for a girl like Maggie.

"I don't believe Philip was the least bit interested in Maggie," she voiced her thought to Peter. "Well, anyway, Mr. Bye, that's why my company is so scarce. Goodness, what are you frowning about?"

"Well, I'm mad to think you swallowed that Frenchman's insult. To think of your taking lessons from him after that!"

"But, Peter, he didn't insult us. He can't help this stupid prejudice. 'In my country, Mademoiselle Maréchal,'—he always calls me that—'you'd be an honor to any class.' He says I've got a great future. That if there's anything that will break down prejudice it will be equality or perhaps even superiority on the part of colored people in the arts. And I agree with him."

"But to be set apart like that!"

"What do I care?" asked Joanna, the practical. "You've

got to take life as you find it, Peter. The way I figure it is this. If all I needed to get on the stage was the mastery of a difficult step, I'd get there, wouldn't I? For somehow, sometime, I'd learn how to overcome that difficulty."

"You bet you would."

"Very well, then. Now my problem is how to master, how to get around prejudice. It *is* an awful nuisance; in some parts of this country it is more than a nuisance, it's a veritable menace. Philip says he's going to change all that some day. First, I'm going to get my training up to the last notch, then I'm going to watch for an opportunity and squeeze in."

"You'll never get it."

"Oh, yes, I will. Some white people are kind, some of them are so truly artistic that they'll put themselves to great trouble for the sake of art. Look at Bertully. It works him much harder than it does us to hold those extra classes."

"Bertully's one man in a thousand. Besides, he's a foreigner. Where'll you find a white American like that?"

"You blessed pessimist. I know of people like that already. That's how Helena Arnold got to Bertully in the first place. A Miss Sharples—why, they're the people your Aunt Susan works for, aren't they? Your aunt told Miss Sharples about Helena, and Miss Sharples took her, herself, to Bertully."

"That was awfully decent, I must say. Of course, the Sharples are Philadelphia Quaker stock. Not that that makes much difference. The white Byes were Quakers, and see how they left us stranded, though my father told me old black Joshua Bye practically coined them their money. Not many people like those Sharples."

"There doesn't need to be. The point is there's *one*. Miss Sharples' family, by the way, may have been Quakers, but there's nothing Quakerish about her. Helena says she goes with the Greenwich Village group all the time, and for all their craziness, they've got some mighty big ideas."

"Can't get anything to eat, if you're colored, down in their dinky old restaurants."

"Awful, isn't it? Well, we'll let some other colored person pound away at that side of it. Me, I'm going to break into art. The public wants novelty, and *I* want fame. I've got to have it, Peter."

"You talk about going on the stage as though you had a signed contract in your hand. How'll you get the stage-presence?"

"I'm to go on a recital tour next fall among colored people. I'm used to singing in the choir. If I can stand before them I can stand before any audience in the world."

"Yes, we are mighty critical."

"I should say so. Get up, Peter Bye. We've got to go home."

They started on the long trip back.

"But see here, Joanna," Peter pleaded when they reached the house, "you will give me a little more time, won't you? I don't have to work in the morning, you know. And I don't work Wednesday nights. Promise me that, won't you?"

"Yes," said Joanna, her heart warming to his glowing beauty. "We'll remember this summer, Peter, the last before we go off trying our wings for further flights."

That was an enchanted season. Peter used to call for her in the morning, and the two would go off exploring. Joanna liked the foreign quarters, but she had never cared to stand around too long in those teeming, exotic streets. She was too conspicuous, attracted too many inquiring glances. With Peter she felt safe to stand for long moments watching the children play, to enter queer dark shops, to taste strange messes. Sometimes she spoke to the women about their dresses, their headgear. One Spanish woman, grown used to the sight of this dark American girl and the good-looking boy at her side, took them into her quarters one day and showed Joanna how she dressed her hair. Another time she taught her an intricate Spanish dance.

"I'm going to do a dance representing all the nations, some day," Joanna told Peter.

They planned for Wednesday nights very carefully at first, but gradually as the torrid weather increased, Joanna's desire for the theater and other indoor forms of amusement yielded to the desire to be cool at any cost. Central Park claimed them then, and later Morningside, since it was just a few moments' stroll from the Marshalls' new house.

Morningside was usually crowded. The seats were always taken when they arrived.

"I wonder what time the people come," Joanna murmured. But they didn't mind. The grass, the sloping hillside, was good enough for them. Joanna would sit down, her dainty summer dress spread around her, her splendidly poised head turned at first so she could see the passers-by. She was forever studying types, and eyed them with a grave deliberation.

"You'll get your head knocked off yet, Joanna," Peter would remonstrate, "staring at people so."

He liked it better when later on in the evening she turned toward the slope of the hill and looked down at the city, laughing in its myriad twinkling lights. Her face at that time took on a grave wistfulness which he could not analyze. Joanna herself could not define the feeling which prompted that expression.

Peter, leaning on his elbow, would lie beside her, his curly black head bent toward her, one slender brown hand touching her dress ever so lightly. He would have given the world to believe she was thinking about him, but he knew she was not. He would have been astounded if he could have dreamed of the maze of her thoughts. Joanna was really most human at moments like these. Through her mind was floating a series of little detached pictures. She saw a glittering stage, Peter, herself, some little children. She felt a hazy, nebulous, mystical joy.

Peter adored her at moments like these, but he was afraid of her, too.

One night she astonished him. "Peter," she said suddenly, "sit up. So. I'm tired. I've had a hard day. Do you mind if I rest my head on your shoulder?"

Would he mind if she offered him a king's estate?

He was too ecstatic, too—yes—scared, to speak. He sat as she directed, he stretched his thin tense arm around her fine young body. He even put up one hand and pressed her head closer against his shoulder, touched her hair, let his fingers trail ever so lightly over her cheek. Joanna in his arms! Joanna!

She felt him trembling. "Am I too heavy, Peter?"

He could hardly articulate, but she heard his ardent "no" and moved imperceptibly closer.

His breath stirred her thick, dark hair. He let it caress his chin. Its soft heaviness was a revelation to him, a rapture.

She lay so quietly against him he thought she must be asleep. So he whispered, "Are you asleeep, Joanna?"

"No," she whispered back, "only very, very tired."

"Oh, Joanna, Joanna," he breathed, "be tired forever."

Somewhere out of the heavenly silence, a girl's voice, a foreign voice, broke into song high and shrill. Russian, Peter thought. It was just a snatch, poignant and sweet, that died away leaving a faint lingering sadness.

She put her head back then. She opened her dark eyes and looked full into his.

Their lips were so near, so near. In a second he had pressed his against hers, briefly yet with passion. She sat up and drew a little away from him, dazed. But he put his arms around her and held her close. Presently they walked home, speechless. When they came to an arc-light, they looked at each other's faces, eager to study and to reveal these new selves. Their glances met and clung with a sweet enchantment. Something leaped, something fluttered within their hearts, like a fettered, struggling wing. And it was beautifully, it was magically, first love!

CHAPTER XIII

THE vacation sped as vacations will. Peter played in the awful cabaret, saved his money and adored Joanna. Joanna practiced trills, danced, thought of Peter and allowed him to adore her. As the early September days spread their golden haze over Harlem and Morningside Park, she actually shivered a little when she realized that when the month was over she and Peter would be miles apart.

It is hard to say just how much Joanna cared for Peter at this time. Certainly the boy worshipped her. He dreamed wordless dreams of her at night sitting in the noisy cabaret. His visit to her was the one objective point in his day. When the inexorable moment of separation came it cost him actual physical pain to bid her good-by.

Joanna was hardly like that. She had a very real, very ardent feeling for Peter. But it was still small, if one may speak of a feeling by size. Her love for him was a new experience, a fresh interest in her already crowded life, but it had not pushed aside the other interests. At nineteen she looked at love as a man of forty might—as "a thing apart." This was due partly to her hard unripeness, partly to her deliberate self-training. Joanna had read of too many able women who had "counted the world well lost for love," until it was too late. "Poor, silly sheep," she dubbed them.

She could not, it is true, bundle up her thoughts of Peter and say, "I'll think of you to-morrow at three," but she did achieve a concentration in her work that made it almost impossible for him to remain too long in her thoughts. And at nights when he tossed sleepless on his bed, dreaming fragrant dreams and seeing golden visions, she was sleeping the perfect sleep of healthy weariness.

The last days were hard for her, however, as they were for Peter. For Joanna was doomed by her very make-up to a sort of perpetual loneliness. Sylvia had her own interests, she had Brian and many, many friends. She was the most popular of all the Marshalls. Alec and Joanna had never been thrown much together. Philip, once her great confidant, was usually away from home. And on his return he was apt to relapse during these days into a rapt sadness.

It followed, then, that while Joanna was Peter's sweetheart, his heart's dear queen, Peter was at once her lover whom she didn't need very much—at least she did not realize that need—and more than that her companion and friend whom she needed greatly. The prospect of the days stretched long and dreary before her. Even the concert tour, a remarkable booking for one so young, did not entirely console her.

The two talked about it on the day before Peter left for Philadelphia. They were in Van Cortlandt Park in a little tangled grove. It was noon and the September sun streamed down on them making the green wooden bench on which they sat pleasantly warm. But the leaves about them were going a little sere; in the shade the air felt chill, and the sunshine, though warm, was thin and white.

" 'The summer is ended.' " Joanna quoted softly; she sighed. Peter looked at her, there were tears in her eyes.

"Dear, beautiful Joanna," said Peter, and his own beautiful face was full of the woe of parting, "how can I leave you to-morrow? Janna, don't send me away, tell me I'm not to go." He put his arms around her and she clung to him.

"Peter, you must go, you must, really. We—we can't go on like this. We've got to prepare ourselves while we're young for the future."

"Yes," said Peter and his ardor chilled a little at the touch of her cool practicality. But a moment later her light touch rekindled him.

"You love me, Janna? You know I love you?"

"Yes, Peter dear, but we mustn't say anything more about it."

"I know, Joanna, I'm not going to worry you any more just now, but you'll let me speak sometime?"

"Yes, oh, yes!"

"Dearest girl! Kiss me, Joanna."

She touched his lips with a light, lingering kiss. He looked at her, his face haggard with his gusty, boyish passion.

"Ah, Joanna, I'll never forget that kiss."

Neither would she, her heart told her. It was the first time she had ever kissed him.

They walked through the deserted park, their arms frankly about each other, like children. The dry grass and brittle leaves crackled beneath their feet, the air hung over them like a thin, misty veil. Joanna sang a bit from an old Italian song:

> "If from Heaven we could but borrow
> One day longer of fond affection
> It would lessen then our sorrow,
> Give fresh joys for recollection."

She hummed a line here, then her voice rose again in the thin, shimmering air:

> "—The future, dark and lonely!
> Dearest Loved One, dearest Loved One
> Parting makes these joys so dear!
> Ah!—"

"Don't, Joanna; it's too sweet. You'll make me cry."

"I know it. Oh, Peter, go away and come back great and when you come back, speak to me."

She went with him to the train next morning and to his amazement no less than her own, broke down and sobbed into her handkerchief.

He bent over her. "To think of your crying for me, Joanna! Good-by, good-by, my sweet. Remember, I'll be back Christmas."

He vanished through the gates, was borne out of her vision. A strange exaltation possessed him. He was sad, but his sadness was as nothing to his joy, his sense of satisfaction. Joanna loved him. She had been unusually capricious since that night in Morningside Park. But now he was sure of her. He smiled steadily from Manhattan Transfer Station to North Philadelphia.

His cousin Louis Boyd met him at Broad Street Station and took him to his great-uncle Peter's in South Eighteenth Street. The old man almost cried over him.

"You're Meriwether's son, but you're more like your grandfather, Isaiah. He was darker than you, but he held his head high like yours, and you're going to do what he wanted his son to do. It's good to see you, boy."

He registered at the University the next day, consulted catalogues, met professors, wrote a glowing letter to Joanna. By the end of the week he was desperately homesick. He would have gone over to New York if he had not been so ashamed, and if he had not been expected to dinner at Louis Boyd's.

"Tell you what's the matter with you, fellow," said Louis when Peter had told him of his nostalgia, "you want to meet a few girls. We'll start out after dinner."

Peter did not think this would help much. He wanted Joanna, though he said nothing about that to Louis. Astonishingly, however, the cure worked.

Louis seemed to know half of colored Philadelphia. "Mighty

nice girls in this man's town, I can tell you. They'll take to you, Peter, because, of course, you're a Bye. Mentioned your name to old Mrs. Viny the other day and she told me to be sure to bring you around. She'd like to meet an 'old Philadelphian,' even if he had been living a while in New York."

The girls deserved the nice things Louis said about them. They were pretty, nicely dressed and a shining contrast to the dingy streets and old-fashioned houses in which most of them lived. Peter was pleasantly struck, too, by the apparent lack of aspiration on the part of most of them. They seemed to be pretty well satisfied with being girls. A few were able to live home, many sewed, a number of others taught. There was no talk of art, of fame, of preparation for the future among them. Peter spoke of it to Arabelle Morton, the last girl to whose house Louis took him.

"Well, of course we want to get married, and we're not spoiling our chances by being high-brows. Wouldn't you like to come and play cards next Friday night, Mr. Bye? There'll be just two tables, then afterwards we might dance. I'm sure you'd like it."

Peter thought so, too. He liked Arabelle already and her friendly shallowness. He wrote to Joanna:

"Tell you what, Jan, I think I'm going to like Philly very much. Being Isaiah Bye's grandson seems to help me no end. They actually consider me an 'old Philadelphian' and on the strength of that alone I've had four dinner invitations from elderly people to meet other 'old Philadelphians.' Some of them old enough, too, I'll say. However, the dinners are fine and come in very handy for a struggling student. I don't board at Uncle Peter's, you see.

"There're lots of jolly girls here. Of course, they're not like yours and Sylvia's crowd, bent on climbing to the top of a profession— well, Sylvia wasn't that way so much—but they're a very nice bunch and they have been most kind to your humble servant. . . .

"Do you remember that day in the Park? Joanna darling, what are you going to say to me when I come back Christmas?

"PETER."

"N. B.   These x's are kisses."   [There was a long string of them.]

His letters to Joanna reacted to his own advantage. He felt he must be able to tell her truthfully of his success in his studies, of his ability to fit into this new life. Joanna was interested in him with a deep personal interest such as she had never exhibited before, and he meant to keep it alive. These were with one exception the most wholesome, most formative days of Peter's life. He had youth, he had inspiration, he had the promise of love, with much hard labor to keep it.

Many of the colored boys lived in West Philadelphia. They had a fraternity, and though according to their laws he could not be taken in during his freshman year, it was plain that this honor would be extended to him as soon as he became a sophomore. He was pretty well liked, and was constantly receiving invitations to spend the night across the river. One or two of the boys lived in the dormitories and he was frequently offered a chance to see something of this side of college life.

But his steadiness surprised himself. He got his meals in a restaurant on Woodland Avenue, worked faithfully in the Library between classes, and completed the rest of his assignments at night in his Uncle's sitting room. The old fellow loved to see him there. He pictured in Peter the restoration of the Bye family in Philadelphia.

To eke out his scanty bank account, he played three nights a week in a dance hall at Sixteenth and South Streets. Saturday afternoons he did track work. Friday and Sunday he spent at Arabelle Morton's or at Lawyer Talbert's on Christian Street. This latter and his family consisting of two sons and two daughters, were the relatives with whom the Marshalls stayed on their visits to Philadelphia. He found them very enjoyable. One of the boys was an undertaker but with a disposition far less lugubrious than his calling. The other was in the Wharton School of Finance at Pennsylvania and was to read law later at Harvard. Both girls were young and both were engaged. They were very much in love, but as their fiancés were studying medicine at Howard University, they welcomed Peter with much acclaim.

Thanks to them and Louis, he was soon enrolled in the social calendar, and if he chose to be lonely, it was his own fault.

At Christmas he went back to New York; Joanna met him at the station and took him home in her father's car. Joel was one of the first ten colored men in Harlem to possess an automobile. The distance between his house and his business rendered it almost a necessity, and he was old enough to deserve release from the noise of the subway and the weary climbing to the elevated.

Joanna had grown very good-looking, Peter thought. More than that, she looked even distinguished. Her purposefulness gave her a quality which he had missed in the Philadelphia girls. His ardor had not cooled in the least, but he had had to force it into second place. Now it surged uppermost in his heart again.

He was glad that he had been in another city, had seen so many other girls. It only confirmed his conviction that Joanna was the only woman in the world for him. He hoped she possessed the same singleness of desire for him.

"There's lots going on," Joanna told him, sitting arm in arm with him in the car. "Sylvia and Brian are to be married Easter, so mother's formally announcing it now. There'll be luncheons—not for you I'm afraid, Peter. Then our dancing class is giving a benefit for the Pierce Day Nursery. There'll be fancy dancing on the stage, in which your humble servant will star. And we're to have a Christmas tree at our house and a house party. I'm asking you now, Peter. Isn't it great being grown up?"

"You bet. Which of these functions comes off first?"

"Sylvia's engagement party."

"So she and Spencer are actually going to pull it off. They've waited a long time, haven't they?"

"Yes, that's because Brian insisted on getting a good start before he married. Sylvia would have married him the day after they became engaged. But I think Brian's right."

"They're both right, but Sylvia's way is the best. That's the only attitude for anyone to have towards marriage. I'm afraid you lack it, my child. You want to begin with a mansion and three cars."

"You mean thing! I don't care about money as money one bit and you know it. But I do care about success. And a house or a car usually implies that. Any girl likes her man to look well in the eyes of other men."

"This man's going to look well." He yearned toward her. "Kiss me, sweetheart."

"Sir, you insult me. People shouldn't kiss unless they're engaged."

"Then be engaged to me, dearest Joanna. Great Scott, are we here?"

Joanna evaded him after that. Christmas was Tuesday, but as he had saved his cuts for Saturday classes, he had managed to come away the preceding Friday night. On Christmas morning he caught her before daybreak. They had arranged to go to an early service in a large Episcopal church where Joanna had recently been engaged as a soloist. He was waiting for her in the dark hall.

"Good! There you are, Peter. We must fly."

"Not until you've told me you love me."

"I love you, Peter. Come on."

"No, sir, put your little arms around my neck. So. Now

say, 'Dear Peter, I love you and I'm going to marry you.'"

"Oh, I can't say that. Let me go, Peter."

"Not one step." He held her so close that she had to poise herself against him, breathlessly, exquisitely. A clock in the house boomed five.

"Peter, ask me to-night."

"I'm asking you now. Answer me this minute, Joanna. Not one step will we stir till you do." He shook her gently. "Say it, darling."

She still had her arms around his neck. "Dear Peter," she began, her voice breaking a little, "I love you and I'm going to marry you."

"You've got a smudge on your face," he told her solemnly.

She burst into hysterical tears at that. "I never thought I'd become engaged with a smudge on my face."

"I know you didn't. I'll try to overlook it." He got down on his knees and kissed her hands. "Darling Joanna, I'll love you always."

Between them, they wiped away the traces of the smudge and of her tears. Then they found their way out, and walked through the dark silent streets singing "Joy to the World," like a pair of Christmas waifs.

The lovers found it hard to see each other. There were too many things going on for that. Peter could have found time, but Joanna, he realized with a pang, seemed to think of nothing but her dance. When she wasn't at a party, or dressing, she was at a rehearsal. The affair for the Day Nursery was to come off New Year's Eve.

Monsieur Bertully's seven pupils danced, swayed, pirouetted. Their slim silken limbs flashed and twinkled through a series of poses and groups until one thought of an animated Greek frieze. At the end the seven girls appeared as school children. Joanna as their leader was teaching them a game. Peter watched her flashing in a red dress across the stage, dancing, leaping, twirling. The orchestra struck up something vaguely familiar. Why, it was Joanna's old dance, "Barn! Barn!" She swayed, she balanced, she stamped her foot.

"Stay back, girl, don't you come near me!"

Miss Sharples was there with a group of Greenwich Village folks, Helena Arnold told them afterwards.

Peter had to leave on New Year's Day. It was bitterly cold and the Marshalls had dinner guests, but Joanna went to the station with him. She didn't cry this time, Peter noticed. She didn't tell him that it was because of the pain raging at her heart.

"I'll have to get used to his leaving me," she told herself stubbornly. "I've got it to stand, for years and years. Talking about it won't do any good."

She had fixed up a box of delicious sandwiches and other goodies for him, and there was a little letter in the box. But Peter didn't know that, so in spite of her wan face he felt aggrieved as he stepped on the train, for she had barely pressed his hand and her lips were cold.

She cried herself into a headache on her way back.

It was bitter in Philadelphia, too. Peter got off the train at West Philadelphia. He would call on some of the boys on Sansom Street.

"They're all out I think," the landlady, Mrs. Larrabee, told him. She gave him a friendly smile. "You can run up, though, and see." She was right, they were out, but the rooms were warm and comfortable.

"I think I'll stay up here and thaw out," he called down.

He sat in a comfortable chair, smoked a cigarette or two, read a few pages in a novel. Then he remembered Joanna's box, and opened it. There was the letter on top.

"Dear Peter," he read, "isn't it awful to have to separate this way? I have a secret I was saving for you. I'm to sing in Philadelphia very shortly. Aren't you glad? I love you, Peter.

"JAN."

His spirits went up, up.

"Good-night," he called to Mrs. Larrabee. "Happy New Year."

It wasn't so cold after all, he thought. Anyway, it wouldn't do him any harm to stretch his legs a bit. He'd swing across town through the University grounds and take a car on Spruce Street.

The car jolted down over the bridge, turned one corner into a dingy side street, then another, slid ponderously into Lombard Street. It stopped to let the Twentieth Street car go by. Idly, Peter glanced out of the window. On the corner stood a woman, neatly, even carefully dressed. Something about her dejected pose made Peter look at her closely. She turned just then, and the street light fell full on an old-gold, oval face, haggard and disillusioned. Peter saw it was Maggie Ellersley.

CHAPTER XIV

POOR MAGGIE! How relentlessly and completely had her illusions flown!

She had enjoyed the ride to Atlantic City. Her husband had surrounded her with magazines, fruit, candy, even books. She had had a wonderful dinner and when they got to Atlantic City, he took her to a very respectable, clean boarding-house. It was nice to be protected, she realized that. And, when, the day after they were married, he gave her seventy-five dollars, and told her to send part of it to her mother, her spirits, which had not yet recovered from the shock of the past two days, rose considerably.

She thought Mr. Neal remarkably kind and gentle. And he was always clean. On the whole, while she was not the least bit in love with him, she considered he did pretty well, though she did wish he knew a little more about English grammar. His deliberate incorrectness made her ashamed of him and because he was so kind to her, this feeling on her part made her a little ashamed of herself.

He was the soul of generosity. Besides giving her money, he had taken her to two of the best stores, and bought her whatever she wanted. He would have liked to buy her a complete outfit, but the prices made her demur.

"Wait till we get to New York again. We can do better there." But she did let him buy her a few things: There were a blue silk dress, a white satin skirt, two or three smart, delicately tinted blouses, a wonderful wrap, light but warm; tan and white shoes and stockings.

Atlantic City was a revelation to her. She had literally never been out of New York City, except once to a funeral in Brooklyn in company with the lugubrious Mis' Sparrow. This fairyland by the sea with its colored lights, its human kaleidoscope, its boardwalk, its shops! She did not know the world held such as these.

But she was more interested in the Atlantic City that lay on the north side of Atlantic Avenue. There were many cottages here, a score of restaurants, a good drug store, all of them patronized by colored people. They were the kind of people Maggie wanted to know, she could see that at a glance. In the restaurant which she and her husband most frequented, she sat and watched the happy, laughing faces. They were like one big family although they came from Washington, Philadelphia, and Baltimore. She realized then how completely she had depended on the Marshalls and their immediate entourage. Cut off from them, she had no way of meeting these people, she possessed no background.

Some of the visitors seemed to know others hailing from the most remote places. One woman said, "Oh, there's Annie Mackinaw, she's been in San Francisco for five years you know, I must speak to her." Surely, Maggie thought, her husband must have met some of these people somewhere. But although an occasional man nodded to him, even came up and spoke, not one brought over his wife or daughters. The women looked at Maggie, a little curiously; once she thought as she passed a large party at a table that they stopped talking with that queer suddenness which made her sure they were discussing her. They looked at her clothes, appraising them, but she could never catch their direct gaze.

She sought to find solace in the theaters, of which she was very fond. This was an opportunity, plenty of leisure and a willing companion ready and able to take her whenever and wherever she wished. But Atlantic City theaters make no secret of their unwillingness to serve colored patrons. After being told at the ticket office that there were no more balcony seats, only to see them calmly handed out to the next white person in line; after enduring an evening in the poorly venti- lated gallery with a feeling of resentment rankling in her breast; above all after seeing how these mischances awoke her husband's passionate but futile anger, she desisted. He had a terrible, devastating temper, which left her speechless and cowering even though it was not directed toward her. Better do without the theater forever, she thought, than be the cause of awakening his savage wrath.

She returned to her survey of the colored visitors. Her husband found some friends and went off on mysterious trips with them, from which he returned amiable and pleasant and usually with some small gift for her. In his absence she sat on the piazza watching happy groups go by, or sat alone in the pavilion far down the boardwalk, where the colored people bathed. In time she came to know the characteristics of certain groups, could even tell from what city they came.

Philadelphians were not as a rule as strikingly dressed as the folks, say, from Washington, but they had a better time. They seemed bound by some kind of tie, family, perhaps— which made it possible for them to group together incongru- ously but with evident enjoyment. Old women and young girls, young girls and elderly men, young men and almost middle-aged women, laughed and bathed and gossiped like brothers and sisters. These were the hardest to approach; it was impossible to invade their solidarity. They made the status of the outsider very clear.

The Baltimore people were somewhat like these, only gayer. They were clannish, too, but more willing to let down bars. Clearly they were a cross between the Philadelphians and the gay Washingtonians who played about in very distinct groups, superb in their fashionable clothes and their deep assurance.

Maggie's landlady introduced her to one girl, a Miss Talbert from Philadelphia, who came up on the piazza one day to inquire for a former boarder. She was brown, not pretty, rather plainly but well dressed, with a beautiful manner. An atmosphere of niceness hung about her.

She acknowledged the introduction pleasantly. "You're from New York, Mrs. Neal—I wonder if you know my cousin Sylvia Marshall?"

Maggie could have jumped for joy. "She's my best friend."

Things went a little better, then. Miss Talbert asked her to go in bathing, introduced her to a few people, beckoned her over to her table at lunch. But she and her party were staying for only three days more, and Maggie was almost as badly off as ever when she left.

Her husband took her down to the pavilion the next day, and left her there. A sharp-faced old woman wearing a plain sad-colored dress and a formidable false front, beckoned to her.

"What does your husband do?" she asked the girl, looking at her over sloping glasses.

Maggie, confused, said he was in the motor-business. The old woman turned incredulously away.

She determined to ask her husband about his work. But he gave her no satisfaction.

"You wouldn't understand it. Too much explaining to it. I make money enough for you, don't I, girl?" He laid a heavy hand on her frail shoulder.

He thought he'd go to Philadelphia to live. "Feller told me of some good prospects there. We'll just room for a while. If we don't like it, we can go back to New York."

She was satisfied. She didn't want to return to New York, she realized. Her mother could make out with the money which, Neal had assured her, she could send regularly. And it made her sick to think of the Marshalls.

Without regrets she mounted the train with him one day

and went to the big, sprawling city. Its size, its long stretches
of streets appalled her. The awful silence which seemed to
descend over the town when she got below Walnut Street
frightened her. One could be very lonely here, no doubt.

The "rooming" of which her husband had spoken proved to
mean the second floor of a house in South Fifteenth Street.
There were three rooms and a bath. She liked this because it
gave her something to do. She kept them clean, arranged and
rearranged the charming furniture which Neal gave her, and
prepared their simple meals.

It was the first time she had had a really attractive setting.
And she was soothed, bewitched by its effect. Her rather
simple plan of life contained, it must be remembered, only
three ideas,—comfort, respectability, and love. This last had
been added to her list very recently. She would have married
Philip any time during the last five years without loving him,
for the sake of the security which he could have brought her.
So it is not strange, then, that she and Neal sailed their little
craft so smoothly. It is true that marriage did not in reality
prove as interesting and picturesque as she in common with
most girls had conceived it to be. But marriage was marriage,
and she must make the best of it. Neal was still kind, almost
fatherly, very generous, clean, and, as far as she could see, had
no bad habits. He smoked one cigar after each meal, and
almost never drank.

"Can't afford it in my business," she heard him say often.
His business! If only he hadn't been so mysterious about
that. Still it must be all right. Men called on him pretty
often and he would see them in the middle room, which Maggie
had turned into a restful living room. Certainly he made
plenty of money.

She had comfort then and she did not feel the lack of love.
Occasionally it occurred to her, it would be nice to be per-
forming some of her housewifely duties for Philip. She

thought he would enjoy doing some of them with her. But perhaps that was because he was young. Things seemed to change so when one became old,—at least elderly. And she did not think Philip would have been out as much as Neal.

Her passion, however, was for respectable company,—for more than that if she had but known it. She wanted friends, impeccable young women with whom she could talk over things, and exchange patterns and recipes, or go to the matinée. Once she met Miss Talbert on Christian Street. The girl greeted her kindly but a bit doubtfully, spoke about the weather. Then came the query:

"What did you say your husband's name was, Mrs. Neal?"

"Why Neal, of course, oh, Henderson, Henderson Neal."

Miss Talbert looked at her a little sadly, exchanged a few more banalities, and went on her assured way.

"I did hope she'd ask me to call," Maggie murmured. "How am I ever to get to know anybody in this great town?"

On the floor above her lived a girl and her brother, Annie and Thomas Mason. The brother played and the girl sewed and kept house. Once Annie got a letter of Neal's by mistake and brought it down to Maggie. She was in her living-room trying to shorten a skirt when Annie tapped.

She stepped to the door. "Oh, come in."

Miss Mason came in, nothing loth. "I got your husband's letter by mistake. He's Mr. H. Neal ain't he?" She held out the letter glancing about the room. "You've fixed it up real pretty here. The last roomers kept the place looking so bad. You going to stay long?"

Maggie didn't know. She was transported at the sight of the pleasant-voiced friendly girl and the North Pennsylvania accent which carried with it something very wholesome and grateful.

Miss Mason was frankly curious. "You here alone all day? What do you do while your husband's to work?"

"Oh, clean, and sew and—and nap," Maggie laughed a little. "Don't you want to come to see me sometime, now, this afternoon?"

Miss Mason thought she "might's well, your room seems bigger'n mine 'cause we've got a piano and you've got a table there. Say, s'pose I was to bring my sewing down, and I could help you even off your skirt."

After that they spent a great deal of time together. They walked in the quiet autumn evenings down dingy Fifteenth Street, past the hideousness of Washington Avenue, down, down the stretch of unswerving street to Tasker or Morris, through to Broad Street which is really Fourteenth. They sauntered back arm in arm under young but fading trees, past the hurry of flying automobiles, under the soft silver of the street lights. Then they turned up Catherine Street, stopped at the bakery for ice-cream or a bag of cakes and so to the house to bed.

It was a pleasant, almost a bucolic friendship. Both girls had rather simple tastes. Sometimes they went further up Broad Street to the theaters, choosing the ones where they met with the least discrimination. Once Maggie took Annie to the Academy of Music. They stood in line for their seats and Maggie looked at the bill-boards. One of them read:

COMING!
THE PHILADELPHIA ORCHESTRA
MR. HUBERT SANDERSON
CONDUCTOR
DECEMBER 27TH, 1910
MR. THOMAS MORSE
WILL PRESENT
MISS JOANNA MARSHALL
MEZZO-SOPRANO OF NEW YORK

She turned away, a little sick.

Maggie usually paid for their outings. Annie's brother

made a pretty fair salary, his sister told Maggie, for he played at private dances for wealthy white people in West Philadelphia, Rosemont, Sharon, Chestnut Hill and various other suburbs.

"But he don't give me much 'cause he wants to leave the country for good sometime. I keep house for him and he pays for the lodgings and for most of our food. I make what little extra I can by taking in plain sewing. Your husband's right open-handed, ain't he?"

"Yes," said Maggie heartily. "He's very generous and very kind." She wanted to change the subject, for Annie was inquisitive—one never knew what she'd ask next.

"Funny, ain't it," pursued Annie, her mouth full of pins—she was at her everlasting sewing, turning up the hem of a bath-robe—"I ain't never seen him yet, no, nor Tom neither."

"Well, you will. Come and walk up to South Street with me. I want to get some postal cards."

It was an aimless existence, but it had its points. Her mother was comfortable, she herself had ease, a husband and a companion.

She went out to market one chilly November morning and came back later than she expected. She had scarcely got in before Annie appeared, an unusual flush on her yellow, freckled cheeks. Annie had reddish, crinkled hair, which she wore brushed stiffly back from her high forehead into a hard, ungraceful knob; "rhiny" hair, Maggie knew Sylvia and the boys would call it. She could imagine how they would talk about Annie in their pleasant, unmalicious way. Joanna would strike her attitude and imitate her accent. Annie broke into these reminiscences.

"I been down here two or three times a'ready. Kind o' rawish like."

"Yes, I think it's going to rain. I'll light the gas-heater

and we can sit here and thaw out. I enjoy a chilly day if it's warm inside."

"Kind o' that way myself."

"Oh, you said you'd been here before. Want to see me about anything special?"

"Oh, aimed I'd come set with you a spell. Me and Tom— now—we saw your husband last night."

"That so? Where? How'd you guess it was he?"

"Near Bainbridge Street, then we watched him come in here. Why, Tom knowed him a'ready. I didn't know his name was Henderson. I'd heard of him before myself."

Outside a steady soaking rain had begun to fall in the gray somberness of the November afternoon. The gas-heater cast a ruddy oblong of light on the white ceiling. Maggie, who had been straightening out a paper pattern, crossed the room and threw her slight figure on the couch, huddling close against the wall. She shivered a little in the luxurious warmth.

"Isn't it grand to be indoors? Where did you ever hear of my husband?"

She was becoming drowsy and did not notice at first that Annie had not answered her. When she did, she looked up suddenly to catch the girl's dog-like brown eyes fixed wist- fully on hers.

"What's the matter Annie?"

"Nothing."

"Oh, but there is. Are you sick? Has Tom been unkind to you?"

"Oh, it isn't me. It's you! Oh, Maggie, how could you?"

"What about me? How could I what?"

"Marry him?"

"Marry whom? my husband,—why shouldn't I?"

"Didn't you know?"

"For God's sake speak up, Annie Mason. What is it you

know about him? Has he got another wife? Is he an escaped convict?"

"He's a gambler."

"A what?"

"A gambler. Tom knows him well. And I guess I musta saw him when I was a little girl. He used to live up around Stroudsburg. They run him out of town."

"I'll never believe it." But in her heart she did. That money—why, of course, his long hours, especially at night, his reticence—all this combined to make her recognize the truth.

"You poor thing. Of course you don't want to believe it. That's what I said to Tom. I said, 'That poor thing, she's got no notion of it.'"

It was intolerable, such pity! "Where is your brother, Annie?"

"Who, Tom! Prob'ly up stairs, he don't go out to rehearsal till four."

"Tell him to come here."

Annie went out, whimpering a little, twisting her fingers in the folds of her white apron. She came back followed by a tall thin young man, dark, with kind, soft brown eyes. Maggie noticed that the hair in front of his ears was unshaven to form flat side-whiskers. "Siders" the boys used to call them. They had teased Sandy about them, for he had affected them in his college days.

She was standing by the table holding the envelope of the paper pattern in her hand. "Mr. Mason, what's this you know about my husband?"

"Annie shouldn't have told you, ma'am," he said abjectly. "It was none of her business."

"Well, she has. Sit down, please, and tell me all you know."

"I'd rather stand, thank you, ma'am. Well if I must. Even when I was a little boy, Henderson Neal was knowed to be a card-sharp. There wasn't nobody could stand against him. Used to wait for the men on a Saturday night, white and colored. He'd meet 'em in the bar and treat, and then ask 'em in on a little game. And they'd play, till they was cleaned out. Then he'd give 'em another drink, and clap 'em on the back. Perhaps he'd hand 'em back a dollar. 'Better luck next time old man!' And they'd come back the next Saturday night, the poor fools. Some of them blowed their brains out, they got so far back in their debts."

She was tearing the envelope into bits, but her voice was steady. "You're sure of this?"

"My uncle was one of them that killed theirselves. They was a colored minister come to Stroudsburg and he run him out of town. Then he crossed over to Phillipsburg, then down to Trenton. They made things too hot for him there, too. Then he got in with a white saloon-keeper in the mining districts in Pennsylvania. Finally things got too hot for him and he left the country for a while, was servant to an actor. He come back in about five years with another name."

"An alias," murmured Annie who read the papers.

"But pretty soon he started out again under his own name. You see he got some political protection in New York, and I guess he's got the same here. Most people know about him a'ready. I'm sorry I had to tell you, ma'am."

"Yes, yes, I'm sure. Would—would you mind leaving me now? You, too, Annie—please."

She didn't lie down and moan and cry as she had done— was it less than six months ago?—when she received Joanna's letter. That was child's trouble compared to this. She had wanted so to be decent, and she was a gambler's wife. God! how funny!

Now she must think, she must think. Oh, what was she to do? Leave him, she knew that. But afterwards? She had no money. He had given her her very clothes. Her old ones were at her mother's. Her mother!

"Poor Mamma!" she said again as on a former occasion. "What a hell her life's always been!"

No wonder those people, those men in Atlantic City who knew him didn't introduce their women folks to her.

"I suppose they thought 'You thief! Dressing that girl on other men's money!' "

Pretty soon he'd be home for dinner. She heard him presently coming up the stairs. There! He had stepped on the creaky one. That meant he was—now—just outside the door. He stepped in.

"Nice and warm in here."

She barely allowed him time to take off his overcoat. "Henderson, I know how you make your money. You're a gambler."

He didn't deny it. "Who told you that?"

"The nephew of that man, that Mr. Mason (she hazarded the name) who shot himself in Stroudsburg."

"Where'd you see him?"

"What difference does that make? And I've been living like a queen off stolen money. I want you to know I'm leaving you this instant."

He caught her by the arm. "Don't be a fool, Maggie!"

She could see the blood mounting, as his temper rose, shadowing his dark face.

"That's what I'm trying to do—stop being a fool."

"Where will you go, how can you live? Off my money? You've none of your own."

"I'll make some."

"I'll never let you go. I'll kill you first." He crushed both slender wrists in his brutal hand and she went ashen with pain.

"I wish you would kill me."

He flung her away from him then and she leaned back against the wall, breathing hard.

"I suppose you'll go back to that man, that fine gentleman that didn't want you."

"Isn't it likely he'd want me now?   I was a nice girl then, not the wife of a gambler."

He broke down suddenly at that, sank in a chair, buried his head in his hands.

"What do you want me to do?"

"I want you to let me go."   Her voice was hard.

He lifted a wretched face.   "You wouldn't stay even if I was to do something else—something decent?"

But she couldn't forgive him for dragging her into this abyss, this slough of degradation.

"You couldn't change now, and anyway I wouldn't live with you."

To her amazement he got up, took his hat and coat and started for the door.

"I'll go.   You're not the one to be turned out.   You know I pay for these rooms a quarter in advance.   This here's the beginning of the second quarter.   There's some money in the top bureau drawer."

"I don't want the money.   Take it with you."   She got it and stuffed a handful of bills—yellow ones—in the pocket of his overcoat.   "I don't want your rooms, either."

"You'll have to keep them.   You've no money and you've no place to go.   You ain't got a friend in Philadelphia, and you can't walk to New York.   If you walk around the streets long enough, you'll find there's worse things can happen than being a gambler's wife."   He straightened up.   "If you don't promise me to stay, I'll tag around after you everywheres you go."

"If I stay—for a while—will you promise me not to come back?"

"I promise."

"Pooh, the promise of a gambler!"   She hated him.

"I'll show you. Best not to try me too far though, Maggie."

"Well, are you going?"

He walked out, closing the door very quietly after him. She had not shed a tear, she did not now. Instead she sat, with her brow wrinkled, trying to recall something.

"Oh, yes," she sprang up and rushed to the closet, pulling with nervous, shaking fingers at the garments hanging there. In the pocket of her little poplin suit, the suit in which she was married, she found what she was looking for.

It was an oblong business card, slightly soiled around the edges. She had come across it in Atlantic City and for some reason had kept it. Across the front ran a neat superscription

MADAME HARKNESS
Hair Culturist
270 West 137th Street
New York City

Her glance dropped to the left-hand corner. Yes, she was right, there it was: Branch offices—Washington, D. C., 1307 U Street, N. W.; Baltimore, 1816 Druid Hill Avenue; Philadelphia, 2021 South Street.

She sat all night brooding wide eyed over the purring gas-stove. In the morning she made herself tidy and walked up to Twentieth and South.

CHAPTER XV

SYLVIA was arranging the smallest birthday cake in the world. It bore one very small candle and it was for the very small baby who, propped up in a high chair, sat and watched the birthday proceedings with round solemn eyes. A three-year-old youngster, whose nose just rose above the edge of the table, watched, too, with eyes no less round and far more interested.

"Look at the darlings!" said Sylvia. "They know just what their mother's doing. Aren't my children intelligent, Brian?"

"What you mistake for intelligence is hunger, much more likely," laughed her husband. "I've seen Roger look that way before when there wasn't any birthday cake, but when there certainly were eats."

"You watch them," said Sylvia, "and I'll see if mother and father are ready to come. I had a telegram from Joanna this afternoon, so I know she can't make it." Her voice floated up to him as she ran down the back stairs.

The five years of Sylvia's married life had brought their changes to the Marshall household. Mrs. Marshall had insisted on Sylvia's and Brian's remaining with them.

"Else we'd be lonely," she complained, "what with Sandy gone for good, and Philip and Joanna everlastingly 'on the road,' as they express it."

Alexander and Helena Arnold, after seeing each other constantly and unresponsively for ten years, suddenly fell completely in love on that night of the Pierce Day Nursery dance. Sandy proved himself an impulsive wooer, for he won

128

Helena's consent and would have married her before Sylvia's and Brian's wedding came off.

"Gracious, don't spoil my thunder," Sylvia had begged him aghast.

"Well, I'm the oldest," Sandy had retorted. "It's really my place to marry first."

Helena, unaware of all this, announced that she wanted to be bridesmaid at Sylvia's wedding, so Alec must wait till after. "Think of all the extra clothes I can get. Besides, I couldn't possibly finish my trousseau before."

The two had married the June following Sylvia's wedding and had moved into a house of their own. The household had hardly become adjusted to Alexander's absence, when Philip started on his long tours which kept him away from home a good part of the year.

He had been graduated from Harvard, with honors and with his coveted Phi Beta Kappa key. He had come home, happy though not as radiant, Joanna thought for one, as in the old days. Then he had evolved his new scheme. He proposed that an organization be started among the colored people which should reach all over the country.

"White and colored people alike may belong to it," said Philip, his eyes kindling to his vision, "but it is to favor primarily the interests of colored people. No, I'm wrong there," he corrected himself. "It is to favor primarily the interests of the country."

He was speaking to a group of both white and black enthusiasts. "How shall we start it?" someone asked.

They all liked the plan. He had his project well mapped out, for he had thought of little else for the past three years. There were to be a national board and a national office, supported by local boards and membership. There would be need of organized publicity; he might suggest a magazine or a

9

weekly newspaper. A huge campaign must be got underway, an effort at nation-wide support.

"Its objects will be," he enumerated them on his long brown fingers, "the suppression of lynching and peonage, the restoration of the ballot, equal schools and a share in civic rights."

"A large order," said Barney Kirchner, Philip's classmate, "but I like it. I'll get my uncle behind it." Barney was wealthy in his own right, but his uncle, an Austrian Jew, had built up an immense fortune which had since supported many a notable cause.

The little nucleus worked well. From that meeting grew up all that Philip predicted, rather weak and tottering at first but the five years had seen the awakening of a great racial consciousness. There were still tremendous possibilities almost untouched.

The organization had a magazine, "The Spur," of which Philip was editor. But he was constantly called to exercise his vision and judgment in the field. His observation, his constant scrutiny of his own people helped him here, but he was the born organizer in any event.

Joanna already started on her concert tours, often met him on the "road." Sometimes they were booked at the same place for the same night. Each was the other's supporting attraction.

"Oh, is this Mr. Marshall?" Joanna would gush when he met her train. She put an imaginary lorgnette to her eye. "Any relation to the eminent Miss Joanna Marshall, the world-famous mezzo?"

"Never heard of her. Haven't the least idea who she is. Come along, Silly. Now, Joanna, do be on time and don't stop to primp. Mind, I won't wait for you a minute."

"Not the littlest, teeniest one?" It was hard to say which was prouder of the other.

Joanna was in fine feather in those days. She had youth

and a certain grave beauty which did not strike the observer at first as did Sylvia's or even poor Maggie's. But it grew on one and remained. Young men, though they liked to be seen with a star, were a little afraid of her queenliness, her faint condescension. She took herself so seriously! Her own folks and Peter often teased her about this, but they adored it in her. And she, in turn, adored her little fame, the footlights, the adulation. Even the smallest church in the quietest backwoods, with a group of patient dark faces peering at her out of the often smoky background, had its appeal. At such times, strange to say, she was at her best, gave of her finest. She would come on the stage, trailing clouds of glory, and lean toward them—a rosy brown vision. In some misty colorful robe of Sylvia's designing, her thick crinkling hair piled high on her head as the Spanish woman had taught her, she seemed to say:

"I am no better than you. You are no worse than I. Whatever I am, you, in your children, may be. Whatever you are, I in my father have been."

She was absolutely sincere in her estimation of her art, or of any art. It was only in its relation to the other things of life that she lost her vision and sense of proportion.

She liked most to go to Philadelphia, where she was in great favor. There she had had three great triumphs, once in Association Hall, twice at the Academy of Music. Both she and Peter had thrilled when she came from the Academy the second time. She sent her flowers and her stage-gown home in the car of a friend, while she and Peter were whirled in a taxi out to Fairmount Park.

They had driven to the Green Street entrance, and then dismissing the cab had walked around the drive, up the steps, in front of the mansion and on to Lemon Hill. It was one of those last, warm, almost hot nights of Indian Summer. The slopes of the park lay deserted before them, deep in velvety shadow, with here and there a gold patch bright as day under the watching arc-light.

They sat down on the dry, short grass. "Like that other evening in Morningside, long, long ago. How long, Joanna?"

"Oh, ages! How'd I sing, Peter?"

"Divinely. You looked like an angel, Janna. No, not an angel, more like a siren in that yellow dress. Where'd you get it, dearest?"

"Yellow nothing! That was orange—deep, deep orange. Sylvia planned it out for me. Isn't she a genius? Through me she certainly is teaching these colored people how to dress. We will not wear these conventional colors—grays, taupe, beige—poor boy, you don't know what they are, do you? They're all right for these palefaces. But colored people need color, life, vividness."

"George! I guess you're right. How'd you come to think of it?"

"I didn't. It was Sylvia. I started out in a white dress. You should have seen me looking like an icebergish angel."

"You are one, you know Janna."

"Which? Iceberg or angel?"

"Both. One makes me adore you, the other says 'hands off'."

"Not a bad thing, do you think, considering all the men I meet?"

"I hate them. Sure you don't like any of 'em better than me?"

"No, dear, I like you best."

" 'No, dear, I like you best'," he mimicked. "For God's sake, Jan, can't you say, 'Peter, I love you always'? Say it."

She hesitated, sighed a little. "Peter I love you."

"Why'd you leave off 'always'?"

"Dear little boy, how can I say it? I do when I think of it. But, Peter, I have so much to think about—my tour, my booking, you know, my lessons in French and Italian, my dancing. I still keep that up; I'd really rather do that than sing. Dancing makes me——"

"Oh, damn the dancing!"

"Why, Peter!" She looked at his flushed face in amazement.

"Hang it all, talking to me about dancing, when I'm talking to you about love—*love*, Joanna—and there's nothing to keep us from getting married. Some fellows and girls ball their lives up so they can't ever get them straightened out. But here we are 'all set' as the fellows say. And you talk to me about dancing! Suppose I were to talk to you about *Materia Medica!*"

"I think it would be a good thing if you would."

He was honestly aggrieved at that.

She leaned over and kissed him. "See how brazen I am. That's the second time I've given you a kiss. Oh, Peter, you big baby!"

"Dear Janna, I love you so! Great Scott! aren't girls funny! You can't guess how hard it is for me to be letting all these stupid years go by. Sometimes I've half a mind to chuck it all."

"You'd never get me then."

"I don't suppose I would. Well, I have you now."

"Dear Peter, we must be going home. Cousin Parthenia will rave."

"Pshaw, she knows you're with me. Love me, darling?"

"You know I do, you dear, dear boy."

"Come, sit up on the bench. There, that's it." He knelt before her. "Know what I'm going to give you to-night?" He felt in his pocket. "Like it, Janna?"

He showed her a ring, a tiny gold chased ring, whose facets gleamed like diamonds.

"Peter, it's too beautiful. Oh, I love you for it."

He slipped it on her finger, got up and sat beside her,

kissing her little cold hands. She leaned against his shoulder, —he put his arm about her. A poignant sweetness seemed to flood in on them out of the solemn, mellow night.

Peter was the first to stir. "I must get you home, darling. Oh, Joanna, aren't you too happy? I wonder if we wouldn't be better off if we were resting like this, our arms close about each other, in our grave."

The inevitable separation came the next day. Joanna was cold, almost indifferent. It was the way she had taught herself to endure pain. She hated always to leave Peter, particularly if she were returning to New York. The excitement of visiting other places healed her loneliness. Sometimes she wished she weren't going to see Peter for these brief visits which lacerated her so.

Unfortunately her lover did not understand this. "How can she melt like she did last night and then leave me so cool and composed this morning?" he wondered, staring dejectedly after the departing express. He had not ridden to West Philadelphia with her because he had to be at a hospital at Sixteenth Street at one o'clock and it was now noon.

"She used to cry when we separated." He stood uncertainly a moment on the corner of Fifteenth and Market. "Guess I'll go over to that little Automat on Juniper Street and snatch a mouthful. I won't feel like eating after I see Carpenter start in on that slashing. Golly, what a steady hand he has."

He walked through the City Hall Arcade to Juniper Street, crossed in front of Wanamaker's and forced a passage through the teeming little by-way

The Automat was crowded. "Have to eat standing," he thought, drawing a glass of water and seizing a knife and fork. "No, there's an empty table." He collected his food and began to eat.

Someone put a plate on the table beside him, rested a hand there a moment. Peter glanced at it.

"Colored. What a nice hand! Ought to have a peach of a face to match that."

He looked up. "Maggie Ellersley! I had heard you lived here. I thought I saw you once, why—four years ago—one New Year's night on Twentieth Street. You've been here ever since?"

"Yes, Peter. Oh, it's so nice to see you!"

"Isn't it, though! I mean isn't it great to see somebody from home? I've just seen Joanna off."

Her face stiffened at that. But he was busy looking at his watch.

"Ten minutes more! Look here, Maggie, what'd you drop us all that way for? How's your husband?"

She answered his second question. "I haven't any."

He glanced at her apologetically, ashamed of his levity. "Is he dead?"

"No," said Maggie woodenly. "I've left him!"

"Oh!" he was embarrassed. "I'm sorry, Maggie. Got to run now. When may I see you again?"

His engaging manner brought back the old days. "Peter, you aren't ashamed of me?"

"My dear girl!" He was younger than she and for that reason he adopted a paternal air, patting her on the shoulder. "How can you ask that?"

"Would you come to see me to-night, Peter? Come to dinner?"

"Try me. What's the address?"

She gave it to him. "That's Fifteenth and Fitzwater."

"Yes, I know. I'll see you at six sharp. Until then, Maggie." He bared his curly head and flashed out the side door.

He tapped at her door at six.

"I didn't hear you ring," said Maggie. "Come in. This *is* nice, Peter."

"I should say so. Jolly little place you've got here." He settled back on the couch, stretched out his long legs. "All these years I've been tramping about Philadelphia, a poor homeless beggar, when I might have been coming to see you. How long have you been alone, Maggie?"

"Four and a half years."

"Four and a half years! Why that's—look here, how long have you been married?"

"Five years last June. I left him almost right away, or rather he left me."

"Deserted you, you mean?"

"No, no, not that. He wanted to stay. I—I couldn't let him." She told him all about it. "Peter, think of it, I'd married a gambler, a common gambler. And I'd wanted so to be decent!" She wept painfully.

He put his arm about her slender shoulders. "There, there now, Maggie."

"It's the first time I've shed a tear about it. Seeing you, someone out of the old happy days, upset me. Sit here, Peter."

"They were wonderful days, weren't they? Remember what a bunch we were? And now we're scattered everywhere. Joanna and Philip romping all over the country; Sylvia and Brian married; Sandy too, did you know it?"

"Yes, I read of it in the *Amsterdam News.*"

"You and I here. Harry Portor—do you remember him?"

"Ye—es, big square fellow, wore glasses. He used to go skating with us, didn't he?"

"Yes, that's the fellow. He studied medicine, too, at Harvard. Went to Washington as interne in the Freedmen's Hospital. I haven't seen him for ages. What'd you leave us for so suddenly, Maggie?"

She couldn't tell *him*, of all people, about Joanna.

"Oh, I don't know, girls are crazy, I think. Well, I'm not complaining. I'm better off than I've ever been. That Madame Harkness—you know whom I mean?"

"The hair-woman—what about her?"

"She's made me supervisor of three of her branch stores, here in Philadelphia, Baltimore, and Washington, D. C. I have my little home here, my salary's good. I make more than enough to live on. My mother doesn't have to do anything if she doesn't want to. And above all, I'm practically free."

"How do you mean free?"

"I'm suing for a divorce. Lawyer Talbert has my case."

"Oh, Mrs. Marshall's cousin. Have you ever seen your—Mr. Neal since he left?"

"About once a year. I hadn't seen him for a long time though, until he came here six weeks ago, just before I started divorce proceedings." Her face changed at the thought of it.

"He didn't threaten you, Maggie?"

"Yes and no. In his way he cares about me, though not as much as for his gambling. He's—he's got it in his head that I care about somebody else, and every now and then he writes me a threatening letter. That's why he came to see me this last time."

"You oughtn't to let him in."

"Oh, I have to. This Mrs. Davis, from whom I rent these rooms, doesn't know there's any trouble, she thinks he's a steward on a boat, and I never have told her differently. She thinks I'm with him when I go away on these trips. Last time he was here, he stayed half the night right on that couch. He had a wretched cold, and it was raining!"

"I should think you'd have been afraid."

"That's why I let him stay. He'd been harboring such jealous thoughts toward me. He—he has an idea that I like another man. And he has a terrific temper. You can't imagine how it smolders and sulks. He wasn't so bad about my sending him away, but since he's had this suspicion I've really been afraid. I expect he'll be really violent some day."

"Well, Great Scott, won't my coming to see you be dangerous? I was just thinking what good times we'd have."

"We will. No, you're all right. He wouldn't be interested in you after he once knew who you were. And there's Thomas Mason upstairs; he's not bothered about him either, though Tom and his sister are in here all the time."

Peter pushed his chair back. "That was a mighty good dinner, Maggie. Mind if I smoke?" He lit a cigarette. "Well, you've had hard luck, haven't you? But never mind, it's bound to break even, sooner or later. That's what I keep saying to myself."

"You in trouble too, Peter? I've been running on so about my affairs. Tell me about yours. Studying the way you have to must be an awful strain."

He noticed gratefully how quick and ready was her sympathy. That was just it. Studying itself wasn't so bad, working wasn't bad. But the combination, the struggle to make ends meet, his few social obligations, and color!

"Why, it's awful. I'm on the rack all the time.

"If you could stop for a year or so and take a little rest, do something entirely different."

He glanced at her, amused but touched. "Joanna ought to hear you say that. She'd faint away. She can't understand anybody's wanting to let up."

Maggie said with a faint bitterness that you must always be top notch for Joanna.

"I should say so. Here, I'll help you with the dishes. Well, —if you really don't want me." She washed and wiped so fast that the room seemed cleared by magic. It had turned cooler and Maggie lit her little gas-stove.

Peter smoked and relapsed into a moody silence, which he broke now and then with an account of his struggles. His

Uncle Peter had died during his third year and the house had been inherited by his daughter, Mrs. Boyd. Of course he couldn't expect anything of her. Her father was only his great-uncle, and she had her own children to look after. He had moved to Mrs. Larrabee's in West Philadelphia, with some of his fraternity brothers. Somehow his money sped. His books were expensive, the cost of his instruments pure robbery.

"I do what playing I can, but I confess I'm up against it," he ended ruefully.

"Lots of the boys do waiting, don't they?" asked Maggie. "Why don't you do that?"

He just couldn't, he told her.

"I never could endure standing around 'grand white folks.' " Both of them smiled at the childhood's phrase. " 'Yes, sir, thank you— Oh, no, sir.' Then some lazy white banker, or some fat white woman that never did a day's work in her life, puts a hand in a pocket and offers you a dime. God, how I hate it! I did it once at Asbury Park, Phil did, too. We both said, 'Never again!' "

"Where do you play?"

"At different dance-halls. They don't pay as well here as in New York, though. What's that, Maggie?"

A thin stream of music, played on a violin, floated down to them.

"That's good fiddling. Is it in this house?"

"Yes. It's Tom Mason, the man I told you about. The very thing for you! He makes barrels of money. Come on, Peter."

She led him, bewildered, up to the third floor, tapped on a door and was admitted to a room much like the one she had just left. A young woman with red crinkled hair and a yellow freckled face sat sewing on a white apron. The young man who let them in had been putting some resin on his bow. Against the wall stood a battered, time-worn piano.

"Hello, Annie," said Maggie. "Hello, Tom. This is my friend Mr. Bye. I've brought him up to hear you play."

"But I can't, Miss Maggie. I've no accompanist." He turned soft brown eyes upon her. "Unless your friend here plays the piano."

"Well, I do admit to tickling the ivories occasionally," laughed Peter. "Let's see your score."

He sat down to the piano, ran his brown limber fingers over the keys, and began to play the accompaniment to a typical syncopated melody, accenting the time with staccato nods of his well-shaped head.

"Oh, great, that's great!" cried Tom after a few minutes. "Wait till I get my violin."

Together they made some wonderful sounds. "Play that passage again, will you?" Tom pointed it out with his bow.

"That's the best accompanist you've ever had, isn't it, Tom?" Annie asked.

"I should say so. Don't suppose you'd ever consent to doin' this sort of thing in public, Mr. Bye?"

"That depends on the price and the hours," said Peter.

Tom told him about himself. He played, had all the work he could do, for the wealthy folks of the town and suburbs. The pay was first-rate. Only he had never been able to keep a good accompanist.

"They're so do-less," he complained. "What's your regular line?"

Peter explained that he was a student.

Mason liked that. "Then you'd be workin' because you'd really need the fun's. Nothin' like having a purpose. Do you think you could go out to Sharon Hill with me to-morrow night and play that? There'd be a few other odds and ends. Though them white folks don't let me play nothin' much but that, once I get started. You might drop in for an hour to-morrow and take a peep at the others. You can do them easy, if you can read that." He pointed to the piece they'd already played.

"Honey-Babe," declaimed Peter. "Well, Mr. Mason, if we can come to terms, I'm your man."

Mason took him aside then, and whispered a few words.

"All right," Peter told him, shaking hands. "That listens pretty. See you to-morrow, say at four. Good-night folks. You coming too, Maggie?"

Downstairs he stopped at the landing. "Maggie, you jewel! How well you've managed! No, I won't come in. You see what was worrying me most was my operating set. The price of those little steel knives and forceps is going to touch the sky pretty soon. Wow! This confounded war is taking everything across seas. Fellow told me to get my order in before Christmas even if I didn't pay for them till next year. But where was I going to raise all that money? Now the way looks clearer."

"I'm so glad, Peter."

"It's me that's glad, Maggie. Best thing in the world for me that I met you to-day. Such a piece of fortune! Cheer up, child! Perhaps we'll bring each other luck!"

CHAPTER XVI

THE house on South Fifteenth Street saw Peter often after that. Mason could have given him work every night if he had wanted it. As it was he gave him enough to cause him to come for rehearsals three and four times a week. Usually Peter terminated his practice with a visit to Maggie, who got home regularly at five-thirty when she was in town.

She appreciated Peter's company, for she had been very lonely in this big city with its impregnable social fortresses. "It's a wonder you come to see me so often, Peter," she told him wistfully. "Being a Bye gives you the entrance everywhere among the oldest of these 'old Philadelphians.'"

"Yes," said Peter cheerfully, "but home-folks are best. And then you make it so pleasant for me, Maggie. Why, I've never eaten in my life anything so wonderful as that dinner Sunday. You certainly have the knack of making a fellow feel comfortable."

She was proud to have him there, he was so handsome and charming, but much more than that, so clearly a personage. She enjoyed being seen with him. He took her out occasionally to the park, to the theaters on Broad Street, once to a bazaar given by some fine ladies at the Y. M. C. A. on Christian Street. She recognized some of the women as among those whom she had seen at Atlantic City. The startled stare of Alice Talbert, who happened to be there that evening, afforded her endless satisfaction. Maggie realized she spoke to her with a sort of wondering respect.

"Wonder what she thought," she said to herself. "Well, she can think anything she pleases." She had not forgotten Miss Talbert's cool reception when she called at Lawyer Talbert's office on the corner of Fifteenth and Lombard. Alice was her father's secretary. She was quite remote on seeing Maggie, until she learned that the latter's business was with the lawyer.

Peter was making money these days, real money he told Maggie.

"I'm better off financially than I've ever been in my life. Why, I could make a real living at this sort of thing. Mason's got a wonderful clientele!" As usual he was lounging in Maggie's little living-room, smoking, watching her move about in her sober house-dress, arranging her accounts and orders. She had bought a little typewriter and had learned to use it. Peter was surprised to find her so methodical. He realized that she would have been a great help to Philip.

He felt a little guilty about coming to Maggie's so often. "But it's so confoundedly uncomfortable in my room. Of course I could do better now, but it's a lot of trouble to move. It's way up at the top of the house, clean enough, but with just a few sticks of furniture in it, a green iron-bed—ugh!— some books and the Bye family Bible. Don't know why I lugged that along with me. I never look in it. Well, so long, Maggie, see you to-morrow or next day."

"All right, Peter. You're sure you won't have me fix a cup of cocoa for you before you go? You poor, neglected boy! Two buttons off that overcoat. Bring it in the next time you come and I'll put them on for you. I'll find some that will match up here on South Street." He said he could attend to it himself, but she told him no, that wasn't a man's job.

"You certainly are some girl!" He took her hand in his for a moment. "I'll bring it with bells. Here, turn me out. I've got to get up at six to-morrow morning. Haven't put my nose inside of Carter's classes this week. Playing out so late with Mason puts me out of commission, you bet."

"Carter, Carter, that's the Professor of Surgery, isn't it?"

"No! no! That's Davenant. I never miss one of his classes. Eat it up in gobs. The old boy's fond of me. Says I'm his pet carver. Wanted to take me to see an operation in a private hospital last week—white of course—but Carter interfered. 'Not the place for Bye, Dr. Davenant,' he said. I hate him with his confounded hypocritical patronage. I'd like to chuck him in a minute."

Her sympathy was instant.

"Well, why don't you, Peter? After all, your music really is in good shape. All this steady practice these long years must count for something. Tom says you're a wonder. He'd like to go into partnership with you, I'm sure. He says there's heaps of money in it."

"Oodles! Absolutely! But nothing doing, Maggie. Too mediocre for Miss Joanna Marshall. But she deserves the best, she's the best herself," he added in quick loyalty. "Well, that was a false start I made before, wasn't it? I'm really going this time. Mr. Peter Bye, exit this way."

He walked up to Lombard Street, thinking. "That girl can certainly see along with you. Nice to meet some one with a disposition like that. Of course I'd rather be a surgeon. But I'm tired of this everlasting digging. I've been nothing but a slave for nearly seven years. And poor as the deuce in the bargain. Good Lord, when I think of all the money I might have made out of you!" He looked at his fine slender hands with their firm square-tipped fingers.

"Ideal surgeon hands," Doctor Davenant had told his assistant.

An idea struck Peter. "I wonder what Joanna would say to that!" He rushed in the house, seized a piece of paper and a pen and told her about it.

"Of course, Jan, I don't expect you to marry me if I can't take care of you. You wouldn't anyway, you're not like Sylvia. That's not a slam, dearest, that's just a plain statement of facts. But I'm making a lot of money right now—guess how?—with my music, playing for 'grand white folks' at all the swell society functions. Of course it takes me out of my classes sometimes, but I don't care, I'm fed up with all that. I've got such a Negro-loving bunch of professors, except my surgical men.

"What say, Joanna, if I quit this, and we get married and I go about the country with you as your accompanist? That ought to suit you, for I don't suppose you ever dream of settling down.

"Did I tell you I met Maggie Ellersley? I see her very often. The fellow I play with lives in the same house she does. In fact, Maggie introduced me to him. She's been no end kind to me. You'll be interested to know she's getting a divorce from that beast she married. See what Philip has to say when you tell him.

"Mind you write me right away what you think about this."

The answer came post-haste.

"What I think about this," [wrote Joanna, infuriated] "is that I don't want and won't have a husband who is just an ordinary strumming accompanist, playing one, two, three, one, two, three. Sometimes, Peter, I think you must be crazy."

A number of irritable and irritating notes followed on both sides until a couple of weeks before Christmas, when both sank into a mutinous silence.

What Peter did not understand and what Joanna never knew he needed explained to him was that she wanted Peter to be somebody for his own sake. She was really paying him a sincere compliment when she told him that she did not want an accompanist for a husband. Like many a woman of strong and purposeful character, she hated a weak man. It followed then that the man who won Joanna must be even stronger, more determined than she.

She did not know much about marriage. She had not only the usual virginal ignorance of many American girls, she had

10

also a remarkable lack of curiosity on the matter. But she knew vaguely that the man was supposed to be the head. How could she, Joanna Marshall, ever surrender to a man who was less than she in any respect? Her dominating nature craved one still more dominant. But neither Peter nor she knew this, she least of all. Youth, egotistic though it be, is notably free from this kind of introspection.

Since American customs of courtship give the girl largely the upper hand, Joanna was instinctively, if unanalytically, using Peter's love for her, and her own desirability, as a whip to goad him on. It was hard for her, too, much harder than Peter knew, or than she realized. For she was beginning at last to feel the tug of passion at her heart strings. It would never have occurred to her to marry Peter before he was in their common estimation "on his feet," she would never have asked it of him, she did not expect him to ask it of her. But unconsciously she was yearning for the day when the two might join hands and enter the portals which lead to the house of life.

Very often she found herself vaguely glad that she had her work. Without it, what would she have done? What *did* girls do while they waited for their young men? Heavens, how awful to be sitting around listlessly from day to day, waiting, waiting! Anything was better than that, even pounding a typewriter in a box of an office. It was this lack of interest and purpose on the part of girls which brought about so many hasty marriages which terminated in—no, not poverty—mediocrity. Joanna hated the word; with her visual mind she saw it embodied in broken chairs, cold gravy, dingy linen, sticky children. She would never mind poverty half so much; she would contrive somehow to climb out of that. But ordinary tame mediocrity!

Besides, colored people had had enough of that. Not for Joanna!

It must not be thought that at this time she had any inten-

tion of relinquishing her work after marriage. But it was for
that reason that she wanted Peter to come out of the herd.
She saw the two of them together, gracious, shining, perfect!
She heard whispers:

"That's Peter Bye, the distinguished surgeon! His wife
is unusual, too, she was Joanna Marshall. You must have
heard of her. Why, she sings all over the country!"

And here was Peter offering her the vision of herself, standing glorious, resplendent in her stage clothes, while he trailed
across to the piano, her music portfolio under his arm:

"That's Peter Bye!"

"Peter Bye? Who's he?"

"The husband of Joanna Marshall, the artist."

She would never endure it.

"And I don't thank Maggie Ellersley the least bit for intro-
ducing him to this music man, whoever he is," she told herself
after she had read the letter. "Tell Philip she's getting a
divorce indeed! How much would any decent man be interested in her after that?"

Poor inexperienced Joanna!

Peter's vagaries were not her only worries. She was under-
going just now what she would have termed a really serious
disappointment. Her dancing, on which she had spent so many
years, so much of her father's and her own money, on which
she had built so many high hopes, was destined, it seemed,
to avail her nothing.

She had been so sure. Her art was so perfect, so complete
that even Bertully, cynic though he was, believed that in her
case the American stage must let down the bars.

"They have but to see you, Mademoiselle, to *réaliser* zat
you are somebody, zat you have ze great gift. And when they
see you to danse, v'la!" He snapped his thin fingers. Joanna,
he told his assistant, Madame Céleste, was the best pupil he'd
ever had.

"You look at her and she is ze child, so grave, so *sage*. In another moment she is like a wild creature, a Bacchante. Onless zey are all fools, these *Américains*, they take her up, *hein* Céleste?"

Madame Céleste nodded a dark, assenting head.

Bertully himself accompanied her. There were three or four managers for whom he had done favors.

They went first to a Mr. Abrams, who received Joanna kindly. "I'm sure of your ability, my dear girl, and you ought to go. You're young. I can see you could be made into a beauty. With Bertully recommending you as he does, you must be a wizard. But the white American public ain't ready for you yet, they won't have you."

He looked at her reflectively a few seconds.

"I know the day is coming, but not for some time yet. That don't console you much, does it? I've got an idea of my own, if I think I can put it over, I'll send for you."

"Courage," said Bertully, helping her into the taxi, "there are some others."

The next manager, David Kohler, was explicit and to the point. "Couldn't make any money out of you. America doesn't want to see a colored dancer in the rôle of a *première danseuse*. How's that accent, Bertully? She wants you to be absurd, grotesque. Of course," tentatively, "you couldn't consider being corked up—you're brown but you're too light as you are —and doing a break-down?"

"No," said Joanna shortly, "I couldn't. Shall we go, Monsieur?"

By the time they reached the third manager, Joanna for all her natural assurance had become a little timid. Bertully's name had gained them almost instant admission to the manager, but it was hard in the short wait to listen to the scarcely veiled comments of the office girls and the other applicants.

"Say, what do you suppose she is?"

"Must be a South American."

"She ain't, she's a nigger or I don't know one."

"Say, she's got her nerve comin' here. Think Snyder'll give her anything?"

"Will he? Not a chance!"

Her cheeks were so flushed when she went in that she really was beautiful. But Snyder gave her one look, checked himself in the act of raising his hat, swung around to the Frenchman.

"This your great find, Bertully?"

"*Mais oui*," the old man began excitedly.

The other calmly lit a big black cigar.

"You needn't wait, Miss. Like to oblige you, Bertully, but I couldn't do a thing for you." He walked across the office, held the door open for them, bent over Bertully's ear. "You'll ruin your trade teachin' niggers, Bertully. Better take my tip."

They rode down in the elevator in silence. Joanna, scarlet to the ears, saw the conjectures written in the eyes of the other passengers as they observed her and the Frenchman's elaborate courtesies. She would take up no more of his time, she told him, thanking him for his kindness; she would go home now. He understood and beckoned her a taxi, into which he helped her with another elaborate display of courtesy, much to the interest of several spectators.

"So silly of me to mind this," Joanna scolded herself. But she did mind it. How could it be possible that she, Joanna Marshall, was meeting with rebuffs? Not that she was conceited. The point was that she had grown up in her own and Joel's belief,—namely, that honest effort led invariably to success. This was probably the first time in her life that she had been thwarted. She was like a spoiled child, bewildered and indignant at being suddenly brought to book.

The week before Christmas a note came from Peter.

"Of course I've been planning as usual to come home, Jan.

But we haven't been hitting it off so well lately. Thought I'd better write and see if you really wanted me to."

She wrote him. "Of course I want you." Heavens, what would Christmas be without Peter!

He told her on what train he was arriving and asked her to meet it. She might have done so, but her day was as usual very full and she had a rehearsal at six—of indefinite length. She would have to cut out something. Too bad it had to be meeting Peter. But he surely would come up to the house at once.

Her accompanist appeared promptly and they put in a hard two hours. Joanna, her ear unconsciously straining for the telephone or the doorbell, was not up to her usual mark. Eight o'clock and Peter not here and his train in at four! Well, he wasn't coming then. She plunged into hard work. Her father came by the door and watched her, thinking what a picture she made in her pretty dress. She had put on one of her old stage frocks, for she usually did better work if she created for herself, as nearly as possible, the atmosphere of the stage. At nine-thirty the accompanist left.

"We went rather slowly at first, but you came out splendidly at the end, Miss Marshall. You were a little bit tired, perhaps."

"That must have been it. Thank you and good-night, Miss Eggleston."

Still no Peter! "Mean thing, I'll fix him for that."

The bell buzzed softly, she could barely hear it. Yes, that was he. She heard her father's voice, "In the back parlor, Bye."

He came in, came toward her. "Well, Joanna, here's the wanderer returned." He bent to kiss her.

She turned him a cold cheek, which to her surprise he kissed without expostulation.

He crossed the room, sat down and looked at her. "H'm, how stagy we are in that get-up!"

He was different somehow, she thought, vaguely hurt by his remark. One of her reasons for putting on the dress had been so that she might please him. She asked him a question to hide her chagrin.

"Where've you been, Peter? I thought your train got in at four?"

"It did, but since you weren't there to meet me, I supposed you didn't care whether I came late or early, or not at all. I met Vera Manning in the station and took her to a movie."

Her spirits went up at that. This was just pique, sheer pique.

"How lovely for Vera! And now I've got to send you home almost right away. I've had a hard day and I'm dreadfully tired. Tell you what, dear boy, come to luncheon to-morrow. We'll have it together, just we two."

She thought after he had gone that he had looked at her critically, impersonally.

"As though he were contrasting me with some one," she murmured.

The next day confirmed her impression. Joanna asked him to praise the luncheon.

"I fixed it every bit myself."

"I should think so, so feminine and knickknackish." His tone said: "I'm used to having my taste consulted."

Joanna did not like the remark, but there was nothing really to be said about it. She sprang up lightly, began to clear away.

"Come on, lazy Peter Bye, don't leave everything for me to do."

He lounged in his chair. "Oh, come, Joanna, I'm used to being waited on, not doing the waiting."

She stared at him then. "Well, good heavens! What on earth has been happening to you in Philadelphia?"

He spoke from a contented reminiscence. "When I have dinner at Maggie Neal's, she's not everlastingly asking me to do this and do that. 'Sit still, Peter,' she says, 'this isn't a man's work.' "

"Maggie Neal has her own methods with her men friends. Personally I prefer to have mine wait on me."

He rose to his feet. "Oh, yes, Queen Joanna must be served."

They finished and went to the parlor. Joanna sang one or two of her songs to his accompaniment. The incident rankled, though she wouldn't let herself speak about it.

"But he certainly is changed," she said to herself in an angry bewilderment.

She had to sing in Orange that night and did not intend to return until the next morning.

"What do we do to-morrow?" Peter asked.

"Remember you said you wanted to hear *Aïda?* I 'phoned them to reserve tickets for us for to-morrow's matinée. But they have to be called for. Better go down there first thing in the morning, Peter."

He twisted around on the piano stool. "You'll be down town to-morrow morning coming from Orange. Why don't you stop for them?"

She couldn't believe her ears. "Peter Bye, you *are* spoilt," she flamed. "You're—why you're absolutely disgusting. We'll never hear *Aïda* if you depend on my getting the tickets. As long as he was well and not busy, there's no man in the world I'd do it for."

"Married women do it for their husbands."

"Sylvia doesn't do it for Brian. He wouldn't dream of asking her. Besides, that's different. And, anyway, we're not married yet. Nor likely to be, if we don't get along any better than this. Whatever's come over you, Peter?"

He shrugged his shoulders. "I think you make a lot of fuss over nothing, Joanna. But all right, I'll get you the tickets. See you at one-thirty?"

She sat a long time in her room after he had gone, her hands and eyes busy with her day's mail, which Sylvia always placed on her writing table. But her mind could not take in the written words, it was too full of something else.

But Peter, Peter of all men to act like this! Both she and Sylvia had always known that Maggie was unexacting. The marvel was, however, that Peter should take so quickly to this kind of treatment. Well, she'd just have to hold him that much closer to the mark. He'd see that there were some girls who knew what was due them.

It was time for her to dress. As she looked into the mirror she voiced her real regret. "Two days of the vacation gone, and we've done nothing but quarrel. To-day he didn't even ask me for a kiss. Peter, you wretch. Just wait till you come to your senses!"

They were a little stiff next day on the way to the matinée, talking politely and impersonally about the weather in Philadelphia and New York, Joanna's concert, and Sylvia's children. Walking up Broadway, however, they thawed a little. Joanna as usual was looking trim. She wore that winter an extremely trig tobacco-brown suit, with a fur turban and a narrow neckpiece of raccoon, the light part setting off the bronze distinction of her face. But Peter was superlative. His financial success with Tom Mason had made it possible for him to indulge in a new outfit which emphasized the distinction of his carriage, set off his handsome face. Several people looked at him on the crowded street. Joanna herself stole several glances sidewise.

He caught her at it. "Joanna Marshall, if you look at me

again like that, just once more, mind you, I'll snatch you up in my arms this minute and kiss you."

"You wouldn't dare."

"I dare you to try it. I'd do it no matter how much you kicked and struggled. Wouldn't the people stare?"

Joanna giggled. "Can't you see the headlines in the papers to-morrow? 'Burly Negro Attacks Strapping Negress on Broadway!'"

"Yes, and the small type underneath, 'An interested crowd gathered about a pair of dusky combatants yesterday. A Negro and Negress——'"

Joanna interrupted: "Both of them spelt with a small 'n,' remember! Here we are at the Opera."

He caught her hand. "Just because you jockeyed me out of that kiss that time, clever Joanna, doesn't mean that I'm going to do without it forever."

In her heart she loved him. "Oh, Peter, be like this always," she prayed.

CHAPTER XVII

THEY enjoyed the opera and sang snatches of it coming home as they walked to the subway. Once in the express train, however, Joanna lapsed into sadness.

"I don't think my voice is as big as that prima donna's, but those dancing girls! I should have been right up there with them! Oh, Peter, I believe I'm the least bit discouraged."

She told him of her trips with Bertully. "I didn't mind those girls calling me 'nigger.' That was sheer ill-breeding. Remember what we used to say when we were children when they called us names?" She recited it: " 'Sticks and stones may break my bones, but names will never hurt me.' What I minded was that they couldn't dream of my being accepted. Thought I had a nerve even to ask it."

She mounted the steps. "Come in, Peter."

After dinner they sat in the back parlor and Joanna went on with her story, Peter listening closely.

"I'm glad you're telling me about this, Joanna," he said seriously. "Now you'll understand my case better. You know how I feel about white people and their everlasting unfairness. As though the world and all that in it is belonged to them! I tell you, Jan, I'm sick of the whole business,—college, my everlasting grind, my poverty, this confounded prejudice. If I want to get a chance to study a certain case and it's in a white hospital you'd think I'd committed a crime. As though diseases picked out different races! I'm a good surgeon, I'll swear I am, but I've got so I don't care whether

155

I get my degree or not. You can't imagine all the petty unfairness about me. Only the other day the barber refused
to shave me in the college barber-shop. Your own cousin,
John Talbert, is a Zeta Gamma man if ever there was one—
that's the equivalent to Phi Beta Kappa in his school, you
know. Do you think he got it? No, they black-balled him
out."

Joanna sat silent, stunned by this avalanche. And to think
she had precipitated it!

"Arabelle Morton's sister, Selma," Peter went on morosely,
"took her Master's degree last year. The candidates sat in
alphabetical order. Selma sat in her seat wondering whom
the chair on the left of her belonged to—it was vacant. At
the last moment a girl came in, a Miss Nelson, who had been
in one or two of her classes. Selma knew she was a Southerner. 'Oh, I just can't sit there,' Selma heard her say, not
too much under her breath. And some friend of hers went
to the Professor in charge of the exercises and he let her change
her place, though it threw the whole line out of order."

He paused, still brooding.

"Another colored girl—can't think of her name—paid for a
seat in one of the Seminary rooms. The white girl next to her,
apparently a very pleasant person, had her books all over her
own desk space and this one, too. They were the best seats
in the room. The colored girl asked her to move them. She
just looked at her. Then this Miss—Miss Taylor, that was
her name, took it from one authority to another, finally to
the professor in charge of the Library. He assigned her another seat. Said the girl had been there four years, and that
anyway, she—the white girl—resented the colored girl's manner
toward her. The damned petty injustice!"

"But, Peter," Joanna argued, "you wouldn't let that interfere with your whole career, change your whole life?"

"Why shouldn't I? There're plenty of pleasanter ways to

earn a living. Why should I take any more of their selfish dog-in-the-manger foolishness? I can make all the money I want with Tom Mason. If you aren't satisfied for me to be an accompanist, I could go into partnership with him and we could form and place orchestras. It's a perfectly feasible plan, Joanna. Why shouldn't I pick the job that comes handiest, since the world owes me a living?"

He frowned, meditating. "Isn't it funny, I felt just then as though I'd been through all this before. It's just as though I'd heard myself say that very thing some other time. Well, what do you say, Joanna?"

"That I don't want a coward and a shirker for a husband. As though that weren't the thing those white people—those mean ones—wanted! Not all white people are that way. Both of us know it, Peter. And it's up to us, to you and me, Peter Bye, to show them we can stick to our last as well as anybody else. If they can take the time to be petty, we can take the time to walk past it. Oh, we must fight it when we can, but we mustn't let it hold us back. Buck up, Peter, be a man. You've got to be one if you're going to marry me."

He shrugged his shoulders. "May I light a cigarette?" But she noticed he did it with trembling fingers. "Just as you say, Joanna."

She rose and faced him, this new Peter—this old Peter if she did but know it, with the early shiftlessness, the irresoluteness of his father, Meriwether Bye, the ancient grudge of his grandfather, Isaiah Bye, rearing up, bearing full and perfect fruit in his heart. Both rage and despair possessed her, as she saw the beautiful fabric of their future felled wantonly to the ground. For the sake of a few narrow pedants!

"Peter, Peter, we've got to make our own lives. We can't let these people ruin us." She felt her knees trembling under her. "We're both tired and beside ourselves. Come and see me to-morrow, will you?"

What should she say to him now, she wondered next day after a long white night. And once she had only to raise her finger and he was willing, glad to do her bidding. Could it be that after all these years she had failed to touch his pride, worse yet that he had no pride? She had been longing so for a cessation from all this bickering, so that they might have time for a touch of tenderness. But she could not afford that now. His love for her was her strongest hold over him. She was sure she could bring him back to reason. Perhaps she had been a little severe last night, calling him a coward.

"I musn't lose my temper," she told herself. Yet that was the very thing she did. The matter took such a sudden, such a grotesque turn.

He came in about eleven, his handsome face haggard, his eyes bloodshot. She was astounded at his appearance.

"Peter, you look dreadful!"

He glanced over the top of her head at his reflection in the mirror, lounged to the sofa, threw himself in the corner of it.

"Guess I'm due to look a fright after staying up all night. Didn't get to bed till five this morning."

She thought he'd been worrying over their quarrel. "You poor boy, you didn't need to take it that hard."

He stared at her. "Take what, that hard? Oh, our talk! That didn't keep me awake. I spent the night at 'Jake's.'"

"Jake's" was the cabaret, a cheap one, in which he had played years ago.

She couldn't understand him. "I thought you had plenty of money without playing there."

"I have. I didn't play there. I was a visitor like anybody else, like Harry Portor; he spent the night there, too. There was a whole gang of us."

Clearly she must get to the bottom of this. While she had been tossing sleepless, he had been in a cabaret, dancing with cheap women, laughing, drinking perhaps.

"You mean you deliberately went there to have a good time and stayed all night? You and Harry Portor and the rest drank, I suppose?"

"I don't think Portor did. He's a full-fledged doctor now, though he's hardly any practice yet. But the rest of us did. There's nothing in that, Joanna, fellow's got to get to know the world."

Her anger rose, broke. She lost her dignity.

"I suppose Maggie Ellersley taught you that, too."

"What's that?" His handsome face lowered. "Say, how'd Maggie Ellersley get into this? No, she never taught me anything. But I can tell you what, if a fellow were going with her and went during his holidays to have a spree at a cabaret she wouldn't nag him about it, like you nag me. Yes, about that and about a thousand other things."

She turned into ice. "I'll never nag you again. Here, take this thing!" She drew off the little ring. "I don't want it."

A pin dropping would have crashed in that silence.

His voice came back to him. "You don't mean this, Joanna, —you can't."

"I do. Here, take it."

"You—you mean the engagement is broken?" He ignored her outstretched hand.

She dropped the ring in his pocket. "I mean I can't consider a man for a husband who throws away his career because of the meanness of a few white men. Of a man who sits all night in a low cabaret where every loafer in New York can point him out and say, 'That's the kind of fellow Joanna Marshall goes about with.' "

"Oh, I see, it isn't for my sweet sake, then!"

She pushed him toward the door. "Go, Peter! Go!"

On New Year's morning he came back, humble, contrite. "I was a fool, Joanna. I must have been mad. Please forgive me."

"Of course I do, Peter."

He fumbled in his pocket, held out the ring. "Will you take this back?"

"I can't do that."

"When will you?"

"I don't know if ever."

There was a long silence. He came over and put his hand on the back of her chair, afraid to touch her.

"Joanna, I don't deserve your love. But you still do love me?"

She nodded slowly.

His face brightened at that. "But you won't take back the ring?"

"No, Peter, I can't take back the ring."

He knelt and kissed her hands.

"Good-by, sweetheart, I must go to Philadelphia to-day. Happy New Year, Joanna."

She let him go then. None of their other partings had ever been like this. Safe in her room she cried herself sick. "Oh, Peter," she murmured to herself, "come back like the boy I used to know." She wished now that she had been easier with him.

"And yet if I were, he'd let go entirely. Well, it must come out all right." But her heart was heavy.

The very next day she got a letter. Peter must have written her as soon as he arrived in Philadelphia.

"Joanna, I was wrong," he had written contritely, "I confess I had got away somewhat from your manner of thinking, and I suppose I was a little sore, too,—your life seems

so full. Sometimes I think there is nothing I can bring you.
But I do love you, Joanna. You must always believe that
and I think you love me, too. We were meant for each other.
I am sure life would hold for us the deepest, most irremedi-
able sorrow if we separated. Whether we are engaged or not,
just tell me that you love me still and I can be happy."

CHAPTER XVIII

IF she had only answered the letter, then, that very moment!

But she had said to her impulse: "No, I must wait. I can't let him off too easily." Perhaps, too, there was a little sense of satisfaction at having him again at her knees, suing for her favors, but this was secondary. Joanna was really sick at heart to think that her beautiful dreams of success for both of them might not be realized. She wanted to be great herself, but she did not want that greatness to overshadow Peter.

Somehow the week slipped by, quickly enough, too. There was always plenty to do. Love,—the desire to give it and receive it was tugging persistently at the cords of her being, but she had been too long the slave of Ambition to listen consciously to that. Yet she found herself lying awake nights thinking, thinking, more about Peter than about her singing engagements during the New Year, or about her plan to make her mightiest efforts just now to enter the dancing world. Yet whatever she might ponder by night, she spent all her time and strength by day going to see performances, practicing, inventing new steps and new rhythms.

Through Helena Arnold and indirectly through Vera Sharples she obtained the promise of an interview with one of the season's favorites.

"I'll be able to see you early Thursday evening," the famous woman wrote. "You may expect either a note or a telephone call from me." At one time such a promise would have sent

Joanna into the seventh ecstasy, without impairing her confidence. But recent discouragements, persistent—and for her unusual, phenomena—had rendered her timid. She was nervous. Her assurance wavered. She spent the whole day going through her repertory. Sometimes she danced like a mænad. Then she adopted a slow Greek rhythm, posturing and undulating. She struck attitudes before the mirror, standing in one position for long moments.

"For Heaven's sake," said Sylvia, putting her head inside the door on one of these occasions, "go out and take a walk, Joanna." She was as nervous as her sister.

"Not a bad idea, Sylvia, I believe I will. You can answer the phone. Have you seen my brown cape?"

She came back a little after five, refreshed and soothed.

"No phone message," Sylvia told her, "but here's a note. What's she got to say, Janna?" She came and looked over her sister's arm.

"So sorry not to be able to see you to-night," the noted *artiste* had written. "I'm halfway expecting an old friend of mine and must keep the evening free. I shall try to arrange to have you call, just the same, not this month I'm afraid, but certainly in February." She ended with a meaningless expression of "good wishes."

"Mercy," said Sylvia, "why didn't she say next year?"

Joanna was bitter. "Or next eternity? Sylvia, I wonder if I'm not a darn fool!" She walked upstairs trailing her long brown cape after her.

All her life she had known and seen success. When she was born her father was a successful caterer, almost a wealthy man. It is true that she had seen her own people hindered, checked on account of color, but hardly any of the things she had greatly wanted had been affected for that cause. She had had money enough to have her dancing and music lessons —the very fact that she had had to take separate and special lessons from Bertully meant to her that some special and separate way would be arranged whereby she would become a dancer on the stage.

She did not know how to envisage disappointment.

Strangely enough, the defection of the *artiste* struck home to her more keenly than the reception which she had had from the stage-managers. She refused Sylvia's invitation to come back downstairs and spend the evening with her and Brian.

"We might go to a movie," Sylvia had said tentatively. But Joanna had only made an impatient gesture of refusal, and walking into her room had closed the door very carefully after her.

She did not cry or throw herself across the bed. It might have been better for her if she had. Joanna's creed was that one kept a stiff upper lip even to oneself. She had not had many occasions to try out that creed.

There she sat, stiffly, on the spindling chair in front of her small flat-topped writing desk and brooded over the future which suddenly stretched dull, stale, and uninvigorating before her. She would never be able to stand it.

The thought of her marriage flashed across her mind.

"And Peter," she said to herself aloud, "willing to be ordinary and second-rate! Where is that letter of his? I might just as well answer it now as at any other time."

In spite of her ugly mood a little wave of tenderness welled up in her heart as she read,—"Just tell me that you do love me still,——"

"Oh, Peter, Peter," she murmured, "if I tell you that you'll never change, never push on. If only you could be strong and let me bring my troubles to you."

It would never do to let him know how completely she was discouraged. And equally she could not let him know how dear, weakness and all, he was to her. She would make her love conditional. "If you want me to love you, Peter,——"

She hated that, but some day they would both be glad of it. She actually cried for the two of them as she wrote her stern little fiction:

"DEAR PETER:
"No, I don't love you as you are. The man I marry must be a man worth while like my father or Philip. I couldn't stand the thought of spending my life with some one ordinary.
"But I want to love you, Peter. Write me soon and say you are going to get to work in earnest. Happy New Year.
                                                "Sincerely,
                                                    "JOANNA."

She read it over and over, totally blind to its supreme egotism. Then she sealed it and, sniffling a little—more like a child than like an artist—went to bed.

In the morning she awoke with a sense of impending disaster. The phrase is trite but so, alas, is disaster. At first, as she lay there, her slender brown arms stretched above her tumbled head, she mused to herself about it.

"Let's see why I do feel so rotten? What's the matter?"

She remembered her engagement with the *artiste*. "But that's not what's making me sick," she told herself after a momentary probing of her self-consciousness. Then recalling the letter to Peter, she got up and walked bare-footed across the room to the desk, shivering a little as the chilly January morning air struck at her, billowing her thin nightdress. She thought she would read it again, but the envelope was sealed. It slipped out of her hand and she ran back to bed again, cuddling luxuriously.

"Oh, well!" Afterwards when she rose and closed the windows she promised herself: "If I do send it I'll write him a sweet, sweet letter soon."

After breakfast she posted it. It fell with a heaviness into the box that made her uneasy. "I'll write him again to-night," she thought. "Poor Peter! He'll be disappointed, I suppose."

But the night brought her several offers to sing in Southern schools which she thought she might just as well accept. Apparently nothing was to come of her dancing. She had about a week in which to get ready.

Just before she left, a little surprised that she had not already heard from Peter, she wrote him a long letter, her first long love-letter.

"Dearest Peter [she began]
"You can't think how awfully I want to see you. If you were here to-night I shouldn't quarrel with you one moment."

She quoted lines from one of Goethe's poems.

"Ein blick von deinen Augen in die meinen,
Ein Kuss von deinen Mund auf meinem Munde:

She hesitated a moment, a little aghast at this disclosure of her feelings. "But I might just as well, he deserves it. Dear, dear Peter, if I could just see you!"

She ended, smiling shamefacedly at her own abandon——

"Mein einzig Glück auf Erden ist dein Wille"——

She might have stopped in Philadelphia on her way South, but she couldn't after that letter. In Richmond she received a note from Peter which Sylvia had forwarded.

"My dear Joanna [she was surprised at the formality]
"I have both your letters. I cannot tell you how surprised I was at receiving the first or how much I cherished the second. Joanna, I would give ten years of my life if you had written the second one first. I am very busy now but I am going to write you a final letter very soon.

"Sincerely,

"PETER."

" 'A final letter,' " she quoted to herself. "What a funny thing to say! Oh, Peter! And I wanted, I needed a real letter, a love-letter!" Her natural reasonableness helped her. "It's my own fault. I suppose he feels like I feel sometimes, don't-care-y. But 'a final letter.' I wonder what he meant!"

But she did not puzzle long. Richmond was appreciative and gay. Some one wrote her from Hampton and asked her to do an interpretative dance. Partly because of the interest and excitement, partly because she had forced herself to do so often, she resolutely put Peter out of her mind.

"He'll know when I write him again," she told herself ruefully.

Two weeks, a month passed; she came into her room one day to find a bulky letter from Sylvia. "He doesn't mean it, Joanna, of course, but I had to send it." Thus her sister's note. Puzzled, she read the inclosure, which turned out to be a letter from Peter to Sylvia.

"DEAR SYLVIA:
"I am writing to let you know that I am to be married in June. Joanna told me she didn't love me and so I am going to marry Maggie Neal; she's crazy about me. Tell Joanna not to bother sending back any of the things I've given her.
"Sincerely,
"PETER."

CHAPTER XIX

ONE of the mysteries of the ages will be solved with the answer to the question: Why do men consider women incalculable? Peter had been hurt by Joanna's indifference again and again, she had refused a dozen times to marry him, she had scolded him, teased him, slighted him. Yet she had always come back to his eager arms. In spite of this he had been unable to see in her attitude at Christmas and in the unkind letter which she had written the logical outcome of her earlier acts—all of which by enduring he had tacitly indorsed.

He read the letter in a maze of anger and wounded pride. Before he knew it he had caught up his cap and started for Maggie's house. By the time the long, yellow, crawling car had jolted him over the uneven reaches of Lombard Street and set him down at Fifteenth he was in a fever of bitterness, resentment and self-pity. Maggie hardly knew him when he entered her little sitting-room.

"Oh, Peter," she went up to him swiftly, "something awful has happened."

He showed her the letter, striding up and down the room as she read it.

She lifted her head to say to him: "She doesn't mean it; you know Joanna, always making a mountain out of a molehill."

Instead she heard herself saying: "How could she possibly write such things to you—you've always been so kind."

168

"Too kind," he muttered. "I tell you what, Maggie, Joanna's got no heart, she's all head, all ideas and if you don't see and act her way, she's got no use for you."

"I do think she thinks herself a lot better than any one else," Maggie said slowly, remembering Joanna's letter to her about Philip.

"Well, she is, you know," he put in unexpectedly. "Oh, Lord, what am I going to do without her!"

Genuinely touched, she sat down on the little box-couch beside him and slid her arm around his shoulder. "After all, you've still got me, Peter."

He looked up at her, feeling the surge of a new idea in his heart. If he could only punish Joanna—no not punish exactly, you couldn't punish her, she was always too remote for that—but shock her, let her see, as his boyhood's phrase would have had it, that she was not the only pebble on the beach. Besides, what a revenge to cut loose altogether from the influence of her ideals and ally himself with one whom she would have characterized as having no ideals at all.

Before the thought was even shaped in his brain he was speaking:

"Of course I always have you, Maggie. How—how would you like to spend your future with me?"

"What do you mean, Peter?"

"I mean, Joanna's chucked me. You and I get along famously, you've got your divorce from Neal. Why not marry me?"

It was plain that though surprised she liked the idea. She saw herself suddenly transformed in this inhospitable snobbish city from Maggie Neal, alone and *déclassée,* into Mrs. Peter Bye, a model of respectability.

That he had no money, no accepted means of making a livelihood she understood would mean nothing. He was a

Bye and she as his wife could go anywhere. She would show Alice Talbert! And afterwards when he got his degree!

But because she had once loved Philip she could judge what Peter might mean to Joanna. To her credit she hesitated.

"Joanna probably doesn't mean to let you go, Peter, she's just angry and disappointed. She takes things harder than Sylvia or I. You know she really cares about you, and so do you about her."

But he assured her that he did not. "She's too exacting. Now there's one thing about you, Maggie—maybe it's because you've already been married—you know how to treat a man. Joanna makes you feel as though you were in a strait-jacket all the time. I always feel ordinary when I'm with you."

Neither of them noticed the doubtfulness of the compliment. In the end she accepted him. After all, she owed nothing to Joanna, who certainly had not considered her. How surprised she would be to think that Peter could so quickly find solace in her—Maggie's—arms! And Joanna should learn, too, that he could become a success without everlastingly being pushed and prodded.

Hard on this thought came another. "Peter, you won't have to work so hard now to get through school. I'll help you. You know I'm doing very well with the hair-work."

He dismissed the theme airily, one hand on her shoulder, the other fumbling for a cigarette.

"Oh, I'm going to give medicine up. I'll just keep on with Tom and the music. Heavens, it's so nice to know you won't mind, Maggie. Can't think why I've stuck to the old school as long as I have, when here I am all set with this nice easy job to my hand. Might as well get along with as little trouble as possible. The world owes me a living."

*   *   *   *   *

Afterwards, back in his room with the green iron bedstead and the Bye Bible, he felt a difference, a sense of let-downness. He threw himself across the bed and groaned

"Joanna, how could you?"

She could, that was evident. He was stupefied at the turn in his affairs. Five hours ago he had expected some day to be a physician and to marry Joanna Marshall. Now it seemed that he was going to be a musician and marry Maggie Neal.

"It isn't true," he told himself, fiercely. But it was true. There on the dresser were some cookies wrapped up in a red and white fringed napkin, Maggie's gift when he left her.

"I made them for you, hoping you would come in. Now you'll be in often, often, won't you? Oh, Peter, I'll be good to you. I'll be as unlike Joanna as possible." He did not want her to be unlike Joanna. In fact, he did not want her at all.

He might as well take her, though, for Joanna did not want him. That was it, no matter how many women he unaccountably married, Joanna might be shocked but she would never really care. Or suppose she did care a little while, she would soon forget it with her singing and dancing. Still, he supposed he must tell her. He would write her a gay, mocking letter. "I hope you'll be as happy with your art as I feel I shall be with Maggie. She suits me perfectly."

After he had littered his desk and the floor beside it vainly with a veritable snow-storm of torn bits of paper, he let his head drop on his lean brown hands and went to sleep. Perhaps it would not be exact to say he cried himself to sleep, but there were certainly tears that burnt and scalded behind his eyelids.

His landlady complained of the torn paper the next morning. " 'Tisn't as though you didn't have a nice waste-paper basket ready and waitin', Mr. Bye." As she finished speak-

ing she handed him Joanna's letter containing Goethe's poem.
The tenderness, the real love that blazed in the beautiful lines
overwhelmed him. He could not tell her the truth after a letter like that. So he wrote her, postponing but hinting, he
fondly believed, at the news which he must soon break to
her. A month later, finding himself still unequal to the task,
he wrote to Sylvia.

CHAPTER XX

SYLVIA had written. "He doesn't mean it, of course"——

But Joanna knew better. Even while dumbfounded she stood staring at the note, trying to believe there must be some mistake, her heart, her every sense was telling her it was too true.

Peter had given her up. He was going to marry Maggie. *He had given her up.* That was the important thing. For if he was not to marry her, what difference did it make whom he married?

She had never been religious, she had never been dramatic. Rather she somewhat despised any emphatically emotional display. "People don't really act that way," she told herself.

Yet she dropped on her knees beside the pine bedstead in the sparsely furnished room. Her hands clutched at the counterpane. She could feel her throat constricting. A scalding hotness seared her nostrils, her mouth became dry, her eyeballs burned.

"Oh, God! Oh, Peter!" She repeated the two phrases again and again in a sick agony.

"God, you couldn't let it be true. You know I always loved him, I didn't hide it from you. You knew my heart."

At first she thought she would go to him. Then the fear that he might not want to see her, might even refuse to see her, overcame her. That humiliation she could never endure.

She sat down and wrote him a long letter, her pen flying

173

over the page like something bewitched. It could not move fast enough to empty her heart of all she had to tell. If she could only make clear to him that she had "chastened" him because she loved him. How patronizing, how silly she had been. She said aloud, "How he and Maggie must have laughed at me, setting myself up above them and their ideas as though I were some goddess! Oh, God, why did you let me do it? You knew what I really meant."

Her tears almost blotted out her words.

The post-office was a mile away but she trudged the distance mechanically, seeing nothing, hearing nothing, absorbed and drowned in the black sorrow which overwhelmed her.

Peter's answer, which came in four days, brought no solace. She had never dwelt on any pages as she did on those of his last letter. The curt, stern phrases both cut her and awakened a new respect for him.

With a sense of responsibility which Joanna had never seen in him before, he insisted on honoring the claim which Maggie's complete and unexacting love made upon him. "Even if I wanted to give her up," he wrote in a sort of anguished virtuousness, "I would not, she has been too kind to me. But I don't want to give her up, Joanna. Besides, I've got to consider the public. She has told several people that we are engaged."

Joanna cried aloud: "If you had only been like this before, ever before, only once, I'd have known I couldn't trifle with you. Oh, Peter, you deceived me." The tears stood, great wells of water about her eyes.

She finished her engagement in the quiet Southern city before an audience which wondered vaguely what had happened to make Joanna Marshall different. Somehow she packed her trunk, thanked the persistent youth who had constituted himself her cavalier, and boarded the Jim Crow car. Her cavalier for all his persistence had been unable to obtain for her Pullman accommodations. After Washington she fell to wondering what it used to be like in other days, less than a year ago, when she would be coming up this way, through Baltimore, Wilmington, past Chester, secure in the knowledge that Peter would be waiting for her at West Philadelphia. He would never be there again! How could she endure it? It was not possible that anyone could stand this thing. No wonder people "crossed in love"—she dwelt on the phrase distastefully—killed themselves. She toyed with the idea. Of course *she* couldn't; that sort of relief was not for her. In the first place it was cowardly. With her usual mental clarity she visualized the colored papers of Harlem. There would be notices telling how the "gifted singer, Joanna Marshall, daughter of Joel Marshall, died by her own hand——"

Her mind lingered over it, painting in new details, consciously withdrawing as far as possible from the real cause of her grief.

As the train slid into the long shed at West Philadelphia she pressed her face against the window-pane and strained out into the dusk. Sometimes miracles did occur. Perhaps he was there, perhaps none of it was true. Her tears crept down the glass, the man behind her watching curiously.

Sylvia met her in New York, got her home and finally to bed. Mr. and Mrs. Marshall knew nothing of the matter and Sylvia had told even Brian very little. The two girls said nothing about Peter directly.

"Help me to get to sleep, Sylvia," Joanna said suddenly after a rambling account of her trip. Her roving eyes and twitching hands had already betrayed her need. "Help me to get to sleep or I think I shall go mad."

CHAPTER XXI

JOANNA was in agony. Her life, hitherto a thing of light and laughter and pleasant work, became a nightmare of regret and morbid introspection. She could not blame herself enough. Nothing that Sylvia could say would make her speak unkindly of Peter.

"No, Sylvia, it wasn't his fault, really, it was all mine. Of course I think he was a little stupid not to see that my very interest in him, my constant fault-finding grew out of my wish to have him perfect. And I wanted him to be perfect because I loved him. But if I had ever dreamed how much I was hurting him, I'd never have said a word to him. I'd rather have had him exactly as he was, faults and all, than to lose him altogether."

She suffered intensely, too, from wounded pride. "Just think, Sylvia, he didn't, he couldn't have loved me after all. He just wanted to get married. See how easily he turned from me. Oh, if I had known that was all he wished, I'd have been different. I'd have been just the kind of woman **he** wanted."

Her humble sincerity almost made Sylvia cry.

Another girl in Joanna's place might not have suffered so intensely. But Joanna, poor creature, was doomed by her very virtues. That same single-mindedness which had made her so engrossed in her art, now proved her undoing. Her mind, shocked out of its normal complacence, perceived and dwelt on a new aspect of life, an entirely different and un-dreamed of sense of values. For the first time in her life she

saw the importance of human relationships. What did a
knowledge of singing, dancing, of any of the arts amount to
without people, without parents, brothers, sisters, lovers to
share one's failures, one's triumphs?

She remembered how interested, how faithfully interested
all her family had been in her small career. Even Brian
Spencer, now that her own brothers were away, felt responsible for her, shifted engagements to get her to the station
on time, met trains at ghastly, inconvenient hours of the night.
And Peter had been her slave, her willing, unquestioning slave,
eager to accomplish any task no matter how troublesome, for
a word of appreciation from her.

And without a thought she had taken all this as her due.

She had failed to realize happiness when she saw it. The
bird had been in her grasp and she had let it go. This was
her constant thought. Of course, she still had her own people.
And she was considerate of them now, painfully anxious to
show her gratitude. She tried to stammer out an apology to
Sylvia for her past remissness.

But her sister threw an arm about her and strained her
close. "Don't be so thoughtful, so good, Jan. You break
my heart. I'd rather have you your old thoughtless, impatient
self."

Of course, this expression of gratitude was really only a
gesture to life, to fate. "If Peter could come back to me now,
he'd see how truly I cared about him. God, couldn't you
let him come back?" Joanna, who had hardly uttered a
prayer outside of "Now I lay me," spent most of her thoughts
at this time in communion with God—"You Great Power,
you great force, you whatever it is that rules things." Walking, riding, any action at all mechanical she utilized in concentrating on her "desire to have everything come right."

In the mornings, weak and spent with the wakefulness of

12

her white night, she picked up her little slim Bible and read portions of the Psalms. The beautiful words not only soothed her but brought with them a wonderment at the passion and pain which they revealed. "David, you, too, suffered. Help me, help me now." So intense was her thought that she would hardly have been surprised if she had looked up and seen the Psalmist bending over her.

She hated the mornings even more than the nights. In spite of her wakefulness, she was sure that there were some moments when she lapsed into unconsciousness. But the morning brought with it the promise of another day of pain, of unprofitable preoccupation. Sometimes after she had read her Psalm, despite the fact that she had been tossing, tossing on her pillow, she yielded to an overwhelming sense of apathy and lay there motionless for hours in the security of her bed.

Her mental agony was so great at times that it seemed almost physical.

Her condition surprised Sylvia greatly. "I never had any idea that Jan cared so much for Peter," she told Brian. She had had to share her sister's secret with him. Joanna's persistent sleeplessness had led Sylvia in her protecting eagerness to pretend to Harry Portor that she herself was in need of a sedative and Harry had spoken to Brian about it. There had to be explanations.

Brian was not at all surprised at Joanna's suffering. "A girl like Joanna would be bound to feel deeply or not at all. I knew she must have really cared for Peter, else she'd have chucked him long ago. Joanna did nag at him, but Peter is really the one to blame, for standing for it. If he'd given her a piece of his mind now and then she'd have understood whom she had to deal with; Joanna thought she could treat him as she pleased. Then when he got tired of it he threw up the whole thing without any warning, the silly ass."

"Better not let Joanna hear you call him that," Sylvia interrupted.

He went on unnoticing. "Of course, what Joanna doesn't realize is that she's up against the complex of color in Peter's life. It comes to every colored man and every colored woman, too, who has any ambition. Jan will feel it herself one day. Peter's got it worse than most of us because he's got such a terrible 'mad' on white people to start with. But every colored man feels it sooner or later. It gets in the way of his dreams, of his education, of his marriage, of the rearing of his children. The time comes when he thinks, 'I might just as well fall back; there's no use pushing on. A colored man just can't make any headway in this awful country.' Of course, it's a fallacy. And if a fellow sticks it out he finally gets past it, but not before it has worked considerable confusion in his life. To have the ordinary job of living is bad enough, but to add to it all the thousand and one difficulties which follow simply in the train of being colored—well, all I've got to say, Sylvia, is we're some wonderful people to live through it all and keep our sanity."

Sylvia agreed soberly that he was right.

"Now, Peter," said Brian, warming to his subject, "had a lot of natural handicaps, he was poor, he had no sense of responsibility, he was never too fond of work unless he had some one to spur him on to it. In addition to that he falls in love with a girl who has everything in the world which he lacks, especially comparative ease and overwhelming ambition. Jan doesn't see Peter and herself as two ordinary human beings, she thinks they have a high destiny to perform and so she drives Peter into a course of action which left to himself he would never pursue. I'll bet a month's salary Peter had no intention of studying surgery until he found out he had to do something extraordinary to win Joanna. Now, just when each needs the most sympathy from the other, when Joanna's plans are, I suspect, going awry, and when Peter is suffering most from his color complex, the two let their frazzled nerves carry them into a jangle and bang, Peter flies to the first woman who promises to let him take life easy! Maggie doesn't see life in the large, she's too much taken up with getting what she wants out of her own life. Perhaps she's right."

"I don't see how you can say that, Brian."

"Well, it all depends on one's viewpoint. Personally, I think Peter will get what he deserves if he marries Maggie. She's the one that astonishes me. Of course, if Peter and Jan really are through with each other, he's got a perfect right to marry whom he pleases, but I should think Maggie's old friendship for you two girls would have held her back awhile." A memory stirred vaguely within him. "Or—no, that would really be too rotten."

"What would?"

"Maggie, you know. Remember how suddenly she married Neal? I've always thought Joanna had something to do with that. Just the Sunday before, Maggie had given me a look-in on her feelings for Philip and I happened to tell Jan about it. My, how she raved! A few days later Maggie married her gambler."

This was all news to Sylvia.

"Well, I won't tell Joanna. She's got enough to bear."

Joanna was indeed bearing more than Sylvia could guess. She was feeling the pull of awakened and unsatisfied passion. It is doubtful if she could thus have analyzed it, for she had rather deliberately withheld her attention from the basic facts of life. "Plenty of time for that," she had told herself gayly, a little proud perhaps of a virginal fastidiousness which kept her ignorant as well as innocent. Yet bit by bit she had built up the idea of a shrine into which, not unwillingly, she should enter with Peter some day. She had never even vaguely thought of any one else as a companion. Her whole concept of love and marriage for herself centered about Peter Bye.

And now Peter was gone—and his departure had opened up this sea, this bottomless pit of torment. This, this was life. "This is being grown up," she told herself through endless midnight watches.

CHAPTER XXII

TEN months later Tom Mason leaned back against the red plush of the car seat and jingled some coins in his pocket.

"Tell you what, Bye, we really are cleaning up. I hadn't expected anything like this run of engagements. Now suppose you beat it along to Mrs. Lea's and find out what special arrangements she wants made for the musicians to-night and I'll go on to Mrs. Lawlor and see about to-morrow."

Peter stared moodily at the flying landscape. "I wish you'd come yourself, Mason. I hate to talk to these white people. Their damned patronizing airs make me sick."

"What do you care about their patronizin'? All I'm interested in is gettin' what I can out of them. When I've made my pile, if I can't spend it here the way I please, Annie and me can pick up and go to South America or France. I hear they treat colored people all right there."

" 'Treat colored people all right,' " Peter mimicked. "What business has any one 'treating' us, anyway? The world's ours as much as it is theirs. And I don't want to leave America. It's mine, my people helped make it. These very orchards we're passing now used to be the famous Bye orchards. My grandfather and great-grandfather helped to cultivate them."

"Is that so? Honest?" Tom showed a sudden respectful interest. "How'd they come to lose them?"

"Lose them? They never owned them. The black Byes were slaves of the white Byes."

"Oh, slaves! Oh, you mean they worked in the fields? Well, I guess that's different. Come on, here we are."

Peter flung himself out of the car after Tom and followed him up a tree-lined street. The suburban town stretched calm, peaceful and superior about them. Clearly this was the home of the rich and well-born. It is true that a few ordinary mortals lived here, but mainly to do the bidding of the wealthy. A group of young white girls, passing the two men, glanced at them a little curiously.

"Entertainers for the Lea affair," one of them said, making no effort to keep from being overheard.

Peter stopped short. "That's what I hate," he said fiercely. "Labeled because we're black."

"Ain't you got a grouch, though!" Tom spoke almost admiringly. He told his sister afterwards: "Bye's got this here—now—temper'ment. Never can tell how it's goin' to take him. Seems different since he started keeping company with Maggie, don't you think so?"

Annie admitted she did.

At present Tom patted Peter on the shoulder, and starting him up the driveway which led to Mrs. Lea's large low white house, went on himself to Mrs. Lawlor.

Mrs. Lea received Peter in a small morning-room. She was pretty, a genuine blonde, with small delicate features and beautiful fluffy hair. But as Peter did not like fair types, his mind simply registered "washed-out," and took no further stock of her looks. What he did notice was that she was dressed in a lacey, too transparent floating robe, too low in the neck, and too short in the skirt.

"Something she would wear only before some one for whom she cared very much, or some one whom she didn't think worth considering," he told himself, lowering.

Mrs. Lea, leading him into the ballroom beyond, barely glanced at him. "See, the musicians are to sit behind those palms and the piano will be completely banked with flowers. I'm expecting the decorators every moment. Your men will have to get here very early so as to get behind all this without being seen. I want the effect of music instead of perfume pouring out of the flowers. Do you get the idea—er—what did you say your name was?"

"Yes, I understand," said Peter shortly. "My name is Bye."

"I meant your first name—Bye—why, that's the name of a family in Bryn Mawr, who used to own half of the land about here. There're a Dr. Meriwether Bye and his grandfather, Dr. Meriwether Bye, living in the old Bye house now. Where do you come from?"

"I was born in Philadelphia like my father and grandfather and his father before him."

She stated the obvious conclusion: "Probably your parents belonged to the Bryn Mawr Byes."

"So my father told me," replied Peter, affecting a composure equal to her own. "His name was Meriwether Bye."

She did not like that. She decided she did not like him either—eyeing his straight, fine figure and meeting his unyielding look. These niggers with their uppish ways! Besides this one looked, looked—indefinably he reminded her of young Meriwether Bye. She spoke to him:

"I don't want you to leave to-night before I get a chance to point you out to young Dr. Bye. He'll be so interested." She looked at Peter again. Yes, he was intelligent enough to get the full force of what she wanted to say. "It's so in keeping with things that the grandson of the man who was slave to his grandfather should be his entertainer to-night."

Peter felt his skin tightening. "I'm afraid you'll be disappointed. I'm a medical student, not an entertainer. I came here for Mr. Mason, who is very busy. You may be sure I'll give him your instructions. Good-day, Mrs. Lea."

He rushed out of the house, down to the station where,

without waiting for Tom, he boarded the train. Not far from the West Philadelphia depot he pushed the bell of a certain house, flung open the unlocked door and rushed up a flight of stairs.

In a small room to his left he found the person he was seeking, a short, almost black young fellow who lifted a dejected and then an amazed countenance toward him.

"Am I seeing things? Where'd you blow in from, Pete? Thought you'd chucked us all, the old school and all the rest of it."

"I haven't, I've been a fool, a damned fool, but I'm back to my senses. I'm going back to my classes and I tell you, Ed Morgan, I'll clean up. See here, you've got to do me a favor."

"Name it."

"You know Mason, Tom Mason on Fifteenth Street? I've been playing for him. But I can't stick it any longer. Tom's all right, but I can't stand his customers. Besides, I've got to get back to work. I'm quitting this minute—see. But Tom's got a big dance on, near Bryn Mawr to-night at a Mrs.—Mrs. Lea," he gulped. "Good pay and all that. You can play as well as I can, Ed. Easy stuff, you can read it. You got to do it."

"Do it! Man, lead me to that job. I'm broke, see, stony broke, busted." He turned his pockets inside out. "I was just wondering what I could pawn. And I need instruments— Oh, Lord!"

Peter gave him some money. "Take this, you can pay me any time. Only rush down to Tom's and tell him I can't come. I'm dead—see?—drowned, fallen in the Schuylkill. And see here, old fellow, afterwards we'll have a talk. I want everything, everything, mind you, that you can remember, every note, every bit of paper that bears on the work of these last ten months. And I'll show them—" he seemed to forget

Morgan— "with their damned talk of entertainers." Down the stairs he ran, still talking.

"Mad, quite mad," said little Morgan, staring. "Glad he's coming back to work, though. Now, where'd I put that cap?"

Still at white heat, Peter walked the few short blocks to his boarding house. Once inside his room he shut himself in and paced the floor.

"The grandson—that's me—of the man who was his grandfather's slave should be his—that's Meriwether Bye, young Dr. Meriwether Bye—should be his entertainer, his hired entertainer.

"My grandfather didn't have a chance, but here I am half a century after and I'm still a slave, an entertainer. My grandfather. Let's see, which one of the Byes was that?"

He went to the closet, pushed some books and papers aside and hauled down the old Bye Bible. The leaves, streaked and brown, stuck together. With clumsy, unaccustomed fingers he turned them, until at last between the Old Testament and the Apochrypha he found what he was looking for: "Record of Births and Deaths."

The old, stiff, faded writing with the long German s, the work of hands long since still, smote him with a sense of worthlessness. These people, according to their lights, must have considered themselves "people of importance," else why this careful record of dates?

His lean brown finger traced the lines. "Joshua Bye, born about 1780"—heavens, that must have been his great-great-grandfather. No, maybe he was just a "great," for the black Byes, he remembered hearing his father Meriwether say, lived long and married late.

"Isaiah Bye, born 1830—a child of freedom." How proud they had been of that! Yes, that was his grandfather, he remembered now. And he had made a great deal of that freedom. Meriwether had often dwelt with pride on Isaiah's learning, his school, his property, his "half-interest," Meriwether had said grandiloquently, in a bookshop. Peter could hear his father talking now.

"A child of freedom"—Peter was that but what had he made of it? He wondered what Isaiah in turn had written on the occasion of Meriwether's birth. His finger ran down the page, and found it, stopped.

There it was—"Meriwether," the inscription read, "by *his* fruits shall ye know—*me*."

At first Peter thought it was a mistake. Then gradually it dawned on him—his fine old grandfather, proud of his achievements, seeing his son as a monument to himself, seeing each Bye son doubtless as a monument to each Bye father. Poor Isaiah, perhaps happy Isaiah, for having died before he realized how worthless, how anything but monumental *his* son had really been, except as a failure. And now he, Peter, was following in that son's footsteps.

He remembered an old daguerreotype of his grandfather that he had seen at his great-uncle Peter's. The face, perfectly black, looked out from its faded red-plush frame with that immobile look of dignity which only black people can attain. "I have made the most of myself," the proud old face seemed to say. "My father was a slave, but I am a teacher, a leader of men. My son shall be a great healer and my son's son——"

Peter put the open Bible carefully on the table and took out a cigarette. But he held it a long time unlighted.

So far as he could remember he had never had any desire to rise, "to be somebody," as Isaiah, he rightly guessed, would have phrased it. He saw himself after his mother's death, a small placid boy, perfectly willing to stay out of school. Until he met Joanna. There was his term of service in the butcher-shop and himself again perfectly willing to be the butcher's assistant. Until Joanna's questioning had made him declare for surgery. Once in college his whole impulse had been to get away from it all, not because he hadn't liked the work; he adored it, was fascinated by it. But the obstacles, prejudice, his very real dislike for white people, his poverty, all or any of these had seemed to him sufficient cause for dropping his studies and becoming a musician. Not an artist, but an entertainer, a player in what might be termed "a strolling orchestra," picking up jobs, receiving tips, going down in the servants' dining room for meals. And when Joanna had objected, he thought she was "funny," "bossy."

And as soon as he had broken with her, he had given up striving altogether. He had been nothing without Joanna. He wondered humbly if she had seen something in him which he had not recognized in himself.

How different they had been! After all, Joanna, though she had not had to contend with poverty, had had as hard a fight as he. "She'd have been on the stage long ago if she'd been white," he murmured. "And see how she takes it!"

Well, he would show her and Isaiah, yes, and Mrs. Lea, too, that there was something to him. But chiefly Joanna. Some day he'd go to her and say, "Joanna, what I am, you made me."

His ladylady called up to him:

"Telephone for you, Mr. Bye."

He went downstairs, took down the receiver.

"Hello, this is Mr. Bye, yes, this is Peter. Who's this speaking, please? . . .

"Oh—oh, yes, of course. Why—why, Maggie!"

He had forgotten all about her!

CHAPTER XXIII

I T had been increasingly easy for him to forget her. When he had first broken with Joanna, when he had written her that virtuous letter, Maggie's rooms, Maggie's arms were a haven. She was always ready to listen, always sympathetic. She met his advances half way; if he asked for a kiss he got it at once. There was none of Joanna's half-real, half-coquettish withdrawal. No one could accuse Maggie of a lack of modesty. Peter would have been the first to fight such an accuser, but he found himself half-wishing that she were not quite so easy to approach.

Somehow life grew less stimulating. Presently they were settling down into the cosy, prosy existence of the long married couple. In the afternoons Peter came in—he was usually playing with Tom at night—they exchanged a word of greeting. Maggie gave him a dutiful kiss; there would be a word or two about the weather, his playing engagements, then silence. Presently Peter would say: "Mind if I look over the paper a moment, Maggie? I got up late this morning."

And Maggie's bright answer: "Oh, of course not, I've got my accounts to run over."

Somehow all the easy, "understanding" conversation had vanished. Joanna, Maggie had soon learned, was not a welcome topic. And Peter no longer went to his classes, so there was no possible theme there. Peter to his disgust found himself drawing unwilling contrasts between these seances and similar moments spent with Joanna. Had there ever been any silences? If there were they were filled with

all sorts of tingling thoughts and meanings.   There was
the night when Joanna leaned against him in Morningside Park.
They had said nothing.   But the very air about them was
pulsing.   How long ago all that seemed!   Had it ever been
true?   Why had he never felt like that when Maggie, as she
frequently did, rested her head on his shoulder?

He would shake himself angrily out of his reverie.   "Silly
ass," his lips formed.

Maggie seeing his lips move would ask him interestedly:
"What's the matter, Peter?"

"Nothing at all," he'd tell her contritely.   What should be
the matter with his dear Maggie so near?   Sometimes he put
an arm around her shoulder.   "Look here, I've got an hour
yet.   Like to go out?"

That never failed to please her.   She loved to be seen with
him.   She had a very charming, flattering air of deference, of
dependence when she was out.   It was singularly pleasing and
yet puzzling to Peter.   Joanna now was just as likely to cross
the street as not, without waiting for a guiding hand, a protecting arm.   If she had once visited a locality she knew quite
as much about getting away from it as her escort.   But
Maggie was helpless, dependent.   Strange when they were all
growing up together he would have said she was quite as independent in her way as Joanna, and she was decidedly capable
in her hair-dressing work.   Madame Harkness' business had
increased considerably in Philadelphia and Baltimore.

Peter had often mused over this.

He had known for some time that he did not love Maggie.
But he could not tell whether or not she loved him.   Certainly
she had appeared to at first, and certainly even now she clung
to him.   Her very submissiveness would seem to indicate some
depth of feeling.   He remembered Maggie as being anything
but yielding in their earlier days, and she had never apparently
changed one iota in her resentment toward her husband.   She

was making a remarkably good living from her connection
with Madame Harkness, had bought the house in New York
and was contributing to her mother. She could not be marrying him to be taken care of.

Of course he knew nothing of her *flair*, her passion for being
connected with "real" people—for "class" as he would have
called it. And if he had known this, it would have explained
nothing to him, for he never thought of himself in this sense.
His most frequent source of worry consisted in wondering if
Maggie realized how lukewarm his feeling was for her. Apparently she never suspected it.

Maggie may not have let Peter realize it, but she was completely aware that he did not love her. She understood, had
always understood, that Joanna was the one woman in the
world for him. Having loved Joanna once there was no possibility of his caring about any one else. She had recognized in
Peter's turning to her a manifestation of the state of mind
which had led her at the time of her marriage to turn to
Henderson Neal.

Her acceptance of Peter had been almost spontaneous, yet
it was governed subconsciously by two or three motives. First
of all, while she thought it extremely probable that Joanna
liked, even loved Peter, she did not believe that Joanna would
ever consider marriage with him as important as her art.
Therefore she might just as well take him. Then she enjoyed
the artistic fitness of showing Joanna that a girl whom the
latter did not consider worthy to marry her brother was deemed
worthy to marry her lover. And last and most important,
Maggie saw through Peter a second means of entrance into
the society of "real" people. She had glimpsed this once
through the possibility of marriage with Philip. Instead
Henderson Neal had closed this entrance to her, she had once
believed, forever. She must not fail to take advantage of this
new avenue.

Already she was beginning to reap its value. Miss Alice Talbert, it is true, became colder than ever when Maggie's engagement to Peter was known. She told Arabelle Morton that she considered "Peter done for, ruined, if he married that gambler's wife. Cousin Joanna did well to get rid of him." But Arabelle herself had laughed, had said she wanted to meet the girl who had captured "that good-looking Bye boy." She had come to see Maggie, had invited her to the Morton house. Her good-natured shallowness, her frank determination not to be a "high-brow" and her complete social assurance captivated Maggie. Arabelle was of as unimpeachable standing as Miss Talbert, though her choice of friends was not so exclusive. Maggie was "taken up" by the young women of Arabelle's set and henceforth her lines were comparatively easy. Still she met with an occasional snub from the older women. Mrs. Viny, who turned out to be the terrible old lady who had asked her about Mr. Neal in Atlantic City, refused grimly to recognize her and gave it as her opinion that "Peter's doings would make Isaiah Bye turn over in his grave—yet. You mark my word."

Her hearers got a vision of the dust and nothingness which, for many years, had been Isaiah Bye, slowly shifting its position in the narrow quarters of his tomb.

Maggie had her own plans. She did not mean to have Peter following forever in Tom Mason's train. But after they had married she would bring about a change. She was sure she could coax him. It would never do to let Joanna think, she would tell him, that he could not achieve distinction without *her*. And when Peter Bye became Dr. Bye, the famous surgeon, Philadelphia would find that Mrs. Peter Bye had a long memory.

Only Peter, who at first had agreed to marry in June, now some months later seemed in no haste to marry at all—that was the rub.

When she telephoned him on the day on which he had had
his interview with Mrs. Lea, she made up her mind to hasten
the marriage.

He came to see her the next afternoon full of his scheme of
returning to his classes. Maggie noticed a difference.

"You look as though you'd inherited a fortune or found a
million dollars."

"I have. My senses have come back to me. What do you
think, Maggie? I've chucked all this foolishness with Tom
Mason. My, I bet he's cursing mad. I'm getting down to
brass tacks; went back to my classes this morning."

Surprise and something else altered her face.

"What's the matter, you don't like it?"

"Yes—of course—only, but Peter, can't you see how hard
all this is for me?"

He got up, fiddled with the things on the mantel, turned
about and faced her, the knuckles straining a little in the hand
with which he grasped the back of a chair.

"Just what do you mean, Maggie? What's hard?"

She told him then that his going back to school naturally
meant a postponement of their marriage. "Oh, Peter, can't
you see I want to be safe like other women, with a home and
protection? I met Henderson, Henderson Neal, uptown Saturday—I didn't mean to tell you—but he glared at me. He
made me shiver, I wished you were with me. I'm afraid of
him, Peter, I'll never be safe till we're married."

His level voice answered her: "I can see to your safety,
Maggie; if Neal really frightens you, I can have him bound
over to keep the peace. But we can't marry now, dear. I
want to be able to take care of my—my wife. And if I go
back to my classes, I'll need all the money I can lay hands on.
I've lost so much time that I can't afford to do any outside
work. I'll just live on what I've made with Mason. But

I

that will leave me pretty poor. You see, I've got to have five hundred dollars cold for my instruments."

She looked at him speechless, her gray eyes going black in the pale gold of her face, her hands submissively folded.

He took out his handkerchief and mopped his forehead. "If you don't mind, Maggie, I think we'd better discuss this later. Suppose we think it over for two or three days, and then we'll settle upon something." His voice, infinitely gentle, infinitely sorry for her, trailed off into silence.

She said listlessly: "I think I'll go to New York for a while. I think I'd like to be with my mother."

He ignored the pathos of this. "That would be fine. How soon do you want to go?"

"To-morrow," she told him. "You needn't come to the station with me, Peter, you'd hardly have time to make it. I won't take much, so I can manage."

He felt himself a cad for agreeing with her. "It's too bad I have to go now, but I've got to read over some notes with Morgan. So this is good-by for the present. Aren't you going to kiss me, Maggie?"

She held up her face for her dutiful kiss.

CHAPTER XXIV

JOANNA stood on the steps of the New York Public Library, gazing at the paralysis of traffic which at the bidding of an autocratic policeman had fallen on the massed ranks of vehicles. Subconsciously she thought of a German story, "Germelshausen," in which all the life of the village suddenly ceased, leaving the people statues of flesh and blood. Fifth Avenue coming to life again, she fell quite consciously to wondering where she could get a good dinner. All about her flashed the lights of restaurants, but she was not sure of their reception of colored patrons and being in a slightly irritable mood, she wanted consciously to spare herself any contact which would be more annoying. She needed more than the cup of chocolate and sandwich which she might easily have had at one of the two drug stores near by. And of course she could get something expensive, but satisfying, in the station which towered not far away. But of late the restaurant management in that particular station had shown a tendency to place its colored patrons in remote and isolated corners.

Joanna had spent the morning shopping. In one of the more exclusive stores on Forty-fourth Street she had asked to look at coats. The saleswoman had been very pleasant, but she had seated Joanna well in the rear of the store quite away from the lighted front windows and the mirrors which were so adjusted as to give all possible views of the figure.

Joanna had not noticed this at first but when she did she proposed going toward the front of the store "where there was more light."

195

"Why not come this way?" proposed the still affable saleswoman, pointing to the windows in the rear wall which also let in daylight. Yet when Joanna without answering had walked on to the front, she offered no further comment.

The incident was a slight one, possessing possibly no significance, but Joanna had walked out of the store hot and raging, the more so because she was not completely sure whether the slight was intentional or not. It had not helped her frame of mind to purchase a less becoming coat in a department store where she was known and liked by one of the salesgirls. Gradually she worked herself into a state of contemptuous indifference, but she meant to be careful in selecting a place in which to get her dinner. She had to work too hard these days to bring on her good spirits, she was not going to have them dissipated by galling if petty discriminations.

Well, there was no help for it, she would have to go over to the Pennsylvania station at Thirty-third Street. She was sure of pleasant treatment there. After this solid afternoon of work in the gloomy library, the walk would do her good.

A hand fell on her shoulder, and she turned to find beside her Vera Manning, one of the members of her old dancing-class. This surprised her, for of late hardly any one of Joanna's group had seen Vera. The report in Harlem was that she was passing for white and had no desire to be recognized by her colored acquaintances.

"It's been ages since I've seen you, Joanna," Vera began confidently. "I was sitting in the library waiting for a 'date'— doesn't that sound awful?—and then all of a sudden I thought, 'pshaw, I don't want to be bothered!' Just then you hove on the scene. Where you going?"

"Some place to get a good dinner," Joanna told her, wondering why she looked different from the Vera Manning she used to know. Her clothes showed her usual careful, even modish taste, but her face looked hard—"reckless"—Joanna suddenly decided; that was the word. She went on quickly: "See here, you work somewhere down in this neighborhood, don't you? Where do you suppose I can get something to eat, without walking a thousand miles for it?"

Vera frowned thoughtfully. "You see, I'm 'passing' just now—I know you've heard of it—and so I go into any of these places around here, but I never see any colored people. Of course you could try the Automat."

But Joanna didn't want that.

"Their food's all right when you feel like eating it, but I want a regular dinner—waiter, service, and all the rest of it. Pick out a good place for me and I'll take you to dinner, too. Nothing could be fairer than that."

Vera agreed smilingly that it couldn't. "There's a place over on Forty-second Street. I remember now I have seen some colored people in there and they get decent treatment. We could go there—" she checked herself a moment. "Oh, no, I forgot."

"Forgot what?"

"Look here, Janna, I might as well be frank, we were all of us children together—doesn't it seem ages ago? You know I wouldn't ever try to fool you. But the truth of it is I go to that particular restaurant often with the other girls in my office and of course the restaurant people think I'm—I'm white. See? I don't know just what they'd think if they saw me with you—some one who definitely showed color—or what might come of it. You don't think I'm a pig, Joanna?"

"I think I'd be a pig if I did think so," Joanna told her heartily. "Come on and take dinner with me over at the Pennsy station. It'll be nice to have a talk."

The two girls moved down Fortieth Street in the direction of Seventh Avenue.

"You'd understand it better if you worked among them— white people you know." Vera told her seriously. "Of course

I suppose there must be some decent ones, not the high-brow philanthropists and all that crowd, but people who have too much breeding, too much innate—well, niceness, I guess you'd call it, to make light of folks just because they're different. But that crowd in my office, they never think of being courteous to a colored person. If they want the janitor it's 'Where's that darky?' or 'I saw a coon in the subway this morning wearing a red tie, made me think of Jim here,' always something like that. Of course they don't say it to the man's face. There'd be a fight if they did."

"I don't see how you stand it," Joanna puzzled. "What put it in your head to work with white people, anyhow?"

"Oh, to get away from everybody and everything I'd ever known." They were at the table in the dining-room now and Vera was making criss-cross marks with her fork on the white cloth, frowning absorbedly.

"You know, Joanna, I wasn't like you—not one of us girls was. I was more like Sylvia, I wanted a good time, but most of all I wanted, I expected to marry. You remember Harley Alexander?"

Joanna did remember him, indeed, a tall personable youth about her own color, a companion of Harry Portor, Brian Spencer, and to a less degree of her own brother Alec. But what she especially remembered was that he had been the constant shadow of Vera Manning.

"Of course I remember him, Vera. He's a dentist now, isn't he? Didn't he graduate the same year as Harry Portor?"

"Yes, that's the fellow. Joanna, we really loved each other, and we planned even before he went to college to get married as soon as he came out. But as soon as my mother—you know how color-struck she is—realized we were in earnest, up she went in the air. None of her children should marry a dark man. It only meant unhappiness. If Harley and I

should have children they'd be brown and would have to be
humiliated like all other colored children."

She fell to drawing more designs.

"We had a terrible time. I was completely alone in my
fight. Father always follows mother's lead. Brother Tom
refused to commit himself. Alice is just like mother—she
really liked, I'm sure of it, John Hamilton, but because he was
dark, she let him go for Howard Morris, whom I can't stand.
For a long time I managed to keep it from Harley but the
Christmas of his last year in college, mother told him she
didn't favor his attentions to me, and told him why."

"Goodness," Joanna breathed, "that must have been awful."

"Awful! It was unspeakable. And nothing I could say to
Harley could destroy the effect of what she said. She must
have put it up to him as to whether he thought he could com-
pensate a wife for the estrangement of her family. You know
how Harley was. We had always been a remarkably united
family up to that time. He said: 'If your mother objected to
my being poor I could tell her that I could change that, but
when it comes to my color, I can't do anything with that and,
by God, I wouldn't if I could.'

"So that," Vera ended wryly, "was the end of my young
romance."

Bit by bit she made Joanna see the picture of her life since
her break with her lover. Before then she had worked in her
father's office, but now she was secretary to one of the heads
of a big advertising agency. As she was an unusually swift
stenographer and had a level head, she was getting along
famously.

"Of course they think I'm white. There are a lot of young
men in the office and I flirt with them outrageously. At first
I did it only to annoy mother, she hated it so. You know,
the funny thing is she doesn't like white people any better than

I do—she just didn't want me to marry a dark man because, she says, in this country a white skin is such an asset."

"Do you enjoy yourself going about?"

"Yes and no. When I began I did immensely. You can't imagine—I couldn't—the almost unlimited opportunities that those people have for work, for pleasure, for anything. As a white girl I've seen sights and places, yes, and eaten food that I never even knew about when I used to go out with Harley. And then, too, Jan, you can't imagine the blessedness of no longer being uncertain whether you can enter such and such a hotel, or of getting a decent berth if you're going traveling or of little things like that, the sudden removal of thousands of pin-pricks, not only that, of inconveniences."

"You must be very happy," Joanna said wistfully.

"No, I'm not. They aren't, either. That's the funny part. Oh, of course I suppose nobody is actually happy, but I do think that colored people, when they're let alone long enough to have a good time, know how to enjoy themselves better than any other people in the world. It's a gift."

"I should think you'd drop it all, Vera."

"I would if it weren't for the sense of freedom. It's wonderful to be able to do as you like. Sometimes I think I will drop it, then I think: 'Oh, pshaw, what difference does it make?' Without Harley I'm bound to be unhappy, anyway, even if I do go back to my own. Since I can't have happiness I might just as well take up my abode where I can have the most fun and comfort even though it's making me—well, no saint, I can tell you." She laughed recklessly. "I wish I were like you, Joanna."

"What do you mean?"

"Well, you know—here ever since you were little you've had Peter Bye right at your beck and call—you must have loved him, Jan, he was so everlastingly good-looking, and charming, too, we all thought. I remember he took me to a

movie one Christmas. Then you fussed with him or something
—some of your high-brow stuff I suppose—and you send him
off without winking an eyelash. How do you stand it?"

Joanna was cautious. "Of course I have my work. I do
miss Peter though—sometimes."

"Sometimes! Girl, you aren't human. Well, being heart-
less isn't bad! What do you want to do, go to the 'Dance of
The Nations' down at the District Line Theater?"

But Joanna wanted a chance to think, so on the pretext of
having to return to the Library, she left Vera. She realized
the tragedy of her friend's case, the awful emptiness that had
come into her life. Hadn't her own life been affected in the
same way?

A bus stopped before her and she mounted it, her thoughts
weaving mechanically. She did not blame Vera at all for the
change in her mode of living. In those first few months after
Peter had left her she had wondered often how she could go
on with life. For a long while she had existed simply from
day to day, paying an exaggerated attention to small happenings, making engagements with people whom she had scarcely
noticed before, doing anything to get away from the weariness
of her thoughts. Many a night she had spent meditating on
some *coup*, some reckless expenditure of energy and interest
no matter how silly, how scandalous, so long as it took her
out of herself.

She had even tried flirting, a field hitherto unthought of.
As it was she had been too kind to Harry Portor; of late she
had consciously avoided him because she knew only too well
what he meant to ask of her the next time they were alone.
She hated to hurt him but that seemed inevitable, for her heart
held not the slightest fraction of love for him.

Oh, Peter! Peter!

As she rode up Fifth Avenue under the starry reaches of
the sky, beneath the tender budding of April trees, her desper-

ate longing quickened to a sudden resolve. She would write to Maggie—Maggie, who could not possibly love Peter. And even if she did, she could not love him as she—Joanna—loved him. Why, there had been Philip once, and then Henderson Neal!— Whereas Peter had been the only love of her own life.

She would write to Maggie, very clearly, very frankly and she would beg her to let him go. It all seemed simple enough. And then she and Peter would be happy. She would make him love her again, worship her. And "Peter," she would tell him, "never another unkind word, I'll be a new Joanna, darling."

Her father's house, its windows darkened, loomed up before her. Straight up to her own room she sped, not stopping to enter Sylvia's apartments, although the sound of laughing voices penetrated to her.

Alone at the little flat-topped desk, she took out pen and paper and began the letter—"Dear Maggie"— But that was what she had done years ago,—written to Maggie to give up Philip. That was in the unconscious selfishness of youth. Now was she to write her again to give up Peter? Her courage oozed away, left her helpless. She looked at the pen, put it carefully away on the rack, slipped the sheet of paper back in the pigeonhole. She might go down to Philadelphia to visit Alice Talbert. Yes, she would do that very soon. And then maybe she would see Maggie Ellersley—on the street, or even go and call on her. Undoubtedly it was better to discuss such personal matters face to face.

CHAPTER XXV

WHILE Joanna was sitting at her desk, Maggie Ellersley some fifty blocks away brooded over plans of her own. She had hoped, vainly as it turned out, that her absence from Philadelphia would quicken Peter's need of her. His very real regard for her hospitality and kindness had long since been evident. She knew that he considered the little apartment on South Fifteenth Street his nearest approach to a home in Philadelphia, and she had hoped that the loneliness caused by her departure would induce him to urge her to come back. But Peter's letters had not been in the least melancholy. Once a week he had written to her regularly during the four weeks of her stay in New York, but though he had been kind and pleasant, not once had he expressed a desire to see her, or even a passing curiosity as to the date of her return.

When she had first come back to New York, she had had a feeling of shame and despondency as she thought of her effort in Philadelphia to induce Peter to take a definite stand about their wedding. But her stay here with her mother had dissipated all that feeling. The prosy, uninteresting life which Mrs. Ellersley and Mis' Sparrow led, the troop of commonplace, albeit kindly and dependable roomers made her turn again to Peter for a way out. More than ever she was in the same trap in which she had found herself years ago when as a little girl she walked home with her mother from the dinners which she had eaten in some employer's house. Now, it was true, her surroundings were no longer dirty and she was no longer poor—she and her mother had all the money they needed and almost all that they wanted. Of lowly stock, Maggie had never cared in the least for the possession of riches. But the old loneliness, the old sense of unworthiness, of being nobody was strong upon her.

In earlier days she had frequented the Marshalls' house; plenty of other girls had frequented it, too. It was to be presumed that the Marshalls from time to time had returned such visits. But somehow she had never contrived to be on really intimate terms with those others. They were all polite, more than polite, even cordial to Maggie, and yet she knew that while moving with that group, she was not of it.

The difficulty had been, had always been, that she had no background.

Other girls' fathers and mothers were "somebodies." Alice and Vera Manning's father was a remarkably successful business man, old Joel Marshall was as famous in his way, she guessed, as Delmonico. Even Peter Bye—as poor almost, she correctly imagined, as she herself in the old days—boasted a long, a *bona fide* ancestry. And, besides, he was a man.

From as far back as she could remember she had had one passion, one desire unique in its singleness. And that had been to "be" somebody. And long ago she had realized that the only way out for her was marriage with a man of distinction. The distinction might consist in a career, in family, in business, —it made no difference to her. At first she thought she could achieve her desire through Philip—and she had loved him, too.

She dwelt on this a moment. How wonderful such a marriage would have been! Loving him as she did she would have let her desire for mere respectability sink into second place, discounting the fact that she would have gained it anyhow by such a union. But Joanna had interfered, and then she had married Henderson Neal, a gambler, a *gambler* who had plunged her further back than ever into the obscurity from which she was beginning to emerge.

"What a fool I was to consider Joanna's letter. Philip might, just possibly, have come to like me better—to love me." She reminded herself then, a little spasm of pain twitching across her face, that he had never since her marriage, not even since her divorce, made any attempt to get in touch with her. "And he could have a thousand times," she whispered to herself.

Now here was Peter. She rose from the couch on which she had been lying and walked restlessly, aimlessly around the room. The light from a cluster of electric bulbs on the wall struck at and brought out little flashes of radiance from the silver butterflies which chased each other up and down across the heavy folds of her black silk kimono. Her hair, parted in the middle and brushed to a smooth luster, hung in two thick short braids one over each shoulder. She caught her lip in her teeth, whitening that mysterious redness which was the only note of color in the golden oval of her face.

A mirror caught her attention and she stopped before it.

"Oh, Peter, Peter," she whispered unseeingly to the image in the glass, "dear Peter, don't you see you're my only chance? You've got to help me. It isn't as though Joanna really wanted you, or as though you'd ever go back to her."

Just as Joanna had resolved a few hours ago to cast herself on Maggie's mercy, so Maggie determined to open up her heart to Peter and beg him to remove her forever from the distastefulness of this life.

Her mother tapped on the door and came in, followed by Mis' Sparrow. The two of them, great "jiners," had just returned from one of their innumerable lodge meetings.

"It was a great sight, Maggie. You'd ought to have been there. Can't see why you mope so about the house, anyway. Don't believe you've been anywhere since you've been here this trip—'cept to Madam Harkness'."

Maggie murmured that she didn't care to go out, she had come home to rest.

"Well, stay in the house all you want, chile. Long's I got Cousin Jinny Sparrow to go around with me I ain't carin'. Reckon we've done our share of stayin' in the house in our time, ain't we, Jinny?"

Mis' Sparrow thus addressed admitted she had: "An' I don't propose to do it no more. Come on, Sallie, I c'n see Maggie's got somethin' on her mind."

Maggie protested, but only faintly. She loved and was deeply attached to the two thin wrinkled ladies, but they and she had nothing in common. They lived a separate life from hers entirely, a life which included much attention to churches, strawberry festivals, lodge meetings, bits of gossip, funerals, visits to ladies similarly faded and wizened, and a sort of shrewd indiscriminate charity. Maggie used to envy them their utter and complete absorption in these matters.

"I'm not the one who wants to be to herself, it's you who want to get off and talk over your secrets." She shook a playful finger. Long after they had gone, curled up on her couch, she sat watching, as she used to watch in Philadelphia, the gas-heater cast its ruddy glow on the high white ceiling.

The morning brought her a momentary shock of pleasure. It was the day for Peter's letter. He had written: "I am coming to see you next week." Her spirits leaped at that. But afterwards he explained; one of his classmates had warned him to get his instruments as quickly as possible, there was going to be a great demand for steel, so he was coming to New York to see about the things he had ordered. "I'm in deadly earnest this time, Maggie, and though I don't like my professors any better than I did before, I'm making the most of my return. There's only one thing that would keep me from finishing and that would be war. It seems foolish for a colored man to fight for America, but I believe I'd like to do it.

Only I want to pick up a commission somewhere. Not a chance for a colored fellow at Plattsburg, but some of the boys are whispering of a training camp for Negro officers at Des Moines. This is still *sub rosa,* so don't mention it."

Her hopes rose, fell, rose again as she scanned the letter.

"He must make some definite plans about me, if he's thinking of war."

The next Thursday saw him striding along Fifty-third Street in the direction of Maggie's house. His nervous glance at his watch justified his fear of being late. That was because he had stopped at his Aunt Susan's little apartment to talk over his plans. She was just the same as ever—stout, sane, energetic, ready to be fond of Peter. Before the afternoon was over she was worshiping him inwardly. For her nephew, suddenly conscious of his debt to her and realizing as he climbed the stairs to her rooms that here was his only real home, had taken her at the door into his arms with a burst of genuinely filial affection. She had, as she put it, "scared up" something for him to eat, and the two sitting at the little dinner table had entered into a silent appreciation of kinship such as lonely Miss Susan had wanted ever since her sister's death. Peter had told her of his break with Joanna. "I can't talk much about that, Aunt Susan—maybe some other time——"

Her kind hand on his steadied him.

"For a while I kept on playing ducks and drakes with my life—that was really why Joanna chucked me, you know—but all of a sudden I came to my senses, and now I've gone back to studying and I'll be all right yet, Aunt Sue. You and I'll have a nice little house somewhere. You'll see." He checked himself: "Unless this war intervenes. Of course I'd have to go into that. America makes me sick, you know, like I used to make you I guess, but darn it all, she is my country. My folks helped make her what she is even if they were slaves."

Aunt Susan beamed on him. "Your great-grandfather

fought in the Revolution, Peter, and two of your uncles, my brothers, were in the Civil War. If you enlist you'll only be following their example."

He looked at his watch. "I must go, dear. Do you know, it's as though I had just discovered you to-day." Her hands were in his and he caught them up and kissed them, bending his shapely curly head a little. "If I have to go away suddenly, I'll send you a few of my things, the Bye Bible and all that, you know. But you'll see me again."

He caught up his hat and ran out.

"That Joanna is a fool and a minx," said the old lady ungratefully. "I hope he didn't suffer much. It's a wonder some other girl hasn't got him now."

Peter had not told her about Maggie. "Not worth while," he muttered to himself, taking the subway steps in four leaps. "Maggie's got to let me off. I'll ask her, I'll explain. God, what a cad I feel!" He tugged at his collar. "But she'll be better off. I know she will. Now I wonder why she married that Neal fellow instead of waiting to give Philip a chance?"

He mused over this sitting in the subway train with his watch in his hand. "I shouldn't have spent so much time with Aunt Susan." He had arranged with Morgan and some other students for a comprehensive review at his house that same night. It would never do for him not to show up on time, they were all busy fellows.

Everything depended on Maggie.

He rushed out of the subway and came swinging along the street looking for her number. As he turned abruptly toward the house he caromed into a tall, heavily set man standing idly and yet purposefully at the bottom of the steps. Peter rang the bell, conscious as he did so that the man had received his apologies only with an odd glare. One last glance over his shoulder just before he went in showed the stranger staring fixedly at the front door as though to see who opened it.

Mis' Sparrow let him in. Maggie was in the "settin' room" at the head of the stairs, she told him as she herself went out. He ran up to arrive at a landing so dark that he knocked over a chair. The door was only slightly open, so he knocked.

"Come in," Maggie called listlessly. "Oh, is that you, Peter? I'd been expecting you all day and then finally gave you up. Was that you stumbling on the landing? I'm always at mother to keep the light going there. I don't know why she won't. Here, I'll turn it on now."

But Peter, unwilling to lose more time, begged her not to bother. "Come over here and sit down, Maggie. We've lots to talk about."

He hadn't kissed her, she noticed, observing his nervousness. "What's the matter, Peter? You seem so excited."

"Do I? Well, I've had a full day—early breakfast, the trip, and walking around downtown—and then visiting Aunt Susan and breaking my neck to get here. That's moving pretty swift, isn't it?"

To control her own lack of composure she asked him to let her see his instruments. "My, aren't they shiny and pretty and sharp? And each one with your name on it? That's splendid. No chance of having them stolen."

"No," he replied absently, taking the little leather case from her hand and placing it still open on the table. "No, not a chance. Listen, Maggie, I've—I've got to go pretty soon, must be back in Philadelphia by nine o'clock, I—I want to talk to you frankly for a moment or two, about ourselves."

She sat expectantly. "Maggie, I don't want you to think me a cad—I'm not that really—but even if you do think me one I've come to ask you to release me. We—our affair has been a mistake, I had no business dragging you into it. I am sure you don't love me—why should you love anyone who's trifled with his life as I have? And I—I don't—you understand, Maggie, I have and always shall have the highest regard

14

for you. There's nothing in the world I wouldn't do for you, for a girl of your fine qualities——"

"Except marry her," she thought.

"But I find—it was unspeakable of me to make the mistake —I find I don't love you, Maggie, as a man should love his— his wife. And that's a bad way to start a marriage, don't you think?" He thought he read scorn in her watching eyes, and hastened to fortify his excuse. "You know, I've been in love once, I know what it ought to be."

She said in a level, absolutely emotionless voice, "You want to go back to Joanna."

That name steadied him. "No, not that, Maggie dear. She wouldn't take me back; I'm not worthy of Joanna; she was quite right. I shall probably never see her again until we are both quite old. Not a chance for me there," he ended sadly.

Curiously enough, if he had himself dared to think of returning to Joanna, if he had told Maggie so, she would have released him instantly. It was not part of her plan to interfere with love. But if Peter, who would never love any one but Joanna, were to be left drifting for some other woman to pick up ten, five years from now, perhaps even immediately after the war! He would never be able to do the service for any woman in this world that he could do for her.

He misunderstood her silence. "It isn't as though you cared such a lot about me, Maggie. My leaving wouldn't really mean anything to you."

"It would mean my death," she told him. And indeed it did seem to her that if he left her alone with nothing in her life but Madame Harkness and those two poor old ladies— her mother and Mis' Sparrow—she would die of it. She would die of sheer disappointment at being balked this second time of her constant desire.

Peter stared at her in sick astonishment. "You mean it?"

he whispered. It had never crossed his mind that she cared
for him like this. Subconsciously he thought, "Suppose this
had been Joanna."

Before Maggie could speak again, someone knocked on the
door; one of Mrs. Ellersley's roomers stuck in a tousled head.

" 'Scuse me, Miss Maggie, I heard you-all talkin' in here,
en they ain't no one else in the house. Jest wanted to tell you
I'm runnin' down to the corner a minute en as I mislaid my
key I'm goin' t' leave the latch up, if you-all don't mind."

Maggie stared blankly. "Oh, certainly Mr. Simpson, certainly."

They heard Mr. Simpson shuffling down the stairs and knew
by the sound of the slamming door that he had gone out.

What they did not know was that a moment later a tall,
heavily built man, who had been lounging sidewise against the
wall of a neighboring house, came forward swiftly and ran up
the steps. He tried the door gently and finding to his surprise
that it yielded, walked in and closed it softly behind him. For
two weeks, unnoticed, fingering a door-key in his pocket, he
had kept watch on that house and its inmates, until he had
become acquainted with the hours of the coming and going of
each. He knew Maggie was at home in the afternoons; his
purpose was to wait for a time when all of them should be out
but her. One by one he had watched them emerge, Mrs.
Ellersley and Mis' Sparrow finally within fifteen minutes of
each other.

"Those old birds," he murmured to himself, "they're just
as likely as not to join up somewheres and go to one of their
protracted meetin's."

Gradually the house had emptied itself with the exception
of Maggie and this tousel-headed Mr. Simpson who usually
left later than this. He had not seen Bye come out, but
thought it likely the visitor had left in the quarter of an hour

he had spent in the saloon around the corner where he had swallowed an unaccustomed dram to fortify his intention.

In the hall he stood blinking a moment in the darkness, then as the sound of voices penetrated to him from above he withdrew into the obscurity of the narrow oblong parlor. Evidently the fellow had not gone yet. There was plenty of time, he could wait.

Upstairs Maggie was pouring out to Peter her great obsession.

"I know I am amazing you, Peter, but I can't endure this life, this utter separation from people who mean something. Take me away from it. I'll be eternally grateful to you."

"But, good God, Maggie, what can I do? I'm only a penniless student with my way to make. We'd be poor for years. And, anyway, where do you get the idea that my name carries with it any social asset?"

She murmured something about his long line of ancestors; years ago in her presence his Aunt Susan had spoken to Mrs. Marshall about it.

"You know how your name gave you the entrance into the best families in Philadelphia."

He stared at her. Of all the crazy complexes, this was the craziest. It was indecent, this situation, agony for both of them. He tried to be firm, faltered, was lost.

"You know I think all this is idiotic, Maggie. If you think marriage with me would help you because I know the names of my great-grandparents—why, it's absurd, ridiculous. I had a lot of foreparents—we all did—but they were nobodies most of them, only slaves."

"That's what they all were."

"All who?"

"All the early settlers, weren't they, the white ones, too, indentured servants, outcasts, outlaws, men driven for one

reason or other from their own countries?   But certain ones
of them have always stood out, attained prominence."

Overcome by this interpretation of history, he could make
no suitable answer. He moved over to the little table, picked
up his hat.

"Obviously all this will have to be gone over again. If you
like I'll send my Aunt Susan to see you, she knows all sorts of
people both here and in Philadelphia. If you ask her no doubt
she'll manage to make it very pleasant for you. I really must
go, Maggie. And of course—that is, if you insist on it—
remember that I shall always be at your service."

He held her hand a moment, passed out and ran sideways,
after the manner of men, down the wide staircase.

The front door closed after him.

Maggie walked back through the room. This was her
great interview. Peter had been here; to prove it there was
his box of instruments on the table—she ran out in the hall
again, perhaps she could catch him, for he could hardly have
turned the corner.

An iron hand shot out of the darkness of the landing, caught
her wrist in an agonizing vise. Then some one dragged her
back into the room and she looked up into the raging somber
eyes of Henderson Neal. She had not been frightened at first,
but the sight of that face with its snarling lips and its bloodshot eyes unnerved her. In an instinctive gesture of fear she
threw up her free hand which held the little case. It slipped
from her grasp and some of the knives fell on the floor.

Still holding her he stooped and picked one up.

Her self-control ebbed back to her. Somehow she had never
been seriously afraid of Neal. Her scorn had been too great
for that. One does not fear what one scorns.

She said to him evenly, "Henderson, let me go."

But he pulled her closer to him. "I'll never let you go
again. Either you'll come with me, or I'll——"

"You'll what?"

"I'll kill you." But the thought obviously had just come to him.

"Pooh!" she made a face at him. A trace of her old-time slanginess returned: "What's all the excitement?"

His heavy countenance lowered, darkened. "He actually looks black," she thought to herself.

"You know you can't fool me, Maggie girl. You had me believing you divorced me because I gambled, when what you wanted was to get back to that high-brow feller of yours!"

"What high-brow fellow?" She knew he was confusing Peter with Philip, but she must engage him in talk until Simpson could return.

"As though you didn't know. The one who just left here. Are you gonna give him up, Maggie?"

"I am not." Her cool decision drove him beside himself.

"You think I'm foolin', don't you? I'll show you. I know you're alone in the house. I'll give you just three seconds to tell me you'll come back to me."

"I'll let you kill me first."

She saw him look at the knife, Peter's knife, which he was still holding in his hand. A look of determination settled in his eyes.

Even then she was not frightened. People—the people one knows never do that sort of thing.

With a flash-like movement he leaned closer and brought the keen, glittering piece of steel down toward her. When she saw he was in earnest she threw her arm forward close over her breast. But the knife bit down, down into the soft flesh. Bewildered she saw the red blood spurting, gushing over her arm, her dress, a soft green dress which she had donned for Peter. Now it was turning in spots to a vivid red.

He let go of the arm, looking at her with fascinated gaze.

Slowly she sank, turned her eyes toward him, saw him drop the knife and rush headlong out of the room.

So she was going to die, killed in a brawl with her divorced husband. The fires of her life were to go out, extinguished under the waters of commonness and degradation. After all, what did it matter? Her thoughts took an odd turn as she felt herself slipping, slipping into the blackness of what must be death.

"He must have loved me even more than I loved Philip. What a pity that I have to die without letting Philip know how dearly I loved him."

CHAPTER XXVI

A FEW moments later Mr. Simpson came rushing up the front steps. He tried the door gingerly and found to his relief that it was not locked. That meant Mrs. Ellersley had not yet returned to chide him for his carelessness. Miss Maggie now was different; she would never carry on, no matter what a fellow did. It would be just as well for him to stop at the room at the head of the stairs and let her know he had returned.

The landing was still dark, but long experience had taught him to navigate the troublesome chair. Without mishap he reached the door of the sitting-room. Everything was absolutely silent, still he would just put his head inside to make sure.

He was concluding there was nobody there when his eye caught something protruding from the other side of the table which stood in the center of the room. A chair, too, had been overturned, and scattered about on the floor were several little bright shiny things. He picked one up, looked at the legend on the handle, "Chilled steel, England, Peter Bye."

The name of the maker evidently. Queer doings here. Half afraid, wholly curious, he ventured in further, especially intrigued by that light brown object which protruded from beyond the table and which looked—though this, he knew, was imagination—like a hand. He bent over it, touched it, followed it with eyes and fingers to an arm dripping and scarlet with blood and beyond the arm a face golden and immobile. Beyond the head lay still another of those small strange objects.

Only this was neither bright nor shining; it was red, a vivid red and the handle which he touched with a shaking finger was sticky.

He sprang backwards, his face ghostly under its brown skin, his eyes goggling. This was—Death. "Oh, God! Help! Murder! Police! Miss Maggie!" Down the stairs he tore, his hands twisted and fumbled at the locks. The door opened to disclose Joanna standing on the door-step about to ring the bell.

She looked past him into the dim hall. "Do you know if Miss Ellersley is in?"

His eyes widened in horror. "For Christ's sake, lady, keep out. Don't go in there, she's dead, pore girl, murdered."

"Nonsense! Maggie murdered! What do you mean?"

Stammering and shrinking he told her of his ghastly find. "Don't go in there, lady, don't know nothin' about it. *I* don't mean to."

She caught his arm. "Here, come on, you must take me to it—to her; she can't be left like this. Be a man." But for all her brave words her knees were shaking.

Unwillingly he led her to the quiet form in the green and red-soaked dress. Joanna dropping beside it put her hand on Maggie's wrist. A faint pulse fluttered.

"She's alive. I must get this dress off her arm and shoulder. Got a knife?"

"Ain't they a million of 'em layin' around you, lady?"

Shudderingly she turned from the red one. "How queer! How awful! Hand me that clean one over there." Her eye fell, as she took it from him, on the handle—"Chilled steel, England, Peter Bye"—rested there stricken.

"Ought to be able to trace the murderer awful quick, don't you think, ma'am? This man Bye would know who he sold them knives to."

Without answering she cut away the cloth, used her hand-kerchief—worthless for this—to stanch the blood. "Find me a towel, there must be one somewhere." If Peter had done this she must save Maggie in order to save him. And if this were Peter's work—he did not love Maggie.

Ashamed of her thought she bent closer. "There's a bad cut below the shoulder but the cut in the arm is worse. Have you a large soft handkerchief? Quick, I must stop the bleed-ing. I can't manage with this stiff towel." He was off and back in a jiffy with three handkerchiefs, immense and happily clean, the testimony of Mrs. Ellersley's supervision.

She twisted one of them. "Now a pencil?" Somewhere out of the past floated a memory of Miss Shanley's direction how to make a tourniquet, one of the things Joanna had meant to forget after she grew up. Subconscious memories guided her fingers. "Now where's a bedroom? Help me to carry her there."

She had already dispatched him to a telephone to get, if possible, Harry Portor, whose office was in the San Juan dis-trict. Puzzled by Mr. Simpson's incoherence, the doctor promised to come at once and soon the chug-chug of his little Ford rose above the sounds of the noisy street.

Joanna ran down to let him in, meeting his astonishment as the two climbed the stairs with breathless information. Harry praised her tourniquet. "Good work, Joanna. Fortunately it's a clean cut, no jaggedness. I suppose he was trying to get at her heart. Where's the knife it was done with?" He busied himself with fresh bandages and restoratives.

"I don't know," she told him faintly. Why had she not thought of this? Now she must keep him out of the sitting-room. Her confusion escaped him, but Mr. Simpson hovering in the background had heard the question and slipping out returned with the knife.

"Here it is, doc. I was just tellin' the lady, ought sure to be able to catch that 'sassin; man who sold him the knife's done got his name stamped on the handle."

Harry took it. "H'm, a surgeon's knife." He turned it over. "Where's the name? Peter—why look here, Joanna, did you see this?"

"There's a whole case in the other room, sir."

"Yes, go get it and bring it to me. What do you suppose this means, Joanna?"

She whispered, "Wait till that man goes."

"All right, I'll send him off." He sent the willing Simpson on his return with the case, to the druggist.

"Now, Joanna?"

She had her story ready. "I came to see Maggie about—about Peter, Harry. One of the girls who works at Madame Harkness, saw Sylvia last night and told her Maggie was in town." This much was true. "So I came to see her. Just before I came, it seems, Peter came. She told me about it. I couldn't stand it. And I caught up one of his little knives—he'd left his case here—and cut her. I must have been crazy."

"You must still be crazy to think I'd believe that. You're not a good liar, Joanna. Now tell me the truth, dear. Were you here when he stabbed her?"

She stuck to her story. "He didn't stab her."

The quiet figure on the bed moved ever so slightly, opened its lips, moaned faintly. "What's the matter with my arm?"

Harry leaned over her. "A bad cut, Maggie! How'd you come to get it?" Her attention wandered. "Who's that standing over there?" Joanna retreated further into the shadows. "Who are you? Oh, it hurts me here, too." She laid her hand on her breast.

"I'm the doctor, Harry Portor, you remember me, don't you?"

He could see her make an effort. "You're sure Henderson's not here? It would make him angry to see you. Peter was here a little while ago—we're going to be married, you know. That's why Henderson cut me." Her voice grew stronger. "I thought he had killed me."

Harry cast Joanna a fleeting look. "Wait down in my car," his lips formed. She slipped down the stairs out of the house.

She sat in the car a long time while the street darkened. She saw Mr. Simpson return and hard on his footsteps Mrs. Ellersley. He must have told the news just inside the hall, for Joanna heard a shriek cut short by the closing door. Presently Harry came running down the steps, peering short-sightedly through his thick glasses at her crouching figure.

He said briefly, "A bad business, but she's not in any danger unless there's a breakdown from nervous shock."

The words were meaningless to her, reviewing Maggie's statement: "Peter was here, we're going to be married, you know."

When they got to her house Joanna politely asked him to come in.

"No, but wait a moment. I want to tell you something." He fiddled with the brake a moment. "Joanna, you've been avoiding me lately because you know I love you and you were afraid I'd ask you to marry me. Don't avoid me any more. I've got my answer. When a girl loves a man as you do Peter Bye, so much so that she'll accuse herself for his sake— oh, it makes no difference that he was innocent—well, nobody else need think there's a chance for him. But I'm your friend, Joanna, believe that."

She thanked him sadly. "Good-night, Harry."

Sylvia sent Roger up to her room to tell her that Miss Vera —Vera—"I forget her other name, Aunt Janna," had called up. She would call again the next day.

Joanna thanked him indifferently. "All right, darling, tell Mamma I'll look out for her."

She thought to herself as he pattered down stairs: "Peter and Maggie, here in New York . . . I won't think of them, I'm not going through all that sick agony again. I believe I'll go South to-morrow."

CHAPTER XXVII

THE day's excitement made Joanna sleep soundly, and in the morning she awoke strongly refreshed and rested. No gesture that she could make to Fate would ever restore Peter. She had been willing to make the greatest sacrifice of all—to surrender her pride—and even as she was about to do this, absolute evidence was given that her sacrifice was useless. The whole affair was over, finished, dead; henceforth Peter was to be in her life what other men were to other girls when they spoke of them as "old beaux." That was the way for her to speak of Peter now. She practiced it with stiff lips: "Peter Bye, oh, yes, he used to be an old beau of mine."

Her romance would hereafter lie behind her. From this day on she would dedicate herself to one interest, which should be the fixed purpose of her life; now that she thought of it she would give up the idea of dancing, too. Her former lover and her former ambition alike were unattainable; they had merely been means of enriching her experience. Now she would get down to the business of living; no more sighs, no more backward glances. And the first thing she would do would be to offer her services as a director of music to a colored school in the South. Many a principal before whose school she had sung would extend her a cordial welcome. Even though the school year was almost near its close she might get a chance to map out arrangements for the work of the following year. Her preference would be one of the less-known, poorly endowed schools where there would be lots of work.

She lay there and watched the April sun mounting slowly, slowly up the walls of her room. From outside rose the myriad sounds of Harlem; a huckster calling unintelligibly, some school children on their way to P. S. 89, shrilling their Iliad of school affairs; from far away came the echo of a spiritual whistled meditatively, almost reverently. Over herself crept a sense of peace, of finality, the sort of let-downness that comes to one voluntarily relaxing from difficult strain. She had not known such a feeling since when as girls she and Sylvia had been sent on a vacation trip into the country. The life was lonely for the two citified youngsters and they sought solace in taking long walks,—"voyages of discovery" Joanna called them. Once after a tramp of two or three hours they had come about four o'clock to a little lumpy field in whose center stood a cluster of trees. Breathless and weary Joanna had scrambled over the wooden bars and had lain down on the short stiff stubble in the refreshing shade. All about stretched only sky, earth, and in the distance rows of trees rimming their pasture. There was nothing, no one in the world but herself and Sylvia. She felt her senses lulled by the quiet security into a deep sense of peace.

Now this came back to her and other thoughts, too: their return from the country to New York—her mother and Peter were at the station. But she would not think of that. She must get up, write letters, explain to her father and mother, make arrangements.

Essie, a fixture in the service of the Marshalls, brought her a breakfast of rolls and chocolate. Joanna devoured it.

"You don't look bright, Essie."

"No'm. Got lots to worry about. Them white folks where my girl Myrtle goes to school act so mean all the time, always discouragin' her. 'What's the good of you comin' to high school'? they ses. 'What're you gonna do when you finish?' "

How quickly once she would have rejoined with one of her sweeping platitudes which to her were not platitudes because they represented a fresh and virile belief: "Don't let her become discouraged, Essie; just have her keep on. Success always comes if you work hard enough for it." But to-day, remembering her plans for the stage and her courtship with Peter—both rendered frustrate through this hopeless obstacle of color—she could only murmur: "Yes, yes, I know. White people are hard to get along with. Better times coming, I hope, Essie."

After a bath she slipped into a flame-colored dressing gown and sat down to her letters. Sylvia coming up noiselessly put her head in the door.

"Not dressed yet, Joanna? She'll be here soon. It's 10:30."

Joanna lifted a startled face. "Who'll be here?"

"Miss Sharples, Miss Vera Sharples. I sent Roger up to tell you."

"Yes, he did, but you know how he forgets names. He said 'Miss Vera' and I thought he meant Vera Manning. Wonder what Miss Sharples wants to see me about?"

"One of her pet charities probably. Get a move on. Here, wear your green dress." Joanna, whose thoughts had flown to Peter via Miss Susan Graves via Miss Sharples, took the green dress absent-mindedly, then dropped it with a shudder. Maggie had worn such a dress yesterday, a soft dull green, horribly, fantastically adorned with bright and sticky red.

"No, not that."

"You *are* nervous, Joanna. What do you feel like wearing?"

Together they chose a crêpe silk dress of straight and simple lines. The bodice as flaming as the dressing gown was long, like a Russian blouse. Its end terminated by hem-stitching into a black shallow-plaited skirt. A narrow rope-like cord confined the waist.

"Stunning," Sylvia said, spinning her around. She had designed the dress. "If Brian just wouldn't treat me right we'd run away to Paris, Jan, and set up a dressmaking establishment. You should be my manikin."

A restatement of Roger's imperfect message revealed the fact that Miss Sharples would call at eleven. Sylvia let her in and ran back to tell her sister who was outlining her plans to her father and mother in the dining room.

"There's your 'grand white folks' Janna. My Heavens, where *do* you suppose she finds her clothes? She hasn't a bit of color in her face and there she's wearing a stone gray suit and a gray hat with a brown, a *brown* scarf around it. Her hair is as straight as a poker and she wears it bobbed." Sylvia shuddered.

"Oh well, she's a good sort," Joanna remonstrated, smiling, "and she doesn't say 'you people.' "

Strange how realization falls short of anticipation. Joanna was about to scale the path which led to her highest ambition, but she had no sense of premonition. Instead, she looked at Vera Sharples sitting insignificantly and drably in an armchair, her graying bobbed hair straggling a bit over her mannish tweed coat, her feet encased in solid tan boots. Only her eyes, looking straightforwardly and appraisingly from under the unbecoming hat, kept her from being dubbed a "freak."

Joanna, who had not seen her for some years, thought amusedly as she came with swift rhythmic steps down the long room: "It would be fun to turn Sylvia loose on her and make her dress worthy of her eyes."

The two were standing looking at each other now, Miss Vera still appraisingly. Then the older woman held out her hand. Joanna had neglected to do this, having, like most colored people of her class, carefully schooled herself in the matter of repression where white people were concerned. However, she took the extended hand and gave it a hearty pressure.

"Yes," said Miss Sharples as though checking up the colored girl's points by a pattern which she carried in her head, "yes, you are the one. I was sure I hadn't confused you with anyone else. I haven't seen you for several years, you know, not since that Christmas when you danced for the Day Nursery with Helena Arnold. Do you remember?"

Joanna, slightly nonplussed, nodded yes. As though she could forget that Christmas when she had become engaged to Peter!

Miss Sharples, still pursuing some train of thought known only to herself, meandered on. "I said, 'I know there must be somebody who could do it,' and then I thought of you, but I didn't know your name. So I called up Helena and she told me. Do you still dance as divinely as you did that night, my dear?"

"Better," Joanna told her confidently, "although it doesn't get me anywhere. Would you mind telling me what all this is about?"

Her visitor settled herself comfortably in a chair, crossed one leg over the other, and took out a cigarette. "Mind if I smoke?" Joanna watched her wide-eyed, picturing her father's surprise if he should happen to look in on them.

"It's a long story. You may or may not know that I am one of the directors of the District Line Theater. Lately we've been putting on a production called 'The Dance of the Nations'—dances of the nations it really should be called. Well, we have one woman to represent France, another England, etc.; we aren't featuring Germany or any of her allies. When it came to America we had to have two or three dances represented, one for the white element, one for the black and one for the red. Of course that made the woman representing America practically a star. Well, she's all right as a white American, or as a red one, but when it comes to the colored American, she simply lays down on her job." Miss Sharples' eloquence drowned her sense of grammar.

"You know," she went on vigorously, "art to my eye is art, and there's no sense in letting a foolish prejudice interfere with it. This girl won't darken her face and hasn't a notion, so far as dancing like colored people is concerned, beyond the cake-walk. Well, I told my Board I didn't believe that wa either adequate or accurate. I'd seen Helena Arnold dance, you know, and I'd seen you, and I figured that your way was the right way," she concluded sensibly, "because you were colored. Miss Ashby's contract expires this week and I persuaded the Board to let me try to find someone else. What do you think about it?" She paused, still regarding Joanna shrewdly.

"You mean," said Joel Marshall's daughter, "that you are offering me a chance to dance at the District Line Theater?" She thought: "I know this isn't real."

"Well, yes, if you suit. It would be an experiment. To be frank, my dear, some of the directors are doubtful about the success of a colored girl on the stage, but if you dance as well as you did five or six years ago, I should say there would be no difficulty. Suppose you come with me now, there's a rehearsal at the theater this afternoon. Are you free?"

Was she free? She dashed off to get her wraps and stumbled into Sylvia on the second floor. "Isn't she long-winded? What'd she come to see you about?"

Joanna took her by both shoulders and shook her. "About my dancing at the District Line Theater in the 'Dance of the Nations.' Oh, Sylvia, if I'm dreaming, don't let me wake up."

Down in Greenwich Village on the south side of Washington Square, Joanna found Miss Susan's "Board." They were occupying, scattered around, a large dilapidated room of magnificent proportions and they were talking of art, of dancing with an enthusiasm and accuracy, an amazing precision such as Joanna had never heard equaled.

"Valvinov is good, more than good, excellent in her conception of the dance and the way she carries it out, but her ankles are too clumsy, it makes me sick to look at her legs." A short, stocky young man seated at the piano delivered this dictum. He was very pale, with thick black hair which he wore plastered back from a low square forehead. His hair was long, Joanna noticed,. and ran in unbroken strands from his forehead to the top of his coat collar. He spoke absolutely unaccented English, and his clothes were sharply American, but he was unlike any American the girl had even seen before.

Miss Sharples introduced her briskly. "This is Miss Marshall," she said to the room in general, "the dancer I was telling you of." Joanna inclined her head slightly, but the men all rose and bowed gravely, and the two other women in the room—a Miss Rosen and a Miss Phelps as they turned out to be—bowed also noncommittally but without hostility.

Evidently the place had frequently been used for rehearsals, for there was a narrow platform running across the far end of the room. Here Miss Sharples stationed Joanna. "Just to give them an idea of what you can do, my dear. There isn't much space, but I don't think that will bother you."

"No," said Joanna confidently, "the thing is the music." She glanced at the pale young man who had spoken about the Russian dancer's thick ankles. "Can you play by ear?"

"I think I could manage it," he told her seriously. They were all serious, as unconscious of self and as tremendously interested as though they were assisting at an affair of national moment. Joanna felt the atmosphere enveloping, quickening her. She stepped down from the platform.

"Well, now listen. I'm supposed to have a ring of children

around me. I sing and they answer. At first I'll have to sing both parts, but afterwards you can play their answers. See, this is the way it goes." She sat down at the piano, and ran through the melody of "Barn! Barn!" singing it in her beautiful, full voice.

"That's it, that's got the lilt," a tall, dark man said to Miss Rosen.

Joanna yielded the piano to the pale young man—Francis—everyone called him. He ran over her sketch, filling in with deep, rich chords, while she flew back to the little platform.

"Now then, you've got it. Ready!

"Sissy in the barn! Join in the weddin'!"

Her voice rang out, her slender flaming body turned and twinkled, her lovely graceful limbs flashed and darted and pirouetted. She was everywhere at once, acting the part of leader, of individual children, of the whole, singing, stamping circle.

The Board applauded. "Oh, but that's great, that's genius," cried Miss Phelps.

"If I could only have some real children," Joanna suggested, "colored children. Are there any around here?"

"About five thousand down there in Minetta Lane," Francis told her gravely. "Want me to get you some?"

"Oh, if you only would." He and Miss Rosen disappeared and were back in fifteen minutes with ten colored children, of every type and shade, black and brown and yellow, some with stiff pigtails and others with bobbed curling locks. Most of them knew the game already, all of them took to Joanna and threw themselves with radiant, eager good nature into the spirit of what she was trying to display.

The tall dark man, Mr. Hale, came over to her. "You're

ll right, Miss Marshall, if you're willing, we'll try you. America's got some foolish prejudices, but we'll try her with a sensation, and you'll be all of that. I'll leave you with Miss Sharples and Miss Rosen, our secretary, to make final arrangements, while Francis and I go out to see what we can do about taking on these kids. I suppose you'll need them."

CHAPTER XXVIII

THE District Line Theater was jammed every night now. People came from all over New York and all its suburbs to see the new dancer—Joanna Marshall. Her success and fame were instant. The newspapers featured her, the "colyumists" wrote her up, her face appeared with other members of the cast, but never alone, on the billboards outside the little ramshackle theater. Special writers came to see her, took snapshots of herself and of Sylvia which they never published, and speculated on the amount of white blood which she had in her veins.

Mr. Hale had taken her on in May. The piece ran all summer with Joanna as the great attraction, although not the acknowledged star. Miss Ashby, the girl who danced as an Indian and as an American, was that. From the first she had resented the colored girl's success and had held jealously to all her rights and privileges. But the public, surprisingly loyal to this new and original plaything, never varied in the expression of its enjoyment of Joanna. Now that her changed contract was again about to expire, Miss Ashby announced her inability to remain with the play.

"I've really been violating my principles in staying this long," she told Mr. Hale with meaning.

Even Miss Sharples was overcome at this news. Joanna could be cast without any difficulty as an Indian, a wig and grease paint would accomplish that. But Joanna could hardly pose as a white American. She was too dark.

Sylvia had a suggestion here. "America" was supposed to

come on last as a regal, symbolic figure, but Miss Ashby had paid more attention to the dancing than to the symbolism.

"Why not," asked Sylvia, "have a mask made for Joanna? She could then be made as typically American as anyone could wish and no one need know the difference."

That was the basis on which Mr. Hale worked. On the first night on which the new "America" was introduced, an inveterate theater-goer in the first row of the orchestra insisted on encoring her. Joanna returned, bowed and bowed, was encored.

Somehow the habitué guessed the truth. "Pull off your mask, America," he shouted. The house took it up. "Let's see your face, America!"

Mr. Hale, Miss Sharples, Francis, Miss Rosen and Miss Phelps held a hurried consultation behind the scenes. "There's nothing to be done," Hale said, "quick, off with your mask, Miss Marshall." And breathless, somewhat with the air of a man bracing himself, he led Joanna again on the stage.

There was a moment's silence, a moment's tenseness. Then Joanna smiled and spoke. "I hardly need to tell you that there is no one in the audience more American than I am. My great-grandfather fought in the Revolution, my uncle fought in the Civil War and my brother is 'over there' now."

Perhaps it would not have succeeded anywhere else but in New York, and perhaps not even there but in Greenwich Village, but the tightly packed audience took up the applause again and Joanna was a star.

The very next week Mr. Hale moved the production to Broadway.

Joanna found herself becoming a sensation. Through Miss Sharples, who was besieged with requests to meet her protégée, she came in contact with groups of writers, dramatists, "thinkers," that vast, friendly, changing kaleidoscope of New York dwellers who take their mental life seriously. Occasionally, too, she was invited to grace an "occasion," an afternoon at the house of a rich society woman. Once at one of these affairs she met Vera Manning, who grinned at her impishly and announced to the room that she and Miss Marshall were old friends. They had been schoolmates.

"When I was a child," said Vera impudently, "my mother sent me to public school for almost a year. She said she wanted me to be a real democrat."

She threw Joanna a droll look. When the afternoon was over, Vera asked her to go on to tea with her.

Joanna was perfect: "That's very kind of you, Miss Manning, and I don't know but what I will. There are several things I'd like to interest you in. When I think of the illimitable power for good which you white people possess——"

Once outside the door the two girls went off into gusts of inextinguishable laughter.

Joanna did not like these affairs and soon she adopted the habit of refusing such invitations. She preferred Miss Sharples' artist friends—because among them she sensed attempts, more or less tentative perhaps, toward reality. True, paradoxically enough it was a reality based on art, rather than on living. But the girl was beginning to feel the need of something with which to fill her life. Whether her disastrous love affair, or the frequent discouragements with which she met, had changed or reshaped her vision she did not know. But life, she began to realize, was not a matter of sufficient raiment, food, or even success. There must be something more filling, more insistent, more permeating—the sort of thing that left no room for boredom or introspection.

For in spite of her vogue, her unbelievably decided successes, Joanna frequently tasted the depths of ennui. She saw life as a ghastly skeleton and herself feverishly trying to cover up its bare bones with the garish trappings of her art, her lessons, her practice, her press-clippings.

Miss Sharples put her up for membership in a club whose members were mostly people that "did" something. And Joanna fell in the habit of taking her lunch and frequently her dinner, too, at this club, just to lose herself in the atmosphere which she found there.

Undoubtedly the contact did her good. Joanna, while lacking Peter's singularly active dislike for white people, was not on the other hand a "good mixer." Following the natural reaction at this time of her racial group, she had tended to seek all her ideals among colored people and where these were lacking to create them for herself. As a result of this attitude, injurious in the long run to both whites and blacks, she was hardening into a singularly narrow, even though self-reliant egocentric. She had never met in her family with much opposition to her chosen career, but then neither with the exception of Joel's and that of her teachers had she met with much coöperation.

Now to her astonishment she found herself in a setting where people, without being considered "different," "highbrow," "affected,"—and not greatly caring if they were—talked, breathed, lived for and submerged themselves and others, too, in their calling. She met girls not as old as she, who had already "arrived" in their chosen profession; incredibly young editors, artists—exponents of new and inexplicable schools of drawing,—women with causes,—birth-control, single tax, psychiatry,—teachers of dancing, radical high school teachers.

There were men to be met, too, really eminent men, but Joanna was not much interested. Following the American idea, she had been too carefully trained to care for the company of white men. Between them and herself the barrier was too impassable. Besides, it was women who had the real difficulties to overcome, disabilities of sex and of tradition.

For a while she was puzzled, a little ashamed when she

realized that so many of these women had outstripped her so early; some of them were poor, some had responsibilities. There were not many of these last. It was a long time before the solution occurred to her and when it did the result was her first real rebellion against the stupidity of prejudice.

These women had not been compelled to endure her long, heartrending struggle against color. Those who had had means had been able to plunge immediately into the sea of preparation; they had had their choice of teachers; as soon as they were equipped they had been able to approach the guardians of literary and artistic portals. Joanna thought of her many futile efforts with Bertully and sighed at the pity of it all. Sometimes she felt like a battle-scarred veteran among all these successful, happy, chattering people, who, no matter how seriously, how deeply they took their success, yet never regarded it with the same degree of wonder, almost of awe with which she regarded hers.

She realized for the first time how completely colored Americans were mere on-lookers at the possibilities of life. She spent a few happy months with these people; they made pleasant and stimulating company for her; she herself suspected that she had made good "copy" for some of them. They were for the most part unconscious of race, not at all inclined to patronize, and generous with praise and suggestion. One woman, it is true, told Joanna that she had always liked colored people.

"My father would insist on having colored servants. He preferred them."

Joanna had made an impish reply. "My father employs both white and colored servants. But he prefers the colored ones. However, it doesn't make any difference to me."

Still that had been a rare encounter. Life on the whole smiled on her. Yet she was not happy. But is anybody so? she wondered. She had forgotten to sorrow for her break with

Peter, her life was too full for that, even for a new love. Vera Manning's brother Tom, brought into her entourage by the flood of publicity and popularity that engulfed her, asked her to marry him. She liked him; found him charming and sympathetic, but he was too white and she did not want a marriage which would keep the difficulties of color more than ever before her eyes. What she did want, she decided, was to be needed, to be useful, to be devoting her time, her concentration and her remarkable singlemindedness to some worthy visible end. After all, she had worked hard and striven tremendously—to be what? A dancer.

"Is this really what you wanted me to be?" she asked her father abruptly. They were driving home from the theater, their nightly custom. "Is this your idea of real greatness?"

And Joel, his voice half glad, half sorry, told her that he, too, had hoped for something different.

CHAPTER XXIX

A T first the war presented itself to Peter in a purely personal aspect. It was a long time before he envisaged the struggle as a great stupendous whole. Boyishly egotistic, he saw it simply as the next big moment in the panorama of his life following on his break with Joanna and his puzzling relationship with Maggie. And always he saw it in relation to the things which were happening to him like a series of living pictures against a great impersonal background.

Ignorant of Neal's attack on Maggie he had returned to Philadelphia, completed his work and had gone to Des Moines. He sent his books to his Aunt Susan,—all but one little black testament which bore written on the fly leaf his father's and grandfather's and *his* father's names. There was another name, too, "Judy Bye." But Peter could not recall this.

"More ancestors," he said to himself, thinking ruefully of Maggie. He could not bear to think of their last talk: even the thought of his forgotten instruments could not induce him to write to her.

In Des Moines he had met Philip. And from that meeting resulted that first indelible picture. He had rushed forward to Philip, his hand outstretched.

"Marshall! Say, fellow, this is really great!"

He could hear his voice ringing even now. And then Philip's contemptuous rejoinder: "I don't shake hands with any such damned light of love."

He thought he must have misunderstood at first. But

there was the angry scorn in Philip's eyes and there was his hand hanging clenched by his side.

The contemptuous epithet made him flinch. Of course, Philip's bitterness and scorn arose from two sources. Peter had broken off with his sister and had taken up with the one girl in whom he had ever shown any interest.

"But hang it all," Peter said to himself in angry bewilderment. "Why didn't he try for Maggie himself, if he wanted her? But no, first he lets that gambler win her and then he leaves her to me."

Here again ignorance was the cause. Philip did not know of Maggie's divorce until she had become engaged to Peter. Joanna had never told him and he, considering her first marriage as an answer to his rather lackadaisical courtship, had not thought it worth while to make inquiries about her. His own liking for Maggie had taken possession of him so slowly that he had not realized himself until too late what she meant to him.

The result of the encounter was to drive Peter back on himself and to confuse his issues more and more. He did not know which way to turn. More than ever if Philip loved Maggie, he himself wanted to be freed of his obligation. Freedom—htat was what he wanted—from obligations, from prejudice, from too lofty idealism. It seemed to him as though the last two years of his life had been spent in struggling to reconcile ideals. First his efforts to win Joanna and then his need to get away from Maggie. He went through the motions of the long days of drill and preparation, thinking incoherent, unrelated thoughts.

"Poor Maggie, I've got her into this. I can't just chuck her." Responsibility began feebly to awaken within him. "But what does she see in me? Yet she'll die if I leave her. Joanna, you've messed up all our lives. Oh, damn all women! I hope to God I get killed in France!"

Still in a dream he left Des Moines for Camp Upton and left the camp for overseas. He was a good sailor and therefore was free to devote himself to men who were less fortunate than himself. On an afternoon he came on deck with Harley Alexander. The two had become "buddies" in the camp and now on the trip over the long days of inaction were awakening one of those strange intensive friendships between two people, in which each tries to bare his heart to the utmost before the other. Harley had told Peter about his disastrous courtship of Vera Manning and Peter had reluctantly, inevitably returned the confidence.

"Well," said Harley, "I'll be doggone. I suppose Joanna did use to queen it over you, but what'd you go make a door-mat of yourself for? She gave you what you were biddin' for. But now as far as this Miss Ellersley's concerned—I can't seem to remember her, Peter—she's got no claim on you that I can see. If she's any sense at all she knows that you came to her on sheer impulse. If you don't love her, don't you marry her. You'll regret it all your life if you do. Gee, I'm sick of this boat. Don't you s'pose we're ever really goin' to get into this man's war?"

He lurched suddenly and violently against Peter, who dragged him to the rail where he became horribly and thoroughly seasick. There he remained, spent and helpless. Peter tried to drag him back to a steamer chair, but he was too much in a state of collapse to help himself and too heavy for Peter to drag across the deck. A white officer, a lieutenant whom Peter had noticed infrequently sitting near the door, was standing looking gravely on. He came forward.

"Here, let me help you." Together the two men got Alexander into the chair. He was the type with whom any physical indisposition goes hard. Peter noticed he was shivering.

"Wait, I'll get a rug," he said, starting toward the door.

Alexander groaned, "Bye, for God's sake don't leave me. I'm as weak as a cat."

"Oh, you'll be all right," Peter called back, and left him with the white lieutenant standing silently by.

Shortly after his return Harley, declaring himself much better, went below to his room. But first he thanked the lieutenant who bowed with his pleasantly grave air. Peter, about to sink into the vacant seat, looked up and caught the intent glance of the white officer who smiled and nodded and came leisurely toward him.

"May I sit beside you a moment?" he asked pleasantly.

"Yes," Peter replied shortly. He thought: "I know what you make me think of. Of myself that first day I put on my uniform. Now why?" It was true that while there was no facial resemblance, the two men were built almost exactly alike, tall, with broad shoulders, flat backs and lean thighs. Peter was at first glance the more comely, his head was more shapely and his hair so crisply curling gave him a certain persistent boyishness. The other man, a little older and plainer, had nevertheless a certain whimsical melancholy about his eyes and mouth which attracted Peter.

"I heard your friend call you Bye," he said still pleasantly. Peter nodded briefly. "That's my name, too. Bye, Meriwether Bye. I was wondering where you came from."

Meriwether Bye! Peter felt his face growing hot as he remembered the circumstances in which he had last heard that name. "Dr. Meriwether Bye of Bryn Mawr, Pennsylvania, I suppose."

Meriwether without surprise acknowledged this. "You know of me then. May I ask how?"

"I've always known of you indirectly," Peter told him coldly. "My great-grandfather spent all his life working for yours—for nothing. There was a black Meriwether Bye, my father, named after him, though I'm sure," he added with rude inconsequence, "I can't imagine why."

Meriwether looked at him with a sort of gentle understanding. "I've often wondered about those black Byes," he said musingly. "My grandfather, Dr. Meriwether Bye—he's an old, old man now—used to tell me about them. He was very fond of one of them, Isaiah Bye. Isn't it strange that we, the grandsons of those two men, friends way back in those days, should be meeting here on our way to France to fight for our country?"

Something, some aching tiger of resentment and dislike, which always crouched in Peter ready to spring at the approach of a white man, lay down momentarily appeased.

"Friends! Say, that's the first time I ever heard a white man speak that way of the relation between a slave-owner and his slave. You can't guess," he said abruptly, "how I first heard of you." And he told Meriwether of his experience with Mrs. Lea, while the doctor watched him with keen, melancholy eyes.

"I'll wager you were angry, mad clear through and through. You had a right to be. Mrs. Lea," as he pronounced her name his gentle voice grew a little gentler, Peter thought, "didn't realize what she was saying. She's like many another of us, totally unaware of our shame and your merits. I hope this war will teach us something."

He had a nice way with him. "A regular fellow," Peter thought, listening to his quiet, unaffected disquisition on many subjects. He had been literally everywhere, even to Greenland, and had seen all sorts of people. He had a theory that while not all individuals were equal, all races averaged the same. Some men were bound to be superior.

"And the differences between the races are a matter of relativity," he finished. "I confess my own interest in colored people is very keen." He raised a fine hand to disparage

Peter's slight movement. "Yes, I know you are sick of that and the patronage it implies. But I mean it, Bye, and when you get back home you must go out to Bryn Mawr and see whether or not I have tried to express that interest."

"I should think," Peter looked at him squarely, "all things considered, you or your family would have shown some interest in us black Byes. You are rich men, your family is a powerful one——"

"Was a powerful one," Meriwether interrupted him. He had flushed a little. "I suppose you know that my great-grandfather, Aaron Bye, had ten sons. But only four of them had sons and all of them except my father died in the Civil War. Isn't that some compensation? My own father died when I was very young and I grew up with his father. He was the one who told me about the black Byes and how he when a boy used to play about Philadelphia with Isaiah. 'Proud as Isaiah Bye,' I've heard him say. Bye," said Meriwether earnestly, "I tried my best when I became a man to find if there were any of you left in Philadelphia. It seemed to me a monstrous thing to have our family and our fortune— for my grandfather is still a very rich man—reared on the backs of those other Byes." He struck the table with a vehement hand. "That whole system was barbarous."

"I wish," Peter told him, "I had known you sooner." Just to hear this expression of penitence seemed to ease the long resentment of the years.

"Without those slaves," Meriwether resumed, "Aaron Bye would never have got on his feet. His father was just a poor farmer, a Quaker, running away from England to escape religious persecution. He came over and received a grant of land. But he could have done nothing without labor, and free labor at that. He and a friend bought a wretched slave between them, worked a bit of land, then that old Bye bought out the other man's share of the slave; presently he bought a woman. Ah, it's a rotten story." Peter saw melancholy like a veil settle upon his finely drawn features.

"You really feel it? I didn't suppose any white man felt like that. Well, you needn't mind about me or about any of the black Byes," he surprised himself by saying. "After all, it isn't as though we were related. It's just the fortunes of —well, not of war—but of life."

"No," Meriwether returned, "we're not related. Thank God there's none of that unutterable mix-up. I don't think I could have forgiven those Quaker Byes that. But sometimes it seems to me that just because those black Byes and thousands of others like them had no claim, that they had every claim."

After that day they met daily; Meriwether expounding, explaining, unconsciously teaching; Peter listening and absorbing. "I'm surprised," the young white man said, giving Peter a calculating look, "that you were content with being an entertainer."

Peter flushed and explained. It was only a temporary phase in his life. He had been broken-up, crazy. Haltingly he spoke of Joanna and finally of Maggie.

Meriwether thought it a bad business. "Stupid of you not to see that the first girl had your interest at heart. Why, man, by your own account she had brought you out of the butcher-shop to the University. Well, life permits these things." Bit by bit he told Peter of his own love-life. He had loved Mrs. Lea for years even before her marriage when they were boy and girl together, but her hard, uncomprehending attitude toward "lesser peoples" chilled him, really frightened him. He knew he could not live with a woman like that.

To Peter's surprise Meriwether was a fatalist. He had strong premonitions and allowed himself to be guided by them. "From the outset," he told Peter, gravely, "I knew that you meant something to me. That was why I used to watch you so closely. I used to wonder and speculate about you. Something in you made me think of myself. It was as though you, all unrelated even racially, represented something which might have been a part of myself, as though you," he said dreamily, "were living actively what I was thinking of passively. I have often tried to picture my life as a colored man. I think if there had been any of that selfish admixture of blood between the white and black Byes and I had heard of it, I'd have gone the United States over but what I'd have found my relatives, and have claimed them, too, before all the world."

One of Meriwether's strange fantasies was that he would never return from the war. "I knew it when I came away from America. And listen, Bye, when I die," Peter marveled at the sureness of that "when," "I want you after you get back home to go to my grandfather and tell him who you are and how you met me. You are to give him this." He took a little case from his pocket in which were the pictures of a man and woman,—old-fashioned pictures.

"Your father," Peter exclaimed involuntarily, "you can see he's a Bye——"

"And my mother," Meriwether finished. He drew a locket suspended on a thin gold chain from around his neck. "And take this to Mrs. Lea. She loves me," he said very simply. "Here, you might just as well take them now." Peter accepted them reluctantly.

He wished he had a picture of Joanna. Death seemed suddenly very near, very possible. He did not care if he died, but he would like Joanna to know that he thought of her. But he had nothing to leave for her. Yes, there was the Testament. He took it from his inside breast-pocket and showed it to Meriwether. Indeed he looked at it closely for the first time himself. The two heads so like yet so different bent over the old faded script. On the top of the page in a beautiful clear hand was written Aaron Bye, then underneath in crazy drunken letters, Judy Bye.

"I can't guess who she was," said Peter.

A little below a familiar name appeared, Joshua Bye, and above it, evidently written, in the same hand, Ceazer Bye. But through this entry a firm black line was drawn, drawn with a pen that dug down into the thin paper. After Joshua's name came the names Isaiah and then Meriwether.

"My father," Peter explained, feeling somehow very near to him. "I guess I'd better put my name in, too." He wrote it in his small compact hand. "I wonder who those two were, Judy and Ceazer," he mused, smiling a little at the quaint spelling. "I don't seem ever to have heard of them; I thought we started with Joshua." But Meriwether professed dimly to remember some mention of Judy.

"I'm sure I've heard my grandfather mention her name years ago and Ceazer's, too; he was her husband, seems to me. I suppose Aaron Bye gave them the Testament."

The little incident threw them into a deeper intimacy. Meriwether professed himself to be as interested in and as bewildered at the workings of the color question as Peter himself, though naturally he lacked his new friend's bitterness.

"It is amazing into what confusion slavery threw American life," he said, launched on one of their interminable discussions. "Here America was founded for the sake of liberty and the establishment of an asylum for all who were oppressed. And no land has more actively engaged in the suppression of liberty, or in keeping down those who were already oppressed. So that a white boy raised on all sorts of high falutin idealism finds himself when he grows up completely at sea. I confess, Bye, when I came to realize that all my wealth and all the combination of environment and position which has made life hitherto so beautiful and perfect, were founded quite specifically on the backs of broken, beaten slaves, I got a shock from which I think sometimes I'll never recover. It's robbed me of happiness forever."

"I like to hear you acknowledge your indebtedness," said Peter frankly, "but I don't think you should take on your shoulders the penitence of the whole white nation."

"No, I don't think I should, either," Meriwether returned unexpectedly, "but that sort of extremeness seems to be inherent in the question of color. Either you concern yourself with it violently as the Southerner does and so let slip by all the other important issues of life; or you are indifferent and callous like the average Northerner and grow hardened to all sorts of atrocities; or you steep yourself in it like the sentimentalist—that's my class—and find yourself paralyzed by the vastness of the problem.

He slipped into a familiar mood of melancholy brooding. It was at such a time that he spoke to Peter of his willingness, of his absolute determination to lose his life in the Great War. For this reason he had gone into the ranks instead of the medical corps where he would have been comparatively safe. "Don't think I'm a fanatic, Peter. I see this war as the greatest gesture the world has ever made for Freedom. If I can give up my life in this cause I shall feel that I have paid my debt."

CHAPTER XXX

THE interminable voyage was over and Peter debarked to spend still more interminable days at Brest. Dr. Meriwether Bye left immediately for La Courtine, where Peter later caught sight of him once more on his way to the front. The somewhat exalted mood to which his long and intimate talks with Meriwether had raised him vanished completely under the strain of the dirt, the racial and national clashes, and above all the persistent bad weather of Brest.

This town, the end of Brittany and the furthest western outpost of France, always remained in Peter's memory as a horrible prelude to a most horrible war. Brest up to the time that Europe had gone so completely and so suddenly insane, had been the typical, stupid, monotonous French town with picturesquely irregular pavements, narrow tortuous streets, dark, nestling little shops and the inevitable public square. Around and about the city to all sides stretched well ordered farms.

Then came the march of two million American soldiers across the town and the surrounding country. Under their careless feet the farms became mud, so that the name Brest recalls to the minds of thousands nothing if not a picture of the deepest, slimiest, stickiest mud that the world has known. All about were people, people, too many people, French and Americans. And finally the relations between the two nations, allies though they were, developed from misunderstandings into hot irritations, from irritations into clashes. First white Americans and Frenchmen clashed; separate restaurants and

247

accommodations had to be arranged. Then came the inevitable clash between white and colored Americans; petty jealousies and meannesses arose over the courtesies of Frenchwomen and the lack of discrimination in the French cafés. The Americans found a new and inexplicable irritation in the French colored colonials. Food was bad, prices were exorbitant; officers became tyrants. Everyone was at once in Brest and constantly about to leave it; real understanding and acquaintanceship were impossible.

Peter thought Dante might well have included this place in the description of his Inferno. Here were Disease and Death, Mutilation and Murder. Stevedores and even soldiers became cattle and beasts of burden. Many black men were slaves. The thing from which France was to be defended could hardly be worse than this welter of human misunderstandings, the clashing of unknown tongues, the cynical investigations of the government, the immanence of war and the awful, persistent wretchedness of the weather.

The long wait turned into sudden activity and Peter's outfit was ordered to Lathus, thence to La Courtine, one of the large training centers. It was at this latter place that he caught sight once more of Meriwether Bye. He seemed unusually alert and cheerful, Peter thought, and when the two got a chance to speak to each other, this impression was confirmed. The young white physician had the look of a man who sees before him a speedy deliverance.

"He thinks he's going to die and chuck this whole infernal business," Peter said to himself. "Wish I could be as sure of getting out of it as he is." Somehow the brief encounter left him more dispirited than ever. "Come out of it, ole hoss," Harley Alexander used to say to him. "What'd your 'grand white' friend do to you?"

"Oh, you shut up!" Peter barked at him.

His real depression, however, dated back to the time immediately after his company had left Brest. The awful condition of things in the seaport town was general rather than specific, and for the first time since Peter had entered the war he was feeling comparatively calm. His long and intimate talks with Meriwether had produced their effect. He had not realized that any such man as the young Quaker physician had existed in the white world. He had too much sense and too many cruel experiences to believe that there were many of Meriwether's kind to be found in a lifetime's journey, but somehow his long bitterness of the years had been assuaged. Henceforth, he told himself, he would try to be more generous in his thoughts of white men—perhaps his attitude invited trouble which he was usually only too willing to meet halfway.

At Lathus, Harley Alexander met him in the little *place*. "Seems to me you're got up regardless," Peter had commented. Alexander, one of the trimmest men in the regiment, was looking unusually shipshape, almost dapper.

The other struck him familiarly across the shoulder. "And that ain't all. Say, fellow, there's a band concert to-night right here in this little old square. I'm goin' and I'm goin' to take a lady."

"Lady! Where'd you get her?"

"Right here. These girls are all right. Not afraid of a dark skin. 'How should we have fear, m'soo,' one of them says to me, 'when you fight for our *patrie* and when you are so *beau?*' '*Beau*' that's handsome, ain't it? Say this is some country to fight for; got some sense of appreciation. Better come along, old scout. There's a pile of loots getting ready to come, each with a French dame in tow."

"I'll be there," Peter told him, laughing. "But count me out with the ladies. I can't get along with the domestic brand and I know I'll be out of luck with the foreign ones."

Some passing thought wiped the joy of anticipation from

Harley's face. "My experience is that these foreign ones are a damn sight less foolish than some domestic ones I've met. Well, me for the concert."

But that band concert never came off. At sunset a company of white American Southerners marched into Lathus down the main street, past the little *place*. There was a sudden uproar.

"Look! Darkies and white women! Come on, fellows, kill the damned niggers!"

There was a hasty onslaught in which the colored soldiers even taken by surprise gave as good as they took. Between these two groups from the same soil there was grimmer, more determined fighting than was seen at Verdun. The French civil population stood on the church-steps opposite the square and watched with amazement.

"*Nom de dieu!* Are they crazy, then, these Americans, that they kill each other!"

The next day saw Peter's company on its way to La Courtine, a training center, where there were no women. Thence they moved presently to the front in the Metz Sector.

The injustice and indignity rendered the colored troups at Lathus, plus the momentary glimpses which he caught of Meriwether and his exaltation, plunged Peter into a morass of melancholy nd bitter self-communing which shut him off as effectually as a smoke-screen from any real appreciation of the dangers which surrounded him on the front.

In the midst of all that ineffable danger, that hellish noise, he was harassed by the inextricable confusion, the untidiness of his own life. God, to get rid of it all! Once he spent forty-eight hours with nine other men on the ridge of a hill under fire. The other fellows told stories and swapped confidences. But he stayed unmoved through it all, impervious alike to the danger and the good man-talk going on about him.

When the call came for a reconnoitering party, he was one of the first to step forward. He went out that night into the blackness, the hellishness of No Man's Land. He saw a dark figure rise in front of him, heard a guttural sound and the next moment his left arm, drenched with blood, hung useless at his side. Raising himself he shot at the legs which showed a solid blackness against the thinner surrounding darkness. Wriggling on his belly, he pushed forward to where he thought he heard sounds, a struggle. "Something doing," he told himself, "might as well get in on that."

But when he drew near the darkness was so intense that he did not dare interfere. Two men, at least, were struggling terribly but he could not tell which was which. They were breathing in terrific grunts, so heavily that they had not noticed the approach of his smoothly sliding body. Suddenly what he had hoped for, happened. A rocket shot up in the air flared briefly and showed him the two men. One was Meriwether Bye, the other was a German, his hand in the act of throwing a hand grenade.

Peter lurched forward and at that ghastly short range shot the German through the stomach. But he was too late, the grenade had left the man's hand. The earth rocked about him, he could see Meriwether fall, a toppling darkness in the darkness. He started toward him but his foot caught in a depression and he himself fell sideways on his wounded arm. There was a moment of exquisite pain and then the darkness grew even more dark about him, the silent night more silent.

When he came to, it was still dark, though the day, he felt, rather than saw, was approaching. His arm hurt unmercifully. He had never known such pain. He raised himself on his one arm, and felt around with his foot. Yes, there was a body, he prayed it might not be the German. Crawling forward he plunged his hand into blood, a depthless pool of sticky blood. Sickened, he drew back and dried it, wiping it on his coat. More cautiously, then, he reached out again, searching for the face, yes, that was Meriwether's nose. Those canny finger-tips of his recognized the facial structure. His hand came back to Meriwether's chest. The heart was beating faintly and just above it was a hole, with the blood gushing, spurting, hot and thick.

He sat upright and wrenching open his tunic tore at his shirt. The stuff was hard to tear but it finally gave way under the onslaught of teeth and fingers. Faint with the pain of his left arm and the loss of his own blood, he set his lips hard, concentrating with all his strength on the determination not to lose consciousness again. Finally grunting, swearing, almost crying, he got Meriwether's head against his knee, then against his shoulder, and staunched the wound with the harsh, unyielding khaki. His canteen was full and he drenched the chilly, helpless face with its contents. All this time he was sitting with no support for his back and the strain was telling on him.

Against the surrounding gray of the coming morning, southward toward his own lines, he caught sight of darker shapes, trees perhaps, perhaps men—if he could only get to them! Placing Meriwether's face upwards he caught him about his lean waist, buckling him to his side with an arm of steel, and rising to his knees he crawled for what seemed a mile toward that persistent blackness. Twice he fell, once he struck his left arm against a dead man's boot. The awful throbbing in his shoulder increased. But at last he was there, at last in the shelter of a clump of low, stunted trees. With a sob he braced himself against them, letting Meriwether's head and shoulders rest against his knees. The blood had begun to spurt again and Meriwether stirred. Peter whispered:

"Bye, for God's sake, speak to me. This is Peter, Peter Bye, you remember?"

The young doctor repeated the name thickly. "Yes, Peter. I know. I'm dying."

"Not yet. Man, it's almost day, they'll come to us. Pull yourself together. We'll save you somehow."

Meriwether whispered, "I'm cold."

Could he get his coat off? How could he ever pull it off that shattered arm? Still he achieved even this, wrapping it around the white man's shivering form, raising that face, gray as the gray day above them, high on his chest, cradling him like a baby.

The chill was the chill of death, a horrible death. Meriwether coughed and choked; Peter could feel the life struggling within the poor torn body. Once the cold lips said: "Peter, you're a good scout."

Just before a merciful unconsciousness enveloped him for the last time, Meriwether sat upright in the awful agony of death. "Grandfather," he called in a terrible voice, "this is the last of the Byes."

When the stretcher-bearers found them, Meriwether was lying across Peter's knees, his face turned childwise toward Peter's breast. The colored man's head had dropped low over the fair one and his black curly hair fell forward straight and stringy, caked in the blood which lay in a well above Meriwether's heart.

"Cripes!" said one of the rescue men, "I've seen many a sight in this war, but none ever give me the turn I got seein' that smoke's hair dabblin' in the other fellow's blood."

CHAPTER XXXI

CHAMBERY, the capital of Savoy, a town situated toward the south of the extreme east of France, has not always been as well known to America as its more important neighbors, Grenoble and Lyons. Up to a few years ago it was celebrated chiefly because it was the location of the chateau of the old dukes of Savoy and the birthplace of Jean-Jacques Rousseau. Now it is known to thousands and thousands of Americans because during the great War it was metamorphosed into a rest center for colored soldiers.

To the tourist's mind it might stand out for three reasons: as a city in which it is well nigh impossible to get a lost telegram repeated; as a place where one may procure at very little expense the most excellent of manicures and the most delicious of little cakes. And, thirdly, as the scene of a novel by Henri Bordeaux, "La Peur de Vivre," the story of a young girl who, afraid to face the perils of life, forfeited therefore its pleasures.

Certainly Alice Du Laurens, the young woman of Bordeaux' novel, would have been no more astonished to find herself in New York than Maggie Ellersley, whom she so closely resembled in character, was to find herself in Chambéry. The nervous shock which Harry Portor had predicted from her encounter with Neal followed only too surely, but for another reason. The flesh wound itself had been negligible and she might have recovered without the nervous breakdown, had not Mr. Simpson in an agony of remorse at the danger to which he had so unwittingly exposed her, subjected her again with equally complete unconscious thoroughness to another shock. He was always presenting her with flowers, magazines, and journals, his eyes silently beseeching her forgiveness. For Maggie had never betrayed his share in the disaster and had thus made him her eager servitor forever.

Two weeks after the accident he brought her an evening paper. "Just picked this up as I come along, Miss Maggie. But there's some flowers comin' later on."

She took the folded paper listlessly and let her eyes travel over the front sheet. A tiny paragraph leaped at her from the bottom of a column. "Negro Leaps In Front Of Subway Train."

"A Negro, later identified as Henderson Neal, was killed instantly this afternoon——"

They found it hard to quiet her. "I killed him," she moaned to Harry Portor, hastily summoned. "His death is as much due to me as though I had poisoned him. I did poison his life."

Portor was at his wits' end. She was too weak to be sent away from home by herself. Her mother could not leave the house, for Maggie's illness had decidedly crippled her resources. And once more they were dependent on lodgers for their livelihood.

Once Portor spoke to her of Peter, thinking to comfort her, but the allusion only made her worse. "Peter! I was getting ready to ruin his life, too. Oh, how awful everything is. If I could only see him again!"

It was all very odd, Harry thought, wondering if Joanna could interpret this. The situation was too complex for him to handle.

It was her first cry of penitence, and as she lay there day after day reviewing her life she came to understand and to analyze for what it was that quality of hers, that tendency to climb to the position she wanted over the needs and claims of others. Now that she had no strength, now that life stretched around her a dreary procession of sullen, useless days, she realized the beauty inherent in life itself, the miracle of health and sane nerves, of the ability to make a living, of being helpful to others.

"Why, Henderson, even Henderson—if I could have taken him back that first time, I might have changed him, got him to work at something profitable and interesting. Maybe," she thought, for the first time since her marriage, "we might have had a child. And what difference did it make if I didn't go with those—'dickties?' I could have had a nice time; I used to have nice times, lovely cosy times with Anna and Tom."

That brought her to the thought of Peter. "Of course, he didn't want me. And I never loved him. He always did and always will love Joanna. Whether he gets her or not, she's the woman for him. He needs her as I need Philip." She lay quite still then, concentrating, probing her inmost spirit. "As I need no one," she said to herself aloud. "If I ever get well again I shall be what I want to be without depending on anybody. And I shall always be content."

Who shall explain the relation between mind and spirit? She grew better after that, began to sit up and, joining one of her mother's myriad committees, engaged in the preparation of outfits for the men overseas. Very slowly, almost reluctantly her interest in life came creeping back with her strength. She grew to be like the little girl she had been long, long ago, before her overpowering desire got possession of her. But she needed the stimulus of an occupation which would take her out of herself.

"If I could find something which would make me forget everything that is past, Harry," she told the young doctor. He had fallen into the habit of taking her on his rounds two

and three times a week. The air did her good and the occasion gave him a chance to study her.

"It will turn up, the right thing always does," he com-
forted her. "You know you are lots better already."

"Yes, so much better than you can guess," she returned,
leaving him slightly mystified at the peculiar expression with
which she was regarding him. He would have been more astonished if he could have read her thought. "Once," she said
to herself, "I might have tried to make him like me, tried to
get him to marry me and lift me out of my obscurity. My, I'm
glad that's over."

Once on her return from one of these trips her mother came
rushing to her. "Guess who's here, Maggie? But, pshaw,
you'd never guess. John Howe, do you remember?"

John Howe who had come to her rescue in the early days!
"Now you just set still," her mother fussed about her, "and
I'll bring him up. He's the Reverend John Howe now. I'll bet
he'll do you good."

Ministers for some reason are either fat or lean. John Howe
ran to the lean type. He came in looking very much as usual,
to stay only "five minutes," he told Mrs. Ellersley.

He stayed five hours and Maggie poured out her heart,
her first liking for Philip, her marriage, her discovery of her
husband's "profession," her engagement to Peter and her in-
sensate determination to hold on to him.

"And then Henderson killed himself. Oh, John, I've been
a wicked, wicked creature."

"Not as bad as all that, Maggie, but life has been as unkind to you as though you had been. That's the trouble,—
whether you burn yourself intentionally or not, you get hurt
all the same. And it's all over now, you've quite decided to
let—to break with this Bye fellow?"

"You were right at first. To let him go. Yes."

17

"H'm, what do you suppose he'll do then, go back to this other girl?"

"It sounds so funny to hear you talk of her that way, so slightingly, almost," said Maggie, a little surprised.

"Well, of course, she's nothing to me. Daresay she's a nice enough girl, though she sounds a bit priggish. Do you think she'll take him back?"

"Oh, I hardly think so. You see, she's the only one of us who's kept on and got what she wanted out of life. She's on the stage, a dancer, the success of the season! Peter's just barely through school, if indeed he did get through, and, anyway, he's still as poor as a church mouse. And I'm just Miss Nobody. The thing is—if Peter wants to go to her, he can."

"And what will you do?"

"I don't know. I can't guess. Something I hope very different that will take me as completely out of myself as though I had been transposed to a fourth dimension. Can't you think of something, John?"

"I don't know, I believe I have a sort of idea. Are you pretty strong now, Maggie?"

"The Doctor says I'm as strong as I'll ever be without change of interests and surroundings. Let's hear about your idea."

"No, that's enough for to-day. Besides, I'm not sure enough of it." But he came back the next day fortified. The Young Men's Christian Association had decided to send a few colored women workers among the colored men at the front. Two had already gone, but more were needed. If he could get the position for Maggie it would prove just the change she needed. Did she think she could go?

"Me," Maggie breathed, "go to France! To help the poor boys! Oh, I'd love it, John."

It was the thing for her. Of course, its accomplishment

took time and much handling of red tape, but it did come to pass and Maggie, leaving behind her an apprehensive mother and cousin—for the day of submarines was not yet over—set sail for France. She landed at Brest, from Brest she went to Paris, where she was summoned to Chambéry to help Mrs. Terry, the colored worker, in charge of the leave-center in the Savoyard capital.

Maggie was taken out of herself completely. The voyage, the danger, the foreign language and new customs went to her head like wine. The need of the men overwhelmed and staggered her. They were pathetically proud of her—and of Mrs. Terry, too,—glad to be allowed a sight of her bright face, to exchange a word. To be permitted to dance with her sent any one of them into a delirium of ecstatic pride. They were brave fellows, conducting themselves as became soldiers, persistently cheerful in the face of the hateful prejudice that followed and flayed them in the very act of laying down their lives for their country. For a time the Negro soldiers had been permitted to go over to Aix-les-Bains once a week, to reap the benefit of the baths, but a white American woman seeing in this an approach to "social equality," contrived to start a protest which resulted in a withdrawal of this permission and the black men were confined strictly to Chambéry.

A new sense of values came to Maggie, living now in the midst of scenes like these. The determinedly cheerful though somewhat cynical attitude of "the boys" in such conditions seemed to her the most wonderful thing she had ever witnessed. It was as though they said to hostile forces: "Oh, yes, we know you'll do for us in every possible way, slight us, cheat us, betray us, but you can't kill the real life within us, the essential us. You may make us distrustful, incredulous, disillusioned, but you can't make us despair or corrode us with bitterness. Call us children if you like, but in spite of everything, life *is* worth living, and we mean to live it to the full."

So many impressions, so many happenings crowded in on Maggie during those days that she failed to differentiate between the strange and the unusual, the calculable and the unexpected. So that on the night when a new detachment of men filed into the canteen and she glanced up to find that the tall lieutenant to whom she was handing a cup of cocoa was Peter, she did not feel at first astonished. Afterwards it came to her that, subconsciously, she had noticed how subdued, how cautious his greeting to her had been. His manner toward Mrs. Terry, whom he had known slightly in New York, seemed by contrast almost effusive.

"That," she told herself later, angrily, "was because he didn't want to encourage me. How he dreads me! Poor Peter. I'll put him at his ease."

She was to make arrangements the next day for a trip to Lake Bourget. On her way to the station she spied Peter sitting, a desolate and lonely figure, in the little parkway that ran through the broad street. He did not see her advancing and she had a chance to examine him. His face, still handsome, was thin and lined and his eyes were hopeless. She held out her hand.

He let it drop after a brief pressure.

"I was thinking of you, Maggie."

"And I of you. How wretched you look, Peter!"

He told her, then, of his wound and of his stay in a hospital in Toul. "My arm is all right now. I've even been in another engagement. In a month at the most, I expect to return to the front again."

"Do you dread it?"

He looked at her in surprise. "Dread it? My goodness, no. I think I prefer war to ordinary living. It is so quick and decisive. Of course, there are some tiresome delays. We were held up for six weeks at Brest and the transportation overseas was very slow. But I didn't care, I made a fine friend on account of it. I wish I'd met him sooner." He didn't tell her the name. That, he thought morosely, would only start her off again on his social standing. "He was killed," he ended hastily.

"I'm so sorry. That's why you're so dismal."

"Perhaps, and then, I don't understand anything more. Life is all a maze and I can't find my way out. I hope I get killed in my next engagement."

She bit her lip at that. How blind she had been! "Well, I'm going to obviate one difficulty for you, Peter. I've decided not to marry—anybody. I think I want to try life on my own. No, don't say anything. You can't very well thank me and there's no use pretending you're sorry. It was a bad business, Peter, and I'm glad it's over."

Before he could speak she had left him. His wound and the loss of Meriwether, his constant brooding, had wrought in him an habitual dejection. But he was conscious of a slight lifting of the pall which hung over him, a loosening of the web.

They saw very little of each other in the five or six days before his departure. Maggie was rather glad of this. She wanted no reminders to spoil her feeling of having begun everything anew with a clean slate. Her new-found independence was a source of the greatest joy. Each night she mapped out afresh her future life. When she returned to America she would start her hair work again, she would inaugurate a chain of Beauty Shops. First-class ones. Of her ability to make a good living she had no doubt. And she would gather about her, friends, simple kindly people whom she liked for themselves: who would seek her company with no thought of patronage. She would stand on her two feet, Maggie Ellersley, serene, independent, self-reliant. The idea exalted her and she went about her work the picture of optimism and happiness.

The boys called her "Sunlight." They all liked her and she was kind to them. Some of them were fine fellows, well educated and successful. It was Maggie's greatest secret triumph that in these particularly favorable conditions she felt no impulse to attempt to realize that old insistent ambition.

On the utmost peak of the Mont du Nivrolet, which towers east of Chambéry, directly opposite the *Chaîne de l'Epine*, gleams an immense cross twenty-five meters high, visible from all the surrounding country. At sunset it stood out boldly and Maggie, looking at it daily at that hour, came to regard it as a sort of luminous symbol of faith. "Oh, God, you have brought me peace; perhaps some day I shall know happiness."

CHAPTER XXXII

INTO the midst of her new-found content came Philip. At first she could hardly believe it. She supposed vaguely that he had enlisted but she was and had been out of touch so long with the Marshall family that she knew nothing definite of his movements. It had been years and years since she had seen him, had in any sense been connected with him. What a long stretch of time and events since she had received Joanna's letter that fateful Sunday!

He was very much changed, not only older and graver, but weak, physically. He had been wounded twice and had been gassed slightly. "I've been discharged from the hospital as cured, Maggie, but I'm afraid I'll never be any good again." He smiled with infinite gentleness. "There was so much I wanted to do." Fortunately his "Leave" had followed on his stay in the rest-area at Nice.

He had been in Chambéry for half of his *permission* then, and the first embarrassment attendant on their meeting had worn off. Still, both avoided discussion of the old days, glancing way from possible points of contact. He seemed to Maggie to be wasting by inches and even Mrs. Terry, who had seen many cases of gassed men, thought he had come out of the hospital too soon. Maggie, her old love mingled with a new tenderness awakening in her, spent as much time with him as she dared. She did not want him to be ill, but she adored his weakness, it gave her her first chance to wait on him, to mother him, to pay back, instead of always taking,

263

something of what the Marshall family had brought into her life.

He said to her one day seated in the little parkway, "Why did you leave us so abruptly, Maggie? Why did you marry Henderson Neal?"

Peter had asked her the same question years ago and now as then she could not answer: "Because of Joanna's letter." So she sat silent a moment.

"Well, Maggie?"

"Because I was a fool, Philip. I was a silly, silly young girl. Without the sense to know what I wanted. Without the patience to wait for it if I had known. All youn girls are silly, don't you think? All, that is, except Joanna. She always knew what she wanted and see, she's got it. Wonderful Joanna! Do you know, Philip, I think I'll have a career, too, a business one! A chain of Beauty Shops."

How wonderful to be able to talk like this without false shame to a Marshall! How wonderful life was! How beautiful to be experienced!

Philip said rather indifferently:

"I'm not surprised at that. My father always said you had one of the clearest heads for business he'd ever seen. I used to be overwhelmed myself at your ability to handle people and things. You were always so sure of yourself. I remember once telling Sylvia and Joanna that you could afford to go about with people that I didn't care to have them meet. Your early experiences rendered you safe. I believe I told them that when they were speaking to me of your husband, Mr. Neal. I didn't know he was going to be your husband then, Maggie."

So that was what Joanna had meant so long ago. Strange how time dissolves mysteries. Strange how, after deciding to take life as one finds it, life comes fawning to one's hand.

Several days elapsed before another talk could be managed.

Then they met in front of the *Statue des Eléphants*. Philip, examining that marvel with meticulous care, asked her indirectly about Peter.

"How will you combine the sort of business you contemplate and your marriage? Seems to me you'll have to be away from home a lot. Somehow, I don't picture you as a 'new woman,' Maggie."

So he was interested! And she had done nothing, not one little thing to lead up to it. "Oh, God, let me be happy now," she breathed. "You know I meant to play the game straight and I really do love Philip." Aloud she said joyously, "I'm not going to be married, Philip, at least not to Peter Bye, if that's what you're talking about. That was all a mistake. We both realized that."

She glanced at him, hoping to meet an answering joy in his face, but found instead a deepening mournfulness.

"Philip," she said very gently. "What is it?"

He lifted a haggard face. "Listen, Maggie, I can speak now. I loved you long, long ago, when we used to go off on those catering jobs for father. Do you remember? But I didn't know it, I didn't think about it, until you married. Somehow I had always thought there would be time enough and that, anyway, matters would adjust themselves. And when I heard you'd married that fellow, I was so amazed, thrown off my feet. I said to myself, 'You poor weak fool, of course, she'd prefer a man, a real man who, no matter what his character, would have gumption to go after the woman he loved.'

"I'd have come to you, but I thought you must love him; I had heard the girls mention seeing the two of you together and I concluded it was an affair of long standing. To ease myself, to put you completely out of my mind, I plunged into this public work; I wouldn't even mention your name. And the first thing I knew you had left Neal and were engaged to Bye. I couldn't understand that, Maggie, since you had grown up with Joanna and Peter, but that's all over now. I cursed Bye out at Des Moines, I remember."

Maggie, reviewing all that had preceded Peter's departure for Des Moines, shivered a little. "Perhaps some day I can tell you all about it, Philip. It was mostly my fault."

"It doesn't make any difference whose fault it was, Maggie; everything is too late now. You don't suppose I'm going to ask you, a beautiful woman, just on the threshold of a successful future, to marry me. My dear, I'm a wreck. I may live a year and I may live a half century. But I'd always be good for nothing, sitting around, ailing, getting on your nerves. I wouldn't be able even to run your cash register for you, Maggie. These gas cases are absolutely unpredictable."

"I don't care," she told him stubbornly. "You haven't asked me but I'll tell you. I love you, Philip, I always have. And nothing would please me more than to nurse you. Why, I love you, my dear. Manage my cash register! We'll get you home and Harry Portor will fix you up and then you'll take up your magazine again. I'll be your secretary, your assistant, your whole force."

But Philip was adamant. "You don't know what you're saying. No, Maggie, after I leave here I'll never see you again. I had my chance to win you once and I let you go, threw you into the arms of Neal. That was bad enough. But I won't chain you to an invalid's chair for life."

For the first time since she had known him she recognized in him a faint bitterness.

"You know, Maggie, I've never made any kick about being colored. Rather, I looked at it as a life work ready and cut out for a man, for me, and I rushed rather joyously into it to do battle. Now as I look back, I think I realize for the first time what this awful business of color in America does to a man, what it has done for me. If we weren't so persistently persecuted and harassed that we can think, breathe, do nothing but consider our great obsession, you and I might have been happy long ago. I'd have done as most men of other races do, settled my own life and then launched on some high endeavor. But do you know as a boy, as a young man, I never consciously let any thought of self come to me? I was always so sure that I was going to strike a blow at this great, towering monster. And all I've done has been to sacrifice myself and to sacrifice you. And the ironic joke of it is that in the defense of the country which insists on robbing me of my natural joys, I've lost the strength to keep up even the fight for which I let everything else of importance in the world go. I've been simply a fool."

She tried to comfort him. "You've been everything that is fine and brave and noble, Philip. And don't think your suffering, as you call it, is due only to being colored. Life takes it out of all of us. I have never spent five minutes in trying to help our cause. Your unselfishness and Joanna's persistent ambition have always amazed me. I have been a selfish, selfish woman, always—looking out for my own personal advantage, grasping at everything, everybody—who I thought might make life easier for me. You don't really know me, Philip. I've pursued a course exactly opposite to yours. And yet I never knew a moment of happiness from the time we were all children together until I came here to Chambéry to help these boys." She thought deeply. "Sometimes I think no matter how one is born, no matter how one acts, there is something out of gear with one somewhere, and that must be changed. Life at its best is a grand corrective.

"But now we've found ourselves, Philip. You have learned ordinary personal consideration and I have learned unselfishness—to a degree. It is not too late for us to be happy—together, Philip."

"How we complement each other," he mused. His eye fell

on his wasted hand. "Ah, but, Maggie, it is too late. Everything is too late."

On the last day of his stay she came to him. "You love me, Philip?" He gave a quick assent. "And you know I love you and you still won't marry me?"

"Don't torture me, Maggie. You've no idea what it means to be tied for life to a peevish invalid. I—I never expect to see you again, my dear."

"Then," she said, and the last tatters of her old obsession, that oldest desire of all for sheer decency—fell from her, "then I'll be your mistress, Philip. For no matter where you go I'll find you and stay with you, you'll never be able to send me away from you. You'll make me the by-word of all New York but I won't care, Philip, for I love you. Oh, Philip, Philip——"

They were in the chapel of the old Dukes of Savoy and the ancient caretaker, having stayed away the length of time which Philip's *pourboire* warranted, came in, but went out again, quietly, smiling.

For Philip had risen and drawn Maggie to him. "You really mean it, Maggie, my Maggie! Oh, my little yellow flower, I'll never let you go."

She looked at him starry-eyed. "You don't seem so weak, Philip."

Outside, the cross on Nivrolet, a luminous symbol of **faith**, **pointed** steadfastly to heaven.

CHAPTER XXXIII

THE War was over, the men were coming home. All Harlem was delirious with excitement. Everything conceivable must be done for "the boys," for those boys who having fought a double battle in France, one with Germany and one with white America, had yet marvelously, incredibly, returned safely home. There were all sorts and conditions of black men, Harvard graduates and Alabama farmhands. These last had seen Paris before they had seen New York and they blessed the War which had given them a chance to see the great capital.

There were parties, dances, fêtes, concerts, benefits. Everybody who possessed the least discernible "talent" was called upon; Joanna among them. She surprised even her most intimate friends by her graciousness. Night after night, when the performance was over, she appeared, splendid, glowing, symbolic before those huge dark masses in some uptown hall. The "boys," starved for a sight of their own women with their dark pervading beauty, went mad over her. She was indeed for them "Miss America," making them forget to-night the ingratitude with which their country would meet them to-morrow.

At none of these assemblies did Joanna find what she was looking for—a sight of Peter. She had gone at first out of sheer graciousness—a willingness to do something for these brave men. But later, there was another reason; something happened which led her to expect to see Peter at any moment, at any turn. She met Vera Manning.

"Vera, you imp! Telling those people that you had gone to school with me to learn democracy; I nearly died! Where've you been this long while? How wonderful you look! And how different!"

"Oh, Joanna, Joanna, I was coming to see you! First of all I've been South. I got sick of going about with those white people, so I cast about for something to do. You remember they mobbed some colored soldiers in Arkansas because they'd worn their uniforms in the street? Well, it made me sick, it made me think of—of Harley. So I rushed to a newspaper, Barney Kirchner is the manager—wasn't he one of Philip's friends? And I told them: 'I'm colored, see, but nobody would guess it; send me down there. See if I can't get a line on those people.'"

"Mercy," said Joanna, "what an idea!"

"And they sent me. And, oh, Joanna, it was wonderful to see how our folks, those colored people, trusted me and shielded me when they found I was one of them. And those white bullies, thinking I was one of *them*, told me the most blood-curdling, most fiendish tales. I really got an investigation started. Mr. Kirchner has taken it up. Oh, Joanna, I'm glad I'm colored—there's something terrible, terrible about white people."

She had seen a side of life which had first amazed, then frightened, then incited her. Joanna had never seen her friend like this, so roused and quickened, so purposeful. "It was as though at last I had found some excuse for being what I am, looking like one race and belonging to another. It made me feel like—don't laugh—like a ministering angel. Oh, I hated myself so for having spent all those foolish months, years even, away from my own folks when I might have been consecrated to them, serving them, helping them, healing them. You can't understand just how I feel, Janna dear. You've always had a definite something before you to make out of your life. I tell you I feel as though I had found a new heaven and a new earth."

"Wasn't it awfully dangerous, Vera?"

"Awfully, and funny, too. Exciting! I'll never be able to get back to Little Rock again. They found me out, suspected me. I really had to make a quick get-away. Something so rotten happened, I just couldn't control myself."

She told her friend that she had finished the investigation on hand and was quietly preparing to go. It happened that on her last night at the hotel where she was staying, the hotel management was approached on the subject of having sold liquor to two young white women, the questionable guests of three or four white men. Vera, secretly amused to realize that she had been staying at such a resort, thought nothing of the disturbance until she learned that the colored bell boys were charged with aiding and abetting the women in violation of the law.

"So I followed it up, Joanna. And what do you think happened? When the case came up for trial, the girls who had been taken up on charges of assignation were adjudged not guilty, but the two bell-hops were held for serving liquor under orders, and aiding in a crime which this same court says never was committed. Isn't it all too absurd! I made so much row about it that they became suspicious. A colored woman whom I had never seen before passed me on the street and handed me a note, in which she told me that my actions had made 'them' highly suspicious of me. Some one suggested that perhaps I was a 'yaller nigger passin',' and if so I'd better look out. So I got out. Oh, there was plenty of excitement, but it was worth it. I'm going to play the same game somewhere else, just as soon as I can. Do you know, I'm—I'm almost glad that I am forced to devote the rest of my life to it."

"Forced to devote your life to it," Joanna repeated, bewildered. "Why, what do you mean?"

A subtle change came over Vera's face. It was almost as though one could see her marshaling her inner forces, her spiritual resources. Despair, resolve, pride, courage—her friend could descry each in turn. Then she laughed her old confident laugh.

"Well, it's like this, Janna. I've had a message—indirectly —from Harley. He—" she bit her lip, "he isn't coming back to America. He managed to get his discharge in France and he's made up his mind to live there. Isn't it great for him? It means he'll have to start his training all over again, but he says he'd rather do that than waste his life bucking this color business any more. And there's all sorts of work for a dentist in those little French towns. Just imagine old Harley's being free to come and go as he pleases. No more insults for him, no more lynching news. Why, it'll be life all over for him, won't it, Jan? And I can't blame him," she broke off breathlessly, "once I might have thought the thing for him to do was to stay with his own folks, but life cheats us colored people so. I wish I had understood that earlier. White and colored people! No wonder Peter used to rave as he did." She ended astoundingly: "I suppose you and he have made up."

"Who?" asked Joanna stupidly. "Peter and—and me? Why, I haven't seen him. Why, he's going to marry Maggie Ellersley!"

"Marry Maggie nothing! Here, here's an Automat. We'll be all right in here. Miss Maggie Ellersley is going to marry your brother. Didn't you know it?"

"No, but I'm glad of it, glad of it. How'd you know all this, Vera?"

"Peter told me, of course. I've seen him. He's the most perfect darling in his uniform! You ought to hear him raving about France, but silent as the tomb about the War. He says the colored soldiers were all sold—fighting for freedom was a farce so far as they were concerned. But France is all right if the white Americans don't get in too much propaganda. I've been meaning to write to you, to tell you you'd better go over there. No end of chances for you on the French stage. You might even get in French opera. Are you sure you haven't seen Peter, sly thing?"

"Of course I'm sure. There was really no reason why I should. Mr. Bye and I haven't seen or heard from each other for three years, now."

"Mr. Bye! Well, good evening, Miss High and Mighty. If I see him I'll tell him I saw you."

"You'll do nothing of the kind. Stop all this raving, Vera, and explain to me about Harley. Are you going to France, too?"

Vera looked at her with a too perfect astonishment. "I going? Joanna, how did you ever get credit for being so brilliant, you're really quite thick-witted. Don't you see Harley's and my ways are going to lie separate forever? He is going East and I am going—South." Her gayety forsook her. "Joanna, don't let me cry in this awful place. I got it out of Peter. I made him tell me. He says Harley is bitter and cynical. He says, over and over, Peter told me: 'Look at these little French girls, they're really white and they don't seem to hate me. And yet a girl of my own race hesitates to marry me merely because she looks like white.' She pressed her hand hard against her quivering mouth. "It seems he can't forgive me. Peter told me so I could be prepared for anything I might hear. Oh, Janna, this terrible country with its false ideals! So you see why I'm glad there's the South to go to—I've got to choose between life and death. Even if I should lose my life in Georgia or in one of those other terrible places where they lynch women, too, I'll save it, won't I? I must go. Kiss me good-by, dear Janna."

18

She was off in a moment in her pretty, modish costume, leaving Joanna in a maze of pity and tenderness for her friend, and of sick bewilderment for herself.

Peter was free; he was, presumably, home, and he had not come near her. Some of the old pain surged up. She was walking presently along teeming Lenox Avenue. Some young girls passing turned and stared. "That's Joanna Marshall. You know, the dancer." A dark colored girl wearing Russian boots and a hat with three feathers sticking up straight, Indian fashion, came along. Lenox Avenue stared, pointed, laughed and enjoyed itself, Joanna's admirer with the rest.

This, this was fame—to be shared with any girl who chose to stick feathers, Indian fashion, in her hat. An empty thing —different, so different from what she had expected it to be. It had not occurred to her that it would be the only thing in her life. Probing relentlessly into an evasive subconsciousness she evolved the realization that in those other days she had expected her singing, her dancing—her success in a word—to be the mere integument of her life, the big handsome extra wrap to cover her more ordinary dress,—the essential, delightful commonplaces of living, the kernel of life, home, children, and adoring husband.

This was too much like examining the bones, the skull and skeleton of living and then every day tricking it out with the one thing which could lend it the semblance of flesh and color, though always with the vivid knowledge that death lay hidden beneath.

If her gift were only something useful! Even Vera Manning, a mere butterfly, had turned the trick, had used her one specialty, her absence of color, to the advantage of her people. But she—of course it did mean something to prove to a skeptical world the artistry of a too little understood people —but she could do that only in New York. After the season closed here she was to have a brief showing in Boston, in

Philadelphia and in Chicago. Even there, as here, she would have to appear in independent theaters. The big theatrical trusts refused her absolutely—one had even said frankly: "We'll try a colored man in a white company but we won't have any colored women."

Her manager, who liked and respected her, had told her only last week that he had nothing in view for her after the brief tour. He felt there was money in the South, but the southern newspapers had started to editorialize against her already. "A negress," a Georgia newspaper had said, "in the rôle of America. Shameful!"

"We might get a showing among colored patrons, Miss Marshall. But the South is in an ugly mood just now. Those hoodlums might break the show up. I'd hate to expose you to it. God, what a country!"

It was just possible that she might get a booking in a high-class vaudeville house. "And later on we'll write a play around you. It would take mighty little to make a fine actress out of you. That's a fact, Miss Marshall. And after we've had a run here we could cross the pond."

This, this, was her great success. She loved and hated it. But she would not have been human if she had not wished for Peter to see her in her triumph, empty though it might prove to be.

CHAPTER XXXIV

PETER had seen her. His first free hours in New York were spent sitting segregated in the portion of the balcony set apart for colored people, watching Joanna in the "Dance of the Nations." And the result, of course, was to make her seem farther than ever out of his reach. She was more wonderful, more mysterious than he had conceived possible. "And why you should think she would look at you! What if she did write and tell you she didn't mean it? Look at the letter you sent her in reply. Do you suppose a woman like that would stand being thrown down and picked up again?"

He was living with his aunt until he could open an office. Fortunately, he had saved up his pay and his aunt had used very little of his allotment. As soon as possible he would get out his shingle. His first impulse on receiving his *congé* from Maggie had been to come back and have at least a talk with Joanna. But after seeing her on the stage he rejected that idea completely.

"But I'll work like fury. I'll really get ahead. And then I'll go to her and tell her I owe it all to her. And I'll explain to her, as Meriwether Bye said, that all my training and instincts have been against me. And then," he finished to himself lamely, "we'll always be friends."

He passed the state-board examinations with a flourish. Then to get an office. He thought it best to consult Harry Portor about this. The latter in his own office greeted him, he thought, none too cordially, ignored his hand.

"Thought I'd look you up, Portor. Gee, what enthusiasm! Nice greeting to give a fellow who's just been making your home safe for democracy."

"Oh, can that stuff, Bye. What I want to know is this. It's none of my business but I happen to be interested. What are you going to do about Maggie Ellersley?"

"Wha-at! Well I'll be——" Had he been in her train, too? Was this why she had given him his freedom? His face clouded.

"You're right, Harry, it *is* none of your business. May I ask how you horn in o this?"

"Well, if you've got to know. I'm, I'm deeply interested in Miss Joanna Marshall and—and——"

"Hold on, I thought you were speaking of Miss Ellersley." Their politeness was wonderful.

"Now see here, Bye, tell me, are you going to marry Miss Ellersley?"

"I am not."

"Well, by God! you dirty cad, what do you mean by getting engaged to one woman after another and not having any intention of marrying either?"

Peter controlled his rising anger. "I don't want to quarrel with you, Portor. Miss Ellersley told me in Chambéry that she didn't want to marry me, she'd made a mistake."

"And Miss Marshall," said Harry, his face clearing, "have you told her yet?"

"No, I haven't. Miss Marshall found out she'd made a mistake three years ago. I don't make good with the ladies, Portor. And I'd like to know how the devil it concerns you?"

"It concerns me," said Harry miserably, "because I'm pretty sure Joanna loves you, and I want you to make her happy, or else get out of the way and let me try to do it." And he told Peter how Joanna, thinking him guilty, had yet declared herself Maggie's assailant.

Peter's natural surprise at Neal's attack on Maggie vanished into stupefied amazement at the news of Joanna's generosity. "She did that for me? Joanna?"

"Yes," Portor told him. "Where're you going, man?"

Peter had snatched up his cap. "You get into that little Ford I saw standing out there and drive me up to her house. I can't drive a Ford. Does she still live home?"

"Still with her father and mother. But they've moved on One Hundred and Thirty-eighth Street. Joanna, I believe, wanted a whole floor for a studio, and as Sylvia's children are growing up, she and her parents got out. The kids are always over at Joanna's, though."

They were silent after that. Harry let him off at Joanna's corner. "Well, good luck, old man," he said insincerely.

Sylvia's boy, Roger, let Peter in. "I know who you are," said the tall lieutenant. "You are Brian Spencer's son."

"Yes, I am, but I don't know you. And you'll have to tell me your name if you want to see my Aunt Joanna. She might not be at home."

"Yes, that's what I was afraid of. See here, son, I knew your Aunt Joanna before you were born, and I'd like to surprise her. I've just got back from France. Understand, Buddy? I've got a German helmet around to my house——"

"Well," said Roger, shamelessly, "you go right up those stairs; 's that helmet got a plume on it?"

Joanna had been singing Tschaikowsky's "Longing." Now she was sitting still reading the words over and over:

> *Nur wer die Sehnsucht kennt,*
> *Weiss was ich leide,*
> . . . .
> *Ach! der mich liebt und kennt—*

She mused over the last line: "Peter, I'm afraid you never really knew me or loved me."

He called to her softly from the door of the studio, "Joanna".
She turned swiftly on the stool and saw him.

"Peter!"

What could they say? Does anyone believe that two people
who have loved dearly and have been parted can say anything
adequate at such moments? Certainly all the explanations,
the pleas for forgiveness that Joanna had meant to utter if
they should ever meet again, left her. She only sat and held
his hand and called his name again and again. But he was
silent.

Both became terribly self-conscious, indeed, were very near
weeping. Peter told Joanna long afterwards that he did not
dare speak for fear of bursting into tears. Peter, who had
been in two terrible engagements, and had brought back Meriwether Bye from No Man's Land!

He told Joanna about Meriwether during those first incredibly beatific days after they had met again. But Joanna was
too astounded at the happiness which flooded the very atmosphere about them. Almost as though she were taking a
deep sea bath in bliss.

"I used to think," she told him, "even if Peter does come
back, we never can

'recapture
that first fine careless rapture.' "

"I don't think we have, dear," he told her wistfully, "for
with this happiness is the memory of that awful bitterness that
lay between us. There was nothing like this that first time."

He persuaded her to go to Philadelphia, to Bryn Mawr in
fact. "I've got to give these pictures and the locket to Dr.
Meriwether Bye and to Mrs. Lea. I'm so sorry for them. To
think we're alive and have each other——"

"And their Meriwether is dead. Oh. Peter, if it had been
you!"

"Yet I used to long for death, Joanna. I used to wish I'd get done in at the Front. Did you pray for me?"

"Yes, sometimes. But I didn't think you'd die. I used to think, though, that you'd never come back to me. I didn't see how Maggie could ever let you go. She's married Philip, you know."

"Yes, I know. I told Vera, hoping it would get to you." He mused over some mysterious memory. "Well, Maggie certainly is some girl. How's Philip?"

"Better, oh, lots better. He has a fighting chance and it's all due to her. He's in a sanitarium and she's with him. She should have married him long ago. It's my fault she didn't." And she told him about the letter.

"Gosh!" Peter exclaimed inadequately, "don't you do funny things when you're kids? Well, here we are at Bryn Mawr. You want to wait here in the station? I don't think I'll be long. If I am I'll send for you. I don't mind going here myself, but I don't want you to go in until I know how they're going to treat you."

"Oh, go along," laughed Joanna, "I've been in a million of their homes. Thought you were all over that nonsense."

He was back in a quarter of an hour, very serious. "The old gentleman is ill, got bronchitis and they're afraid it might turn into flu. So I left a message and the pictures and my address. Your address, rather, Joanna dear, since I don't know just when I'm going to move. Now we'll go to Mrs. Lea's. She's just the next station up the line."

They boarded the local. "I wish you could have seen that old butler, Janna. He knew my grandfather. And the moment he saw me, he knew I was a Bye. Gave me the funniest look. 'Why,' he said, 'you'se the spit of both families!' Funny, isn't it, Joanna; those two families, the black and the white Byes, lived so long together that they developed similar characteristics, like husbands and wives, you know. And they say white

and colored people are fathoms apart! Even I noticed that
Meriwether Bye and I were built alike. I'm afraid we weren't
much alike spiritually. Well, here's where we hop off again.
I'm afraid I'll be longer this time. Mind waiting for me,
darling?"

"Never, if you'll only promise to come back to me," she
whispered.

Nothing had been said as yet about a new engagement. But
he kissed her in the Sunday quiet of the tiny station and held
her close.

When he came back at the end of an hour she could see he
was deeply stirred.

"Hard on you, wasn't it, Peter?"

"Yes, and on her, too. Poor little thing. I don't pretend
to understand white people, Joanna, but I can't imagine what
Meriwether, that big, fine idealist, could have seen in that
little ball of fluff. Self-centered, narrow and cruel—cruel,
Joanna! Oh, such people! Do you know what she said?"

"I can't imagine, Peter."

"I gave her the locket, and she said with the tears stream-
ing down her face, 'To think that the Lord would let Meriwether Bye be killed and would let his nigger live!' "

Joanna fell back against the red plush seat. "She didn't,
she couldn't!"

"You wouldn't think so. And then she told me, 'Go on, tell
me every word he said.' And I did, all I could remember. He
had said to me one day, 'I love her and she loves me,' and I
told her that and she leaned back and moaned—moaned, Janna.
I wanted to pick her up in my arms and comfort her, and if I
had, do you know what would have happened to me——"

"Don't, Peter."

"Well, this is Pennsylvania, so probably I'd have got off
with imprisonment, here, but if it had been in Georgia, and
I'd have dared to touch her— —"

She put her hand over his mouth, "Peter, you shan't say it."

"Darling, all the time I was there I was thinking: 'Suppose this were Joanna and I were Harley Alexander, or someone, telling her about Peter Bye!"

They were very sober after that.

At the West Philadelphia station Peter remembered a restaurant on Market Street, where he had eaten in his student days. "I guess they'll still accommodate us. Where do you think I'm going to take you after we eat?"

"I can't imagine, Peter."

"Out to the Park, darling. I used to dream of this in France, when I was in that hospital."

Philadelphia, since the War, has changed for the worse in her attitude toward colored people. But these two contrived to get a decent meal after which they set out for the Park. It was October again, mellow and beautiful. Joanna, tingling with memories of the past, asked Peter nervously to tell her more of Meriwether Bye.

"He was a wonderful man, Joanna, a real, real man and he made me see life from an entirely different angle. He said white men in their fight for freedom in America had had tremendous physical odds to face and that black men had helped them face them. Now it was our turn to fight for freedom, only our odds were spiritual and mental obstacles, infinitely more difficult because less tangible. 'And just as you black men helped us, Bye,' he used to say, 'there're plenty of white men to help you. You don't know it; for one thing, you've shut your mind to us. Oh, you're not to blame, lots of us aren't to be trusted; most of us, I'm afraid. But we're ignorant and incredulous. Show us what manhood means, Bye.' "

"He must have been wonderful, indeed, Peter."

"Yes. And yet the queerest chap. You know I told you he had made up his mind to die. That was the difference between us. I wanted to, but he had made up his mind to it. And he told me: 'I knew as soon as I saw you on the ship that my job was finished, but you would have to carry on. You'll have to finish up my life, Peter.'"

Joanna felt tears in her eyes.

"Darling, he told me something else. He said I was a fool ever to have let you go. My dear, I'm going to try to finish up Meriwether Bye's life, to be the man that he would have been. But I can do nothing without you, Joanna." Suddenly they were back in the full tide of their love of long ago. He knelt beside her, kissing her hands. "Sweetest Joanna, will you take me and make a man out of me? All that is decent in me already is your work. Are you going to marry me, Joanna?"

An ineffable solemnity hung around them.

"Tell me, Joanna."

"Of course, I'll marry you, Peter. Dear, don't think I don't understand how hard things have been for you. I was such a stupid, before, when we were young. I didn't allow for the difference in our temperaments. Why, nothing in the world is so hard to face as this problem of being colored in America. See what it does to us—sends Vera Manning South and Harley overseas, away from everybody they've ever known, so that they can live in—in a sort of bitter peace; forces you to consider giving up your wonderful gift as a surgeon to drift into any kind of work; drives me, and the critics call me a really great artist, Peter, to consider ordinary vaudeville. Oh, it takes courage to fight against it, Peter, to keep it from choking us, submerging us. But now that we have love, Peter, we have a pattern to guide us out of the confusion. When you left me for Maggie, I used to lie awake at night and think of all the sweet things I might have said to you. Oh, if you've suffered half as much as I have, you've suffered horribly. I learned that nothing in the world is worth as much

as love. For people like us, people who can and must suffer—
Love is our refuge and strength."

He kissed her reverently. "Yes, thank God, we've got Love.
That is the great compensation. We've tried everything else,
dear: you, your career; and I, my self-indulgence. And we've
found what we wanted was each other. But you're right,
Joanna, it is frightful to see the havoc that this queer in-
tangible bugaboo of color works among us. Vera and Harley,
you and I, aren't so badly off. We're intelligent, we can choose
our own native land and prejudice, or freedom and a strange,
untried country. We see clearly just what we're keeping and
what we're letting go. But when I think of the millions of
Negroes, not as lucky as we—there's Tom Mason, remember
the fellow I used to play with in Philadelphia? I heard from
him this morning. He's made his pile and he wants to leave
the country. But his sister can't and won't stand the idea of
taking up a new life with strange people and a new language.
'Why should I give up my country?' she wails. 'It *is* my
country even if my skin is black?'"

"'*Entbehren, sollst du,*'" Joanna quoted softly. "If you're
black in America, you have to renounce. But that's life, too,
Peter. You've got to renounce something—always."

"Yes, you do. Unless, like Meriwether, you renounce life
itself. Of course, that is the great burden of being colored in
this day. You've got to make the ordinary renunciations
which life demands, and you've got to make those involved in
the clash of color. . . .

"I'm afraid you'll have to give up your career, dear
Joanna——"

"Of course, of course, I know it."

"For, if there should be children, I want, Oh, Joanna, I
hope——"

"You want them to be different from both you and me,
Peter."

"Not so different from you. You were always so brave, so plucky. But, Joanna, if they are like me they'll have so much to fight, and they'll need you to help them."

"We can do anything together, Peter."

"And, Joanna, of course you know we will be poor at first——"

She broke out crying then. "Oh, Peter, you won't ever say again that I'm different from Sylvia."

CHAPTER XXXV

MAGGIE and Philip had returned from the sanitarium to New York, but Philip undoubtedly was dying. Peter and Harry Portor were at his bedside every day, but not because of their ability to help him. They were simply three friends together. Philip never spoke to Peter of the incident at Des Moines, though it is probable that he thought of it many times, but the young doctor seemed so serenely unaware of any former misunderstanding that Philip, with a deep sense of relief, let the whole incident slide out of his mind.

Joanna, meanwhile, was experiencing a little private purgatory of remorse and grief. As she saw Philip's joy in Maggie, his complete and unbounded satisfaction in her presence, she became more and more overwhelmed with the awfulness of that old unconsidered act of hers, the sending of the letter which had caused Maggie to marry Henderson Neal. Maggie had never told her this, but she was pretty sure that such was the case. The mere fact that Maggie had never spoken about it to Peter, even in the days of their engagement, led her to suspect that her sister-in-law had attached more significance to it than she had cared to show. There was only one thing for her, if she was ever to know any peace, and that was to confess to Philip.

She went to see him in the late October weather. On the way she had passed Morningside Park and the gorgeous autumn sights and colors had brought back to her in a sudden heady rush the memories of the old days,—partings with Peter, concert tours and meetings with Philip, talks, dreams, ambitions, all the activities of her assured, confident, determined youth. If she might only relive a few brief scenes—the night she had dismissed Peter, the time she had spent in writing that cruel letter to Maggie—how different her memories would have been!

Philip was in excellent spirits. He seemed quite reconciled to dying and even spoke of it with a cheerfulness and familiarity that never failed to bring a rush of tears to Joanna's eyes, though this she was careful to conceal. "Just think of the luck I'm in," Philip would say, "I never expected to come home at all. If Maggie hadn't found me there in Chambéry and taken pity on my lonesomeness, I'd probably be lying in a French cemetery this moment with one of those little white crosses standing above me. As it is, I'm seeing you all again and I have Maggie. She has promised to stay with me always. It's all right, Joanna, old girl, I've had a good run for my money and except for Maggie I'm not so sorry to chuck it all. Just think, it might have been my luck never to have found her again at all."

He said something like that to Joanna on this afternoon. Sobbing she fell on her knees beside the bed. "Oh Philip, if it hadn't been for me, you'd have found her long ago."

He was suddenly attentive, his eyes bright and keen in his thin sharpening face as she told him about the letter. With infinite gentleness he let his hand rest on that proud dark head which life had taught so hardly to bow.

"Dear Janna, dear little sister, don't blame yourself one moment. It was all my fault. If you'd left a hundred letters unwritten, I should hardly have moved any more quickly. In those days I was so taken up with the business of being colored! After I'd adjusted that I thought I'd arrange my life. Ah, Joanna, that's our great mistake. We must learn to look out for life first, then color and limitations. My being colored didn't make me forget to provide myself with food and raiment. I shouldn't have allowed it to make me forget love." His grasp on her hand tightened.

"Learn this, Joanna, and tell the rest of our folks. Our battle is a hard one and for a long time it will seem to be a losing one, but it will never really be that as long as we keep the power of being happy. And happiness has to be deliberately sought for, gained; even that doesn't solve the problem, but it does make it easier for us to fight. Happiness, love, contentment in our own midst, make it possible for us to face those foes without. 'Happy Warriors,' that's the ideal for us. Only I realized it too late."

That was his last long talk with Joanna. Usually he gave all his attention to Maggie who was with him always, supplying and anticipating his wants and radiating an ineffable peace. Her hand was in his when he died.

His father, remembering his intense patriotism as a child, said with a touch of bitter pride: "He died for his country."

"It was what he always wanted to do," Sylvia said gently. But Joanna knew that Philip's real desire envisaged *living* for his country—to save her from something worse than war.

His death diffused a gentle melancholy over the others. It was the first serious rent in the fabric of the Marshall family. Old Joel took to indulging in long, deep reveries. Mrs. Marshall, quite dry-eyed, took out all of Philip's baby things, wrapped them up to send away and quite suddenly put them back in their places. Her interest in Sylvia's children took on an almost feverish intensity. Sylvia herself and Joanna and sometimes Sandy had many talks, wistful with reminiscences.

Maggie alone remained calm and almost cheerful. "Not because she's unfeeling," Joanna explained to Sylvia, "but because she is so satisfied."

Sylvia raised an eyebrow. "Satisfied and Philip dead?"

"Yes, because so easily he might have died without their

ever having come together. But they did. Oh, Sylvia, you and Brian have had such a simple, easy, jog-trot time of it, you don't know what it means to have your life all broken up like Maggie's and mine have been, and poor Vera Manning's."

Whatever the cause, Maggie spent her days serenely. Secure not only in the knowledge that she was bulwarked by the Marshall respectability, but also by the resolve which she had made before she saw Philip in Chambéry, she started on the project of her Beauty Parlors.

She said to Joel who, she knew, admired her ability: "See if you can't make me as great a success in business as you've been." They spent many pleasant hours in consultation.

CHAPTER XXXVI

JOANNA and Peter married and Peter came at Joel's insistent request to live in the One Hundred and Thirty-
eighth Street house. It was marvelous to see how the
two old people renewed themselves in the youth of their children. Joel was as proud of Peter as he had been of Joanna.
Even Mrs. Marshall's long allegiance to Sylvia wavered a little.

The first child was a boy; "Meriwether," Peter had named
him after young Dr. Meriwether Bye. "I'm going to tempt
providence," he said to his wife. "I hope he'll not be the sort
of Meriwether that my father was. I'll see to it that he isn't.
He's going to be all and more than old Isaiah Bye ever dreamed
of," and he quoted, to Joanna's mystification: "By *his* fruits
shall ye know *me*."

The two possessed happiness; but more than happiness they
had found peace. They were united by the very pain which
each had caused the other. And the knowledge of how greatly
each could suffer created in them a sort of whimsical tolerance.
There is nothing like humor to speed the wheels of life.

Joanna, having come to understand the nothingness of that
inordinate craving for sheer success, surprised herself by the
pleasure which came to her out of what she had always considered the ordinary things of life. Realizing how nearly she
had lost the essentials in grasping after the trimmings of
existence, she experienced a deep, almost holy joy in the routine
of the day. To see about her, her husband and parents, little
Meriwether usually in Joel's arms, gave her, she confessed
almost shamefacedly to Sylvia, "thoughts that lay too deep for

tears." She rarely regretted leaving the stage and although she sang sometimes in churches and concerts and once even went on a brief tour, she almost never danced except in the ordinary way.

Still, as her mentality was essentially creative, she found herself more and more impelled toward the expression of the intense appreciation of living which welled within her. Luckily her training in music offered her some outlet. With her slight knowledge of composition she composed two little songs and glimpsing future possibilities, she began to study that most fascinating of all the sciences—harmony.

The change in Peter was more fundamental than that in Joanna. She at least had always had these possibilities of domesticity. Her desire for greatness had been a sort of superimposed structure which, having been taken off, left her her true self. It was as though her life had expanded on the plan of Holmes' admonition to the Chambered Nautilus:

> Leave thy low vaulted Past—
> Let each new temple,
> Nobler than the last,
> Shut thee from Heaven
> With a dome more vast
> Till thou at length art free,—

Joanna was free.

But Peter had had to undergo a complete metamorphosis. He was a supersensitive colored man living among hosts of indifferent white people. Not only had he to change in every particular his theory of how to maintain such a relationship, but indeed he had to decide what sort of relationship was worth maintaining. At his father's death and during his young manhood he had been absolutely without a notion of the responsibilities which the most average man expects to take upon himself. He looked back with a real shame and chagrin to the many favors which he had accepted without question from his Aunt Susan.

Joanna, clever Joanna, helped him here. She was not only naturally independent, but she was, for all her talent, essentially practical with that clearheadedness which artistic people exhibit sometimes in such unexpected fashion. Perhaps it is wrong to imply that Joanna had lost her ambition. She was still ambitious, only the field of her ambition lay without herself. It was Peter now whom she wished to see succeed. If his success depended ever so little on his achievement of a sense of responsibility, then she meant to develop that sense. To this end, she consulted him, she took his advice, she asked him to arrange about the few recitals which she undertook. In a thousand little ways she deferred to him, and showed him that as a matter of course he was the arbiter of her own and her child's destiny, the *fons et origo* of authority.

So he grew both in the spirit of racial tolerance and in the spirit of responsibility. He wanted to live in America; he wanted to get along with his fellow man, but he no longer proposed to let circumstances shape his career. No one but himself, not even Joanna, should captain his ship. He meant to be a successful surgeon, a responsible husband and father, a self-reliant man.

The memory of Meriwether Bye, never far distant, braced him constantly. The young physician's words and ideas had exercised a singleness of concentration, of influence over Peter such as a friendship of long standing could hardly have hoped to achieve.

For a long time he expected to hear from Meriwether's grandfather. Then as the months and nearly two years rolled by without a sign from Bryn Mawr, Peter decided that the old gentleman wished to spare himself the pain of learning more of the circumstances surrounding his grandson's death.

Sylvia's boy, Roger, captivated by his new soldier-uncle,

spent most of his time at Peter's house serving in the purely impressionistic capacity of office-boy. He came up to the sitting room one summer morning bearing a bit of cardboard between his fingers.

"Meriwether Bye," he pronounced, handing the card to Peter. "Ain't it funny he should have the same name as the kid? But he's no relation because he's white and as old as the hills."

"Meriwether's grandfather!" Peter said in astonishment. "Come on down with me, Joanna."

Together they descended to find an old, old man sitting in an absolutely immobile silence in Peter's office. He rose, a tall, straight, white figure and looked at the two young people, still in silence.

"I'm Peter Bye," the young man said, coming forward. "Won't you sit down? Sit here, Joanna."

Together they sat in a strange, strained quiet, Joanna watching Peter in whom she sensed the rising anew of the antagonism of all the years. There they were, she felt, representing the last of the old order and the first of the new, since Peter's generation was the first to escape the effect of the ancient régime, and he personally had not completely escaped it. How many things this ancient, stately personage who sat regarding them with keen though inscrutable eyes could have told them of the circumstances which had combined to make the two of them what they were! For this old man's whole life and fortune had been reared on the institution of slavery.

Out of the puzzling silence he spoke, in the expressionless, brittle tone of extreme old age. "Yes, I know you are a Bye, Isaiah Bye's grandson. And you were with Meriwether at the end. Tell me about it."

Very solemnly, almost pityingly, Peter began the recital of his brief, dream-like acquaintance with Meriwether Bye. "He had quite made up his mind beforehand that he was going to die. Perhaps you knew. So, I'm sure he was quite reconciled to it; I don't think you need grieve for him. And at the very end I was with him. It turned out that we had been fighting just a few yards apart. I think I eased him a little; I'm a doctor, too," said Peter simply. He put his hand in front of his eyes as though trying to shut out the vision of the pitiful, needless death. "His last words were to you, did I tell you, sir? He sat up suddenly against me, his hand on my arm and called out—Oh, I can hear his voice now: 'Grandfather, this is the last of the Byes.'"

They sat again in a deep silence.

"I'm sorry, Peter continued after a long revery, "that he hadn't married, and had no children. It's hard on you, sir, you who are now the last of the Byes."

"Yes," said the old gentleman laconically, "it is. Now, suppose you tell me something about yourself."

But first Peter told him about his father, Meriwether, glossing over the dead man's faults and irresoluteness and dwelling on his ambition. "So you see, I had always had the idea of becoming a doctor before me. But I'm afraid I should never have realized it if it had not been for my wife, here." He smiled gratefully at Joanna, who smiled back at him with a gratitude of another sort. He had uttered no word of complaint nor of the difficulties attendant on being a colored man in America. She was very proud of him. He was so charming, so handsome, growing daily in independence.

"You have a son," said old Meriwether. "I believe you said you had a son, Meriwether? How would you like me to take him and educate him, bring him up away from all he'd have to go through in this country, let him spend his life in Paris and Vienna. Perhaps he would be a doctor, too. When he became a man he could do as he pleased. And probably, probably, I say, I should make him my heir."

Neither Joanna nor Peter had ever thought of wealth. And

while neither of them envisaged for a second the possibility of parting from little Meriwether, they were momentarily stunned at such prospects, Joanna especially.

"Why," asked Peter, his old demon of dislike and suspicion flaring up in him, "should you at this late date show interest in a black Bye?"

"Because," said Meriwether Bye, getting up and beginning to pace the floor, "because he *is* my heir. Because he *is* the last of the Byes. Because when my brave boy called out 'this is the last of the Byes,' he meant you, not himself. He had no way of knowing it, but he did know it. That queer sense in him which warned him he was going to die, probably told him.

"You've heard of your grandfather Isaiah, the boy that grew up with me?" Peter nodded. "Well, his father, black Joshua Bye, was my oldest brother; my father—he was Aaron Bye—was his father. Joshua was really his oldest child. His mother was Judy Bye, old Judy Bye, whom I've seen often sitting in Isaiah's house, her eyes straining, straining into the future—perhaps she saw this, who knows?"

"My father," said Peter in a dangerously level voice, "told me and told me often that much of Aaron Bye's prosperity had been due to the loyalty and hard work of Joshua Bye. But he never told me that Aaron was his father. And you knew this, have known it——"

"Not while Isaiah and I were boys. Not for many, many years afterwards. My father," the word seemed strange on this old man's lips, "always meant, I think, to do something for his—his son in his will. But he put it off and finally just before his death he told my brother Elmer—his oldest son by his real wife you know—told him about it. But Elmer was all out of sympathy with the idea, and, although he did not tell my father so, had no notion of acquainting Joshua either with his real parentage or with the fact that he should have been one of Aaron Bye's heirs Elmer was one of those men with a sharp dislike, amounting to an obsession, almost, for Negroes, for all unfortunate people. I'm free from it personally."

"Yet," said Peter harshly, "your conduct has differed not one whit from his. How long have *you* known this?"

"Since the close of the Civil War. All my brothers had died but Elmer, and all *his* sons were killed in the war. When Elmer was himself about to die, he told me. He thought the loss of his sons was a curse upon him because he had failed to obey my father's wishes. He left their carrying out to me. I was a young man still. I saw no reason for opening up old wounds. Besides, I did not know what had become of Isaiah's son. Isaiah and Joshua were both dead. I could not see that my father had acted differently from other slave-holders—it was the custom of the country—and at least he did not do as many a white man had done, sell his son into deeper and more terrible slavery. . . . I can see now that whatever slavery may have done for other men it has thrown the lives of all the Byes into confusion. Think of the farce my father's religion must have become to him . . . and I shall never forget Elmer. Sometimes I think the shadow of it fell across Meriwether's life—I meant to tell him. I know he would have made restitution. Now I shall do it for him."

He ceased speaking and looked at Peter curiously, wistfully. "I suppose you find it hard to forgive us. I'm afraid I had not thought until very recently what this might have meant to you,—to Isaiah."

Peter ignored this. "If you made my son your heir," he questioned, avoiding Joanna's startled look, "would you be willing to publish to the world that you were doing it because little Meriwether was your blood relation—no matter how distant—or would this be the gift of an eccentric philanthropist?"

The old man's face grew a dull red. "Surely it would not be necessary—think of my father. What good would it do the boy to know that Aaron Bye's blood flowed in his veins?"

"None," said Peter triumphantly. He turned to Joanna. "See, dear, there is the source of all I used to be. My ingratitude, my inability to adopt responsibility, my very irresoluteness come from that strain of white Bye blood. But I understand it now, I can fight against it. I'm free, Joanna, free."

He walked over to Meriwether Bye, and the two tall straight men—so alike, so different, one young, one very old—gazed for a long time at each other.

"I don't want your gifts," said Peter gently, "nor does my son want them—neither your money nor the acknowledgment of your blood. They come too late." He turned to his wife after Meriwether had left the house. "Thank God, Joanna, they have come too late. Perhaps I might have been like that."

Afterwards the memory of the little black testament returned to him. He found it and showed it to Joanna. "I'll bet that old codger Ceazer knew that Joshua wasn't his son and that's why he scratched his own name out of the book. *He* would have been an ancestor worth having."

Joanna looked at him proudly. "Peter, you are wonderful! Such a man, a great man!"

He sighed a little wistfully. "There spoke the real Joanna. Greatness, even in daily living, will always be your creed, I suppose."

"No," said Joanna, a shameless apostate, "my creed calls for nothing but happiness."

THE END